G000150360

The Dragon of the Red Mist Awakes

Tom McDonald

Dedication

For my mother Alice, whom I sadly miss, and my father Jack for being a tower of strength and a source of wisdom. To my three children, Theresa, Alex and Grace, you can achieve when you have a mind to.

About the Author

Tom McDonald was born in Manchester in September 1959 into a loving family. He was the second of five children and grew up in a normal household with his siblings. His education was average, and he left school at an early age to join the Army. Some nineteen years later, he left the Army, settled down and became a family man with three children. For twenty years, he worked for Her Majesty's Prison Service. Then a serious motorcycle accident changed his life completely. Separating from his family, he took a job that took him far from home. While working in Cyprus during the Covid-19 lockdown, he found the time to sit and write his first novel. He is now working on another book which is due to be published soon.

Contents

Chapter 1

She pushed him hard against the wall of the house, her face only inches from his own. He could smell she had been eating blackberries not long since. When Taw finally looked into her eyes properly for the first time, he saw they were a bright emerald green, with fire in them. At the centre, they were deep black, so black that Taw could see himself. Her low, angry tones were slowly getting through.

'If you ever do that again, Taw, I will skin you like a fish.' With another shove against the wall, Dina released him and walked away.

Dina was only six months older and yet a good three inches taller than Taw. She was slim with long, black hair tied in a ponytail. A pretty triangular face, which lit up when she smiled. As Taw would put it, she had a long neck and long legs. No wonder she could outrun anyone in the village, maybe even in Astel Kingdom; hence she would have caught Taw if he'd run.

Dina lived upstairs from the forge with her brother, Joshua, who was a year younger. Joshua was apprenticed to his father to become a blacksmith, and at fourteen, he was in his second year of a five-year apprenticeship before starting his three-year Masters in the royal forges.

The argument with Dina had started when Joshua told Taw and the twins, Earthie and Jackus, that he knew a way to get into the Palace grounds on Saturday, and not only that, but to watch the knights training.

'No way,' said Jackus. 'How?'

'Well, it isn't easy. Firstly, we distract the guards on the drawbridge; we then sneak past and head down towards the royal forges, then climb over the wall into the gardens and cut across them until we get to the next wall. Once there, we climb over that wall which is into the orchard,' said Joshua.

'The royal gardens and orchard?' Earthie said with a raised voice.

'Are you mad? That's a flogging offence.'

'I know, but we sneak along the back wall, then we just climb on top of the wall at the far end, and we can watch the knights all day.'

'Won't we be seen?' asked Earthie.

'No! We just lie on the wall; the trees cover us,' said Joshua.

'Shall we meet at nine then, by the inn?' suggested Taw.

Everyone agreed.

They met at nine, at the Cross Axes Inn.

'Where's Dina?' asked Taw.

'She's doing stuff for Father,' said Joshua.

'We go on without her then,' said Taw.

Getting past the guards was the easy part. Down past the royal forges the four of them went, then a quick left, and up and over the wall into the royal gardens.

Sneakily they ran along the hedgerows to the bottom, turned right, and again keeping low, they made it to the next wall. Over this wall, and they were in the orchard.

'We follow it along until the next wall, and that's where the knights are training,' said Joshua.

They were about a quarter of the way when Joshua fell badly over a tree root and let out a yelp of pain.

'Guards, guards!' the gardener shouted. 'They're stealing from the royal orchard!'

Before they knew it, they were surrounded by royal guards and were being escorted into the inner keep.

Thankfully, it was the Royal Princess Juliet who was in the throne room and not the Queen or, even worse, the Prince, Prince Marcus. He was known as the best fighter in the kingdom, to be feared by all. He was always the one who would say if someone was to be hanged, and he was always there in his gleaming uniform.

'They were caught stealing in the royal orchard, Princess Juliet,' the guard said.

'What are your names?' she asked.

'Earthie and Jackus Adamis, Taw Sandbite and Joshua Shield, Your Majesty,' Jackus said.

'Sandbite? That must be you,' the Princess said as she looked directly at Taw.

She seemed to be looking right through him, right down to his soul, with a stare. How did the Princess know him? Taw looked pale, and his knees and hands were shaking. That's it, they all thought, we're going to die right here and now.

'You have been caught stealing from the royal orchard, a crime punishable by public flogging or the stocks.'

'But, Your...'

'Silence!' roared one of the guards.

'I am not an unjust princess, so I have an alternative in mind. Do you wish this instead of what the law decrees?'

They all nodded their heads in agreement, not knowing what the Princess had for them as the alternative. They were escorted outside the inner keep and to the drawbridge.

'Right, off you go,' came a voice, and the guard promptly about-turned and left.

They ran until they were far enough away from the Palace, then just collapsed on the grass at the side of the road. They looked at each other, then burst out laughing; even the thought of telling their parents did not dampen their laughter.

They had reached the edge of the town, Rollstream, and stood on the corner by the inn, trying hard to think of a way to tell their parents that they were to report to the Royal Games Master at daybreak on the Prince's Hunt Day for a day's 'bashing'.

Bashing was where a whole group of people would walk in a straight line across the country fields and through the woods, making lots of noise to scare the wild birds and animals out so the nobles could hunt them. The day before Midsummer's Day was the Prince's Hunt; the day after was the Queen's Tournament, where the knights jousted. Archery, staff and other tournaments took place, and a day's carnival was enjoyed by all the following day.

It was during this conversation that Dina overheard them talking and automatically blamed Taw for leaving her behind and getting her brother into trouble again. He did try to splutter a response, but it was too late, and she slung him against the wall.

Grandfather was sitting in the log chair in the garden smoking his pipe. He was an ex-soldier and retired from services to the King. He and Taw lived in a modest house on the east edge of Rollstream. The houses here were provided by the Crown for ex-soldiers, numbering some twenty-odd, on each side of the road leading out of town. Taw's mother had died when he was too young to know, and according to his grandfather, his father had died in a war when he was only a toddler crawling around. Grandfather, or 'Gramps' as Taw called him, had taken Taw in and brought him up. Gramps was teaching them all sums, reading and writing. They spent an hour a day practising sword and shield, staff fighting, sometimes horse riding. Then maybe two hours doing classroom stuff every day, as Gramps said they needed to be able to read and write. But best of all, Taw enjoyed going with Dina in the early mornings, hunting with their bows. He was never as good a shot or at stalking as she was, but it was great.

Although Gramps never worked, they were not without. There was food on the table and in the cupboard. They had clothes, and Gramps had two horses in the stables at Dina's father's. The house cleaner came twice a week to tidy up and do the washing. Gramps was a big man, over six feet tall, wide chest and shoulders, huge hands. The most striking thing about him was not his size; although that was impressive, it was his mop of white hair and his sapphire blue eyes. His hair was neatly trimmed around the ears but longer at the back, and his sparkly blue eyes never seemed to miss a thing.

Everybody in the village knew Gramps; they would say, 'Morning, Sandy,' or 'Day's Greetings, sir.' (Sandy was his nickname.)

On Sundays, they would walk to church in the kingdom. Even the soldiers would ask him whether he wanted a seat down at the front with the other soldiers, but he always declined, and they sat three-quarters of the way back from the front.

'Supper will be ready in just over an hour, so go and do some sword practice for half an hour, then wash for supper.'

'Yes, Gramps,' Taw replied.

'Then over supper, Taw, you can tell me why you were in the Palace keep today,' he said.

Dina had told her father, Henry, the blacksmith. He was a big man with a big bushy head of hair and a beard. His wife had died when the bird flu had struck, just after Josh was born. Dina had said about Joshua and the rest of them being brought before the Princess for so-called stealing from the royal orchard, and the punishment they'd been awarded. Joshua's father was furious and gave him a lashing with a length of leather. He was ordered to bed, to carry out extra chores, and not to leave the forge.

Dina was so sorry she had told her father; she had never seen him react like that and lash Joshua. If she had known, she would never have told Father. She was preparing two pheasants and a pigeon that she had got that morning in Astel Forest. It had taken her less than an hour to get all three birds: one shot each from her trusted bow. Dina had found the bow when she was ten years old and still learning to hunt. It was beautifully made from yew, blackthorn and another wood she did not know. It was dirty and had no string. She had taken it home, cleaned it up and shown it to her father.

'Nice bow,' he said. 'That must have been expensive to make, and the workmanship is second to none.'

It had taken her two weeks to buy a string for it as the others just snapped. Now it fired true and straight; Dina did not miss.

Dina made supper for her father and herself, and off Father went down to the Inn of the Crossed Axes for a few goblets of ale. She took Joshua a bowl of broth and some bread. He was sitting on the bed and had been crying. He looked up, his knees up to his chin, his arms wrapped around his legs. He looked so frail, just a child of fourteen and small for his age. That's why Father thought that working as an apprentice blacksmith would build him up. But there was too much of their mother in him: blond, blue eyes, very pale, timid, a copy of his mother. Whereas Dina was like her father: tall, slim, dark, and full of strength.

'What do you want?' Josh asked her. 'Leave me alone.'

'I'm sorry, Josh,' Dina said. 'I had no idea Father would do that. I have brought you some food. Come on, eat it; you must be starving. Father's at the Inn, so he won't know.'

Joshua took the bowl and bread, putting his legs down and saying thank you.

'Ouch,' Dina said when she saw the welts on his legs. 'I'm so sorry, Joshua, really I am.'

'It's alright,' he said. 'It could have been a lot worse; I could have been flogged or put in the stocks for days.'

'I'll bring some water and herbs and treat the worst of them for you.'

'Thanks.'

Jackus and Earthie were the twin sons of the town's merchant traders, Jack and Sadie Adamis, not hard to miss as they were all pale skin and bright ginger hair. They had a big double-fronted shop, a warehouse, and stables and a wagon yard at the rear, just about the biggest holding in town, next to the Cross Axes Inn. The twins thought it best if they did not tell their parents about the day's events and could come up with some excuse to be absent on Prince's Hunt Day. After all, it was a three-day celebration. First, the Prince's Hunt, then Midsummer's Day, and finally, Thank-harvest day on the Sunaday. Most people were drunk on honey mead, dark ale, rum or whatever else they could get drunk on. Most people failed to recall the whole weekend. Their parents would not be drunk but certainly merry.

Taw was tall for his age, with deep black collar-length straight hair, pale sapphire blue eyes, a little podgy around the middle and the face, but he walked with the pride of maybe a small soldier, a mirror of his grandfather at that age.

'So, boy,' Gramps said to Taw, 'what's this I hear about you and your buddies today? Having a private audience with the royal Princess?'

Taw almost fell over in shock. How did he know? Was he there?

'Erm! We sort of...erm!'

'You were caught stealing from the royal orchard, yes? Tell me the truth, boy!'

'Well, Gramps, if the truth be told, we were not trying to steal from the orchard. We were trying to sneak across the orchard to watch the knights training in the training court, which is next to the orchard. At the far wall, we could climb up and watch them training, but Joshua tripped over in the orchard, and the gardener saw him. He shouted for the guards, and we were caught. Nobody asked us; they just presumed we were there to steal the fruit.'

'I see. So let me guess: you, the twins, Joshua and his sister Dina? Is that correct?'

'Dina was not with us; she was doing stuff at home, cleaning or washing. Normally she would have been with us.'

'The Princess awarded you all a day's bashing on the Prince's Hunt Day. You got off lightly; you could have been flogged or put the stocks. It is not good, Taw. One day, boy, they'll get you proper.'

'I'm sorry, Gramps. I got into trouble again, but it was not my fault that Josh tripped.'

'Be that as it may, you were all in it together, so together you have been punished, and if you're ever going to be a man, you must accept the responsibility for your own actions.'

'Yes, Gramps. Can we still go to the celebrations and watch the knights and the princes joust? The sword fighting, axes, staffs, archery…?'

'That's enough, Taw, at the moment. No, you're on punishment. Time for supper, then an hour's practice, then off to bed with you.'

After their supper of fish and boiled rice, Taw went to gather his wooden sword and shield for practice.

Gramps said, 'We will practise defending and attacking with shield only, so you don't need your sword.'

Taw was trying his best against his grandfather, but he was just too strong and quick. Yet again, he was face down in the dirt, thinking it was better when the twins, Dina and Josh, were here training too. He did not seem to get hurt as much and wasn't face down all the time.

Just as he was picking himself up for the umpteenth time, two soldiers mounted on dark brown chestnut horses approached their home. Taw always admired the way they looked, their armour gleaming in the evening sun, with their royal blue tunics with white piping, white leggings and full-length black riding boots. They halted in front of the garden fence as Grandfather walked to meet them.

The one on the right asked in a deep Astel voice, 'Do I have the honour of addressing Lord James Sandbite?'

'You do indeed,' replied Grandfather. Both soldiers then promptly saluted him. 'Thank you,' said Gramps. 'What can I do for you young gentlemen?'

The soldier on the right said, 'I have a sealed letter for you from Her Majesty the Queen, Lord Sandbite.'

As he handed the letter over, the soldier said, 'Can you please attend the throne room tomorrow at one hour past noon to give your answer to Her Majesty and Prince Marcus?'

'I will be there,' replied Grandfather. Both soldiers saluted again, turned their horses and set off back towards the Palace.

Gramps looked over and said, 'That will be all for today, Taw. Tidy the place up, then get yourself off to bed.'

'Yes, Gramps,' he said. Lord Sandbite? Is Gramps a lord? How, why? A letter from the Queen? In Taw's head were a million questions, but looking at Gramps, now was not the time to ask; it was bedtime.

The next morning, Taw wanted nothing better than to get to the twins and Dina to tell them about the soldiers, the letter from the Queen and that Gramps was actually a lord. Grandfather was having none of it. Whilst having their break fasting of honeyed oats and milk, Gramps spoke to him.

'I need to talk to you, Taw, my boy, and this is very important. Under no circumstances are you to inform anybody that I am a Lord of the Realm, nor of the letter from the Queen. There may come a time when you will be able to, but for now, silence is the key. Do you understand me, Taw?' His face was set, his voice deep and controlled.

Fear struck Taw in a way that he'd never known Gramps to do.

'Yes, Gramps,' Taw said.

The twins, Jackus and Earthie, had been banned from going anywhere apart from the stables or the wagon yard. They were to muck out the stables and to shift the mucked-out mound to Farmer Higgins at Froggetts Farm on the north side of the kingdom. Straight there and back about four times with a heavy load. Their father had an arrangement with Farmer Higgins. Once or twice a week, they would move the horse-mound to his farm, where once a year he would mulch it up mixed with water, then spread it out over all his fields as fertilizer. Everybody knew when this occurred because the smell was disgusting, and if the wind was northerly, it was even worse. It could be smelt as far as the Southern Kingdom.

The twins' father, Jack, had gone to the Cross Axes Inn last evening after he had closed the shop. Shops generally closed as it got dark, according to the local custom. There were some townspeople in, soldiers and visitors, all getting on with their own business, and friends. A group of townspeople, all known to Jack, were sitting at a table in the middle of the inn, chatting, laughing and drinking ale, so Jack sat down with his ale and joined in.

Soon the subject changed to the four brats who had been caught in the royal orchard earlier that day. It wasn't until two ginger-haired boys were mentioned that Jack started to pay attention.

'Two ginger-haired boys?' Jack half-screamed.

Then everyone looked at him, and realisation struck them all.

Jackus and Earthie were the only two ginger-haired boys of that age in the kingdom.

'I'll murder the pair of them! I'll be in front of the Queen myself for two murders when I get my hands on them.' All around the table they laughed, and Jack was soon laughing too as they drank more ale and talked about the troubles they'd got into as children.

Whilst everyone was getting merry, a stranger made his way into the inn and approached the innkeeper, Nalt.

'Do you have a room for a couple of nights?' he asked.

The stranger was wearing a long, waxed riding overcoat and a broad-brimmed hat made of the same almost-black material; his face was old, and he looked tired. His white moustache and triangular beard looked out of place against his lively, piercing green eyes.

'Travelled far, my friend?' asked Nalt, but the stranger did not reply. 'We have a room, sir. Would you like supper? I can save you a place.'

'No,' said the stranger in a rustic voice. 'May I have it in my room?'

'Yes, sir. I'll show you where it is and get the fire lit for you, as it's still a bit chilly in the evenings. The price will be one shilling and two bits for two days; that's two suppers and two break fastings.'

'Thank you,' said the stranger and handed over the coins.

Nalt showed the stranger to his room, and as they entered, Nalt noticed that the old man had a black walking staff with a white knarl in the top, and he carried a canvas bag. The maid came in and was attempting to light the fire while Nalt lit the candles around the room. The stranger laid his bag on the floor and leaned his staff against the chair; then he sat down near the fire that was struggling to catch alight.

'Your food will be served soon, sir, and don't worry; it won't take long for the fire. Will there be anything else?' Nalt asked.

'No, thank you.'

Nalt ushered the maid out and followed her, closing the door. Vantor looked at the pitiful fire before him and thought it would take an hour before it gave off any heat worth having, but it was better than no heat at all. He stood and removed his hat and was just about to remove his coat and sword when there was a knock on the door.

'Supper, sir,' came a female voice.

'Come in,' he said.

The maid set the food down on a small table near the fire. It came with a large mug of dark ale and a quarter crust of bread. She was not pretty but had a nice smile. Typical barmaid: jovial attitude, buxom figure.

'Was there anything else?' she asked with a smile.

'No, thank you,' said Vantor.

She smiled. 'Enjoy your meal,' she said as she left the room.

Vantor took off his coat, his old bones aching after riding too long. He could travel the other way, but he shivered. The fire was still pitiful, so with a word of power, he caused the fire to burst into life.

'Ah, that's better,' he said as he rubbed his hands. Now for some hot food. The gravy was rich, with plenty of vegetables and potatoes, but the meat was in short supply. Still, it tasted good, washed down with an ale. He would have preferred a honey mead, but 'Can't have everything,' he said to himself. The fire had warmed up the room nicely, so it was time for a decent night's rest before attending the Queen's throne room tomorrow.

After breaking fast with Gramps, Taw sat with him at the table. 'Can you tell me at least some of the stuff I should know, Gramps?' he said.

His grandfather looked at Taw, and for a minute, he thought he was looking at himself many, many years ago.

'Before you were born, Taw, your father and I were fighting in a war in a faraway land with the King and other knights of the realm. It was a terrible, bloody war, Dragmen, shadows, war beasts, commanded by a demented winged creature, driven mad by the sparkle crystals of hell. Suffice to say that those of us who survived swore an oath before the Arch Bishop never to divulge what we had encountered whilst there. For to speak about it would strike fear across the kingdom, and to speak the name of the accursed one would call it from the depths, back to devour the earth.

'Your father and I were made Lords of the Realm. We never used our titles, and truth be known, very few people did. We just wanted to be treated as ex-soldiers and respected as such. Your mother, bless her, died not long after you were born. Already weak from childbirth, she caught the black lung bird fever and passed away. She was a gifted member of the witches of Purple. She could sense when your father was in danger and was indeed his shadow shield. When your mother passed, that protection was lost. Eventually, the shadows found your father and, in his weakened state, killed him in his sleep when you were but an infant.

'The sheets or shadows are monks highly trained in the dark magic who have given up their souls to sail as ghost assassins. They were completely destroyed by the Black and Purple witches. Without going into too much detail, I fear something is very amiss and hence the letter from the Queen.

'As I have said, Taw, you must never repeat this, and don't be going around telling folk that I'm a lord. I know you have a mountain of questions, but believe me when I say that now is not the time. But soon, Taw, soon I will answer all your questions.'

Chapter 2

Dina loved the smell of the fresh forest early in the morning. Spring was here, the birds singing, life growing everywhere, the trees, the plants, the wild spray of daffodils and bluebells speckled across the forest floor. This is where I am going to live when I am older, deep in the forest surrounded by nature, she thought. She sat behind a fallen tree downwind of the central dark undergrowth in Astel Forest, waiting patiently. A good hunter knows that patience is a real skill and, if done right, pays off. Dina had scouted the area three days ago and had spotted the tracks of a mature wild boar. It was using the thick undergrowth as cover and would come out and rummage around the forest floor for food. The boar cautiously poked its head out of the bushes, smelt and looked around and disappeared back.

'Wait…' said Dina to herself. 'Patience!'

Again, the boar stuck its head out, looked about and came out some more.

'Wait…' Dina told herself, her bow and arrow relaxed in her hands. Back in it went again; Dina waited. It came out again, this time fully convinced, after sniffing around, that it was safe. It started to rummage around for food and maybe, if lucky, find a truffle. It did not even feel the arrow that struck it through the eye and into its brain. Dina had waited; she drew the string on her bow, checked her breathing, closed one eye, slowly releasing her breath, and then released the arrow. It shot straight and true, hitting its target and felling the boar, causing it no pain at all, keeping the meat tender. There is nothing worse than when a prey survives the first shot; the adrenalin starts to pump around the body, making the meat very tough. More than happy with her morning hunt, Dina set off for home. Most of the meat she could sell, and the rest would last a few days.

The Lord Marshal was not happy; in fact, he was furious.

'Why was I kept in the dark about this? You know I want, and I am required, to be kept abreast of all the dealings with the witches.'

'But dear,' Lady Alice was trying to explain to Edmond, her husband, that she was only a member, albeit a senior member. She had no control over the Mother Superior of the Purple order or the Queen of the Black order.

'Edmond,' she said in a growl of a voice, 'Will you just shut up and listen? The Queen of the Black order, Sienna, and the Mother Superior of the Purple order have sought a truce with the Green order, the monks. This would put an end to six hundred years of virtual war between the orders. No decisions have been made yet, and it is only in its infant stage.

'Much has yet to be discussed and agreed by the senior members and, of course, yourself and the Queen. If we can all agree, we would cover the whole of the mid to north. That would leave the Red witches to the south, but nobody really knows anything about them, and they don't communicate with anyone.'

'But I am the chair of the Witches' and Wizards' Council in place of Vantor. I need to be informed so that I can brief the Queen and the Prince. If I don't know, I can't brief them.'

'You are only an honorary member, dear, you're not a real wizard, and as nobody has heard from Vantor for many a year, there are no real wizards of power anymore – just those so-called upstarts who are playing at being wizards.'

'But I still need to know,' he said under his breath as he was walking out the door.

'The reports, Mother, are the same from our spies in the south; they have lost four locations in the last couple of months, including the Emperor's Palace. It is getting more dangerous down there.'

'I am aware that there are reports of were-beasts and even Dragmen. Perhaps we should think about withdrawing all, except your cousins, the Smith brothers, and, of course, my son and your brother, Harry.'

'Perhaps, Mother, but not yet.'

'We can discuss matters further this afternoon when our guests arrive, and we may have more information to hand.'

'Forgive me, Mother, but I have some things I need to see to personally with the knights and the Lord Marshal before our meeting.'

'Very well, son; until later,' the Queen said.

Prince Marcus was of average height, lean and muscular. His short-cropped, spiky black hair with a tail was crisscrossed with a silver band, and his bright blue eyes were always alert. He was a handsome man, to hear the ladies talk, but none as yet had he taken to. He was full of confidence, well-educated, and some would say older than his years. As he moved through the inner keep, one thing was on his mind: the report that the Emperor was dead, attacked by Shadows or Dragmen in the night. Then the red mist had settled all around the Palace and part of the city. Anyone trying to gain entry or presuming to leave was instantly killed by the mist.

'We desperately need Earl Vantor to return before this red mist descends upon our kingdom, too. Where are you, Eric Vantor?'

The Prince met with the Lord Marshal and several of the knights to discuss other pending matters. The guards were briefed on some who could possibly turn up without invitation but were to be admitted on the Prince's orders, and he gave them a list.

'Taw, get yourself washed and put your good clothes on. You're coming with me,' Gramps said.

'What? Why? No thanks, Gramps, I've seen enough of the Palace and throne room to last all my life,' said Taw.

'You'll not be in the throne room, and I won't tell you twice, boy,' came the answer.

Taw knew it was a waste of time to argue with Gramps when he had his mind set. They set off towards Dina's to pick up the horses. Once there, they saddled them up and set off towards the Palace. Taw did not see Dina or Josh, but Grandfather said hello to Henry, who returned the greeting. Taw thought he would ask Gramps again why he was going to the Palace.

'Gramps, am I going to the Palace to help you with something?' he asked in a merry sort of way.

To Taw's surprise, Gramps answered, 'No, there is something I want you to see, but don't ask me anymore. All will be revealed once we are inside the Palace.'

They approached the Palace, and the two guards looked up. One said, 'State your business.'

Gramps put his hand inside his jerkin, pulled out the invitation and showed it to them.

Both guards sprang to attention. 'Forgive us, m' lord. I was unaware.'

'That's alright, soldier. Where may I find Commander Zarin?'

'He's where he is every day, m' lord – in the training compound.'

'Thank you.'

Taw and Gramps set off.

The two guards looked at each other. 'Did you see that? Old Sandy a lord. Well, I never, just goes to show you.'

They proceeded down the main street until they came to the inner keep and then went off left, continuing to follow around the keep on the cobbled path, their horses' hooves occasionally causing sparks, down past the gardens and along by the orchard.

Gramps chuckled and said, 'You know this bit then?' and chuckled again.

Taw did not reply as they pulled up at a large wall, dismounted and tied the horses up.

They went to a large, arched, oak double door with a huge royal coat of arms above it. Gramps thumped on the door twice. A second later, a viewing hatch opened, and a spotty-faced boy was there.

'May I help you, sir?' he said.

'Lord Sandbite to see Commander Zarin.'

'Is he expecting you, my lord?'

'No. Just tell him, young man, that I'm here.'

'Yes, my lord,' and the hatch slammed shut.

'This is where the squires train to become knights, and the knights train,' said Taw excitedly.

'Yes, it is. Be quiet when we go in and do not stare or wander off.'

There was the clunk of an iron bolt being slid back from the door, and one half opened. A tall slim man, dressed all in black, stood just inside; his hair was grey, tied back in a ponytail with a silver ring. He was tanned and had deep brown eyes. His face was angular with a slightly pointed long nose which made his eyes look like those of a bird of prey. He smiled a big, white-teeth smile.

'Sandy! You old warhorse, you haven't changed a bit,' the man said, walking forward to greet Grandfather.

Gramps stepped forward, and they shook hands in the warriors' grip and patted each other on the back.

Gramps said, 'Well met, Rodge,' which was short for Rodger, of course. Taw suddenly realised who he was; he was Rodger the Rapier King, his unofficial title. Rumour had it he had killed over thirty men in duels, some over certain ladies' misconduct, it was said. His official title was Her Majesty's Sword Master to the realm.

After Gramps and Rodger had exchanged a few words, Gramps said, 'This is my grandson, Taw Sandbite.'

The tall man looked down and said, 'A pleasure to meet you, young man,' and offered his hand in a formal shake.

Taw took his hand and looked at him. There was that look of an eagle, as if he could see right through you and miss absolutely nothing.

'Nice firm hand there, Taw. So, Sandy, what brings you up to the Palace? You never come up anymore.'

'A letter from the Crown,' said Sandy.

'Ah yes, I've been given that pleasure too,' Rodge said as he smiled.

'I was going to ask whether young Taw here could watch the training whilst we are in this meeting.'

'So, you wish to be a knight then, Taw? It's in your blood. Your grandfather here and your father, and they were the best of them. You'll have some big shoes to fill.'

'Grandfather has been training me, sword, shield, staff, archery but says I have long ways to go.'

Both men chuckled, and the commander called over the spotty-faced boy.

'Yes, sir?'

'Take young Master Taw here over to Captain Craig with my compliments, and tell him young Taw here is allowed to watch the sword and shield training this afternoon until we return.'

'Yes, sir. Come with me, Master Taw, please.'

Taw followed the young man. Grandfather and the Sword Master walked towards the gate and out onto the cobbled road.

Captain Craig was sitting waiting for the squires to return after midday meal to resume their training. 'Captain Craig, the Commander's compliments. Would you please allow Master Taw to watch this afternoon's training session?' requested the spotty-faced boy.

The captain was a square-built man, a bit shorter than six foot, with sandy coloured hair and blue eyes. When he stood up, he looked like a house, well-muscled arms and legs and broad shoulders, and gave the impression he could rip anything apart that stood in front of him.

'Master Taw? Master Taw who?' asked the captain in a low, gravelly voice.

'Em... Sandbite. Taw Sandbite, sir,' Taw managed to splutter out.

The captain raised his eyebrows and looked Taw over.

'Captain Craig, sword and shield trainer for Her Majesty,' and held out his hand. Taw took it and thought his hand would be crushed in his. 'I know your Grandfather, and I knew your father. Best men ever to have with you in a scrape – a real hero your father, and sadly missed.

'Anyways, Taw, if you take a seat over here with me, the squires will be here any minute after their mid-day meal.'

Eric Vantor washed himself down in the cool water in the room, looking in the mirror at a wrinkled old face, beleaguered with criss-cross lines. Two green eyes, alert behind the sagging lids that come with age, together, supposedly, with wisdom, knowledge and understanding. Pah! He quickly dressed and headed downstairs for break fasting. After he had eaten his ham, eggs and bread, he made his way back to his room with the taste of the cherry tisane still in his mouth.

He stood listening for a moment. Making sure no one was around, he cast the spell of shielding. Happy now the room was protected, he opened his mind to thought-speak. 'Brothers, are you there? Can you speak?'

'Yes, we can hear you.'

'Have you discovered any more?' Vantor asked his two brothers.

'There is a feeling around each site. We can't determine what. It's like the old Dragmen, the shadows, like someone or something is watching, or coming.'

'Brothers, there are also rumours the Emperor is dead? And that some children can walk in and out of the mist.'

'The Emperor is dead; we think killed by shadows or Dragmen. We are not sure about the children, but will look.'

'Thank you, brothers. I will speak again once I have spoken at the meeting today.'

'Very well, brother; be vigilant. The Cross.'

'You two be very careful if you suspect the Dragmen or shadows are back. The Cross.'

The numbers were shouted out, 'One, two, one,' then 'one, one, two,' as the squires went through the different movements across the arena, with sword and shield. Back and forward they went for a good hour.

Taw started to get a little bored and looked around. 'Where are the knights?' he wondered, but he knew the answer. They only came here on certain days, the opposite days to the squires.

'Enough! Line up in pairs,' shouted the captain.

The squires lined up facing each other in two long rows.

'First pair, begin,' and the nearest pair began a no-holds-barred, full-on fight with wooden swords and shields, which ended when one hit the floor. Then the next pair would start, and again, the next pair and so on.

'Would you like to give it a go, Taw?' the captain asked. 'I know you're a bit young yet. How old are you, fifteen?'

'Yes, sir,' said Taw, 'and I would like to give it a try.'

'Very well, Taw. I will tell him to take it a bit easier on you. Go and get some armour on over there. Alright, positions everyone.'

The squires formed a semi-circle in front of Taw.

'This is Taw, and he has agreed to fight with sword and shield. He is only fifteen, so we'll have Squire Sam Baxter to face him. Remember what I said, take it a little easy; he is only a boy. Ready? Begin!'

Taw did not know what had hit him! Blow after blow hit him like raindrops of rocks, and he backed off under the onslaught.

Taw soon dropped his sword and was down on one knee. The captain called a halt. Taw's head and arm hurt, but he was angrier at himself. Why did he back away and cower? That's not what Gramps had taught him. Deep breath, let your opponent do the work.

'Are you alright, Taw?' said the captain.

'Yes, it just took me a little by surprise,' said Taw as he looked at the other boy, who had a smug grin on his face.

'Swords and shields away,' said the captain.

'Captain, sir, can I have another try? said Taw.

'Certainly. Baxter, are you ready? Taw, you ready? Begin.' Taw faced Baxter, his sword tight in his hand, his shield locked firmly in his forearm. He swung with all his might a right-to-left diagonal downward strike, hitting Baxter's shield with a mighty thud, making him stagger backwards under the blow. Taw felt a hammer blow on his shield, nearly knocking him to the ground, but not this time. Again Taw struck; back and forward they went.

'Stop!' shouted the captain.

Taw's arms were on fire, and he was exhausted.

'That was well fought, the pair of you, especially you, Taw. I can see your grandfather has been training you. Put your armour over there on the racks.'

Sam Baxter and Taw walked over to the racks.

Sam said to Taw, 'That was well fought for a non-squire. My name is Sam, Sam Baxter,' and held out his hand.

'Taw Sandbite,' and they shook.

'Sorry about the first fight; we were always told not to hold back.'

'That's fine; I was trying to take your head off in the second,' said Taw.

They looked at each other and laughed.

'Taw, it looks like your grandfather has not returned as yet,' said Captain Craig. 'Squire Baxter, you look after master Taw until his grandfather returns. Show him around the squires' quarters, as I think he'll be here within a couple of years.'

'Yes, sir,' and they both set off towards the building.

Chapter 3

There was a large oak table across the top and four other tables pushed end to the top one, forming a very large square table. There were six chairs on each of three sides; the top had only three, a large one in the middle and one on either side. There was a silver tray for each side, with a silver jug and goblets. Grapes, apples and cherries were in a small tray next to the water. The Sword Master and Lord Sandbite were admitted to the anteroom after giving their names and invitations to four burly guards dressed in royal blue uniforms. There were other people there that Sandy did not know.

'Take your places everyone, please,' announced Prince Marcus.

Everybody quickly moved to a place around the table. Sandy noticed there were still some empty places. Did some not make it, or were they just empty chairs?

'Her Majesty the Queen,' announced the Prince.

'Please be seated everyone,' the Queen said as she sat.

Prince Marcus remained standing. 'With your kind permission, Mother.'

'Granted.'

'Earl Vantor, it is a real pleasure to see you here. We were unsure whether you would make it. There are seats vacant as some of our guests cannot be here. May I ask...' then the door opened, and Prince Harry walked in.

'My apologies, Your Majesty,' he said. 'I only just arrived minutes ago in the kingdom.'

'Welcome home, Prince Harry, my son,' the Queen said.

Harry walked around the table, kissed his mother's cheek and sat on her left.

Marcus continued. 'Earl Vantor, if I may ask you to secure the room, please.'

Vantor stood, whispered the words of power, and a shimmer went through the room.

'It is done, Prince Marcus.'

'Good, then we may proceed. Prince Harry, as you have just returned from the Southern Kingdom, can you give us a report, please?'

Harry stood. 'The situation is grim, to say the least. Four sites have been taken over by what can only be called a red mist.

'This mist arrives from nowhere, is silent, and anyone trying to walk through it dies instantly. Some have said there is a low humming noise coming from inside, and some have said they hear screaming, but we cannot confirm any of these noises. People are fleeing the city as quickly as they can, but many are disappearing before they can leave, including children. We believe they are taken into the mist, but how and when is another question. We heard of only one child who somehow wandered out, but he is of no sense, as if his mind has been taken. The Palace has been taken over, but as yet no word of the Emperor, whether he is dead or alive. The army and military are in disarray, and some have become bandits, raiding villages outside the city. Some of our spies have also disappeared, vanished. My cousins, the Smiths, are still there, but I think we should think about pulling them all out, Your Majesty. That concludes my report.'

'Thank you, Harry,' said the Queen. 'Has anyone anything else to add?'

'Your Majesty,' Vantor said, rising. 'I have been there myself, and my two brothers are at another site. After arriving at the Emperor's Palace and the city of Darkas, they have confirmed the Emperor is dead, and we believe the royal family too. Something more disturbing is that they suspect that the Dragmen are back, or the shadows. There is no confirmation of this, but there is a feeling around each site that you're being watched very carefully by someone or something, just as the shadows used to do before they attacked in the night. One or two children have been able to wander in and out of the mist, but their minds are missing.

'Since the city of Darkas, and in particular, the Emperor's Palace, is covered, the country has fallen into anarchy. Bandits, robbers, rapists, all just running around the country. We know the Palace at the moment is covered – how long before the city is? Mons Harbour, Taddy City and the mountains of Rajh are all covered; where next?'

Earl Vantor then took a goblet of water. There was a bit of a free-for-all at the mention of Dragmen and shadows. How long before it crosses into our Kingdom? What can we do? Marcus held his hand up for silence.

'Thank you,' said Vantor. 'The first place to be taken was a little island just off the coast of the Southern Kingdom. The village was called Raging Rock; it had about eight hundred people and livestock, mainly sheep. At first, I attempted to penetrate it with mind-thought, but blank – no effect. I then tried minor spells, increasing each time in magnitude, but it again just absorbed it. So I then tried a more powerful spell.

'Just as I was about to release it, I got a thought-back, if you will, that the spell I was about to unleash would backfire on me, so I withdrew. Some of the locals fired an assortment of weapons at the red mist, but again the wall just swallowed them up. A young farmer ran at it to get to his wife. He bounced off, dead. I have been consulting with my brothers, who are investigating the other sites to confirm they are the same, which I think they will do. I would like to mention that I believe that it is the best spell I have ever seen. Only Merlot the Great may know of such a spell, if indeed it is a spell. That is about all, Your Majesty,' said Vantor and sat down.

'Thank you, Prince Harry and Earl Vantor, for your briefings. It seems to me there are a vast number of questions that still need to be answered. Would you agree, Prince Marcus?'

'Yes, Your Majesty. With your permission, Mother, we must have more intelligence before we can even think of defending ourselves. We need to know how the mist travels. Can it be seen? What is going on inside? Who or what is controlling it? These are the most important questions we need answers to.'

'Your Majesty, we have heard that some children have been able to come and go in and out of the mist but have lost their minds. Can we not maybe use the witches to try and mend the children's minds and maybe gain something? Also, is there a pattern or a strategic plan to the locations of the mist?' Lord Sandbite asked.

Sienna, Queen of the Black witches spoke. 'We are unable to help in this situation, but the Mother Superior of the Purple order may be able to assist. They have, over the centuries, been successful in mind reading and control. Maybe the child that first came out, maybe get that child to them. Possibly Earl Vantor could assist in this. I will arrange this meeting once I have spoken to Mother Superior.'

'Thank you, that sounds promising. What else have we to go on?' the Queen asked.

'At this present time, Your Majesty, we have very little more to go on. Might I suggest that we withdraw our spies, with the exception of the Smith brothers, and reconvene after the Midsummer festival? We may be in a better position to try and come up with some sort of plan by then,' said the Lord Marshal.

'Thank you, Edmond. Prince Marcus, anything to add?'

'Edmond is quite correct, not much to act on, but if Earl Vantor and Mother Superior can get something from this child or any of them, it will be invaluable to our plans, Mother.'

'Thank you all for attending today. Please remember, what you have heard here today must not leave this room. Prince Marcus, my son, will take charge of this as of today and will keep me informed.'

'Yes, Your Majesty,' said Marcus. 'Lord Vantor, will you lift the shield please and then come and see me in my chambers in about thirty minutes?'

'Of course, Prince Marcus.' Vantor stood, again whispered the words of power and the shield lifted.

The Queen, escorted by both Princes, left the room.

'Well, Zarin, what do you think of that?' said Sandy.

'I just hope the bit about the *you know who* is wrong. Don't want them coming after me. Remembering what happened to your son, Sandy. They are formidable.'

'Yes, I know, but I'd like to see this mist stuff first hand.'

'Ah! Sandy and Zarin, may I have a quick chat?' asked the Lord Marshal. 'Perhaps here,' he added and pointed to the chairs. They sat and Sandy said, 'What can we help you with, Lord Marshal?'

'Edmond, please, gentlemen. Can you bring us some cool wine?' Edmond said to a passing servant.

'Right away, sir.'

'The Prince and I have been discussing the strength of our army because we may need it before too long. We have a total of two hundred and twenty thousand mounted soldiers, thirty thousand of whom are knights, two hundred thousand bowmen, and four hundred and fifty thousand pikemen or infantry.'

'Your wine, sirs.'

'Thank you,' they said in unison.

'That's every man across the kingdom currently in the army, plus reserves. Our total, with luck, would be close on one million in the field. Our navy, according to Admiral Taylos, is two hundred and fifty-five warships, eighty-eight small attack boats. If we were to commandeer the civilian ships, we could more than double the fleet.'

'I did not think we had that many,' said Sandy.

'I actually thought we had a lot more,' said Zarin. 'Be that as it may, the Southern Kingdom could, before this, field three million troops and an armada of some two thousand warships. There are, or were, two hundred thousand in and around the Emperor's Palace and the city of Darkas. So, a major problem: is anyone running the military? Has it all disbanded, or are there pockets of military still operating as normal in the other cities? Would they want our aid? Or will they become our enemy? Now that the Emperor is dead, is the treaty also?'

'Yes, again, lots of questions and no answers, but I have been instructed by the Prince to conduct a major recruitment drive and triple our army in a year. We will need to start with the knights, as they take the longest. Instead of three years, it will be three months, and twenty thousand at a time. The rest of the army will be found also, some two million recruited. This will be across the whole kingdom.'

'Impossible. Never,' said the two of them. 'How?'

'Sienna, Queen of the Black witches, will instruct her men to train all the bowmen across the country. Every garrison will start training infantry immediately, as many as possible. The Prince has someone in mind already to do this job. No, Sandy, it's not you, before you ask. The Prince did say that he would come and see you personally. Zarin, you will, of course, be in charge of the knights' training. We will meet up again next week to discuss your progress. In the meantime, if there is anything, please just come and see me. Thank you, gentlemen. I must go now and meet with the Admiral. Good luck to you both, you old rogues,' he said as he left.

Sandy left with Zarin, but they parted when Zarin said, 'I need to catch up with Edmond. We'll talk later, Sandy.'

Sandy was deep in thought after that, thinking about the shadows. Also, what did Prince Marcus want to see him about? 'I am getting too old at fifty-five to be riding around in full armour. Maybe it is defence of the city or some other place, or possibly the northern harbour? Taw – damn, nearly forgot he is in the training arena.'

The arena was empty when he walked in, so he continued down to the squires' quarters. Taw was sitting on a long bench, talking to two boys, Sam and Errol. They stood when he entered.

'Hello, Gramps. This is Sam and Errol. They are squires here.'

'Yes. Taw, it's time for us to leave.'

'Bye, Sam, Errol. Hope to see you again.'

'Bye, Taw.'

They walked into the training arena and over to where their horses were now tethered and mounted.

'Thank you, Gramps, for taking me today. I watched them practise sword and shield, and I even had a fight with Sam, who you met earlier. It's a shame that it will be another two summers before I can apply for knighthood and attend the training.'

'Well, Taw, things are changing pretty quickly, and you never know what the morrow brings on the sun's new day.'

'Why did you never tell me, Gramps, that you were a lord? I mean a Lord of the Realm, that's next to royalty, isn't it?'

'It is a long story and a bit of a sad one too, but essentially, in the last war, your father and I ended up in the worst battle ever. We got ourselves cornered and were fighting for our lives and to protect the King. A small group of cat archers – they were called that because they were short, quick and nimble like a cat, and they fired short cross-bow bolts at a tremendous rate – anyhow, they saw us and began firing bolts at us. Your father and the King were hit in the first volley; your father was trying to protect the

King, with the rest of us around them. The cats heard the charge of the knights, so they got away and the battle was won, but not before the damage was done. The King had two fatal bolts in him and died shortly after. Your father had stood in front of the King and had four bolts in him. None were actually fatal but would be soon if not treated. He was gravely injured but fighting to stay alive. But in the night, the shadows found him, and with no protection from your mother, they murdered him. The Lord Marshal, the Sword Master and I had bolts in us, but again, none fatal, mainly in our arms and legs outside of the shields. Your father was made a Lord and myself a Lord of the Realm, but I have never used the title. I am quite happy to live where we do, rather than at some country estate and have folk calling me My Lord, Your Lordship, blah, blah.

'So now you know the most of it. Perhaps we can sit one day and talk all about it. We are just on the edge of town, and it's getting a bit late. How about we stop at the inn and have supper there this evening. Sounds good?'

'Yes, please, Gramps.'

'Come on, Taw. We'll never get anything if you don't get a move on,' shouted Dina. Taw appeared in the doorway with his bow and quiver in hand.

'Let's go, then,' and they set off at a brisk pace for Astel Forest.

'Where were you yesterday? The twins came around ours looking for you.'

'Oh, Gramps had to go to the Palace.'

'What? About you? About you getting caught?' Dina asked.

'No! Er, you don't understand. I was, was... er! You will have to swear on the Cross that you'll not tell anyone else.'

'Yeah! Taw, tell me.'

'No, this is serious. You have to swear.'

'I swear on the Cross not to tell a living soul. There!'

'Firstly, Gramps is a Lord of the Realm.'

'Ha, funny, Taw.'

'No, two soldiers turned up at Gramps's house with an invitation from the Queen to attend a meeting yesterday. They saluted him and called him Lord Sandbite, and then he told me last evening. I was in the training arena with the squires while he was in the meeting with the Queen. I did some training with the squires. It was really good. You would have enjoyed it too, but they don't have girl knights, in the – quiet, not a sound.'

'Hello, off into the woods hunting?' It was Jackus with Earthie in tow.

'Yes,' said Dina. 'What are you two up to?'

'We go to the river for a swim and catch fish while we're there.'

'I wondered how you caught them without a stick or rod,' said Taw.

'Well, we swim out to the sandy bit where it's calmer and wait. Then when the fish swim past, we flick them out onto the bank.'

'But don't you get pulled by the river?'

'No, we just stand there.'

'How can you just stand there? The water would be over your heads. It's over mine there, and I'm taller than you.'

'Don't know. We just can, can't we, Earthie?'

'Yeah, we been doing it since we were little.'

'Whatever,' said Dina. 'Come on, Taw. Let's go and hunt something. See you after mid-day.'

Further into the wood they went until Dina said, 'Taw, you look for tracks and do the hunt, and I'll watch you.'

Taw was soon on some rabbit tracks which were fresh, so he hunkered down and waited, Dina at his shoulder watching.

'Look, there! Now gently bring your bow up and notch the arrow. Breathe, Taw!' Dina whispered.

Slowly he took aim and then fired.

'You dolt, you missed!'

'I don't know how I missed. I did everything right; I'm just not as good as you.'

'No, that's not it; even an average shot should have hit it. Show me your arrows. You see that tree with the big fork near the top?'

'Yes.'

'Fire an arrow at the joint.'

Taw took up his bow and notched an arrow. Slowly releasing his breath, he fired. 'See, I told you. I missed.'

'Now try one of my arrows, here.'

Again, Taw took aim and fired. It hit the tree with a thud where he was aiming.

Dina said, 'If you look at my arrows compared to yours, what do you see?'

'I'm not sure.'

'Your cock feather is not aligned properly. If you re-do them, they will be fine, so you can use some of mine today.'

They set off home with four pigeons, five rabbits, one hare and two grouse, Taw having shot half of them, using Dina's arrows, of course.

'Earl Vantor, please take a seat. It's a long time since we have seen each other. How are you?'

'Getting old, Prince Marcus.'

'Just call me Marcus when we're alone.'

'Getting old. I am tempted to use the youth spell, but I've been around too long now. All of the people I grew up with are dead, long gone. I am, I think one hundred and twenty-two, give or take a year or so.'

'You do look a lot older than I remember. Yes, I was about twenty after the last war. Father had died, and we buried him. Shortly after, you disappeared. Would you like some wine?'

'Yes. Thank you, Marcus.'

The Prince poured two goblets and handed one to the wizard.

'Do you mind if I warm it?' he asked.

'No, not at all,' said Marcus.

Vantor moved his hand over the goblet, and steam started to rise from it. 'I find it warms the bones better,' he said. 'You have become a shrewd young prince, Marcus. How is it you have not taken your father's crown and become King yet, if I may ask?'

'Up until recently, I was not ready, and my mother is better able to manage the kingdom. We saw no need. So now, when she is ready to step down, with the kingdom stable, I will assume the throne. So, Eric, what did you want to tell me outside of the meeting that's so important?'

'You are aware I have been travelling around this world of ours, seeing many different places and wonders. I came to a kingdom called the Chindo Empire. It would take three months to cross on horseback; it is that vast. The people are shorter than us, a very simple race. Strange they are, of a yellowy colour, with the majority having black hair – no straw, brown or any other colour hair – and there are millions of them. Anyway, I was visiting one of their temples – churches, that is. The temple was a huge building, a four-posted turret in the middle, with spirals reaching up to the sky. On each corner, carved in ornate rock, was a huge what we would call a dragon.

'Once inside, there were wooden slats about two feet long and six inches wide, all the way around the outside, apart from a huge rectangle in the middle. In this, there is a picture made up of millions of tiny pieces of coloured stones. The picture is of a gold dragon on a red background. According to the monks, who have shaved heads and dress in orange and red robes, the temple was built some one thousand years ago. There is in their scribings only one mention of a so-called dragon some two thousand years before the temple was built on the site of the old one. This dragon breathed an orangey-red mist that covered whatever it came across. Hence what the monks wear.'

'Eric, that is interesting. How long does a dragon live? It would be over three thousand years old now, then? So, we could be facing a mythical, old-aged dragon?' said Marcus.

'Don't be fooled, Marcus. Dragons could live that long. I could manage a thousand, I think, with magic, so why could not a dragon, from whence all magic was born and drawn? We really don't know, but it fits with what's going on in the south. I would like your permission to send a message to the senior monk at the temple, Zing Fan Tu Wah, to come to the kingdom and bring whatever information he has on this gold dragon. It may be a myth, but we can't take the chance. It will take him near on six months to get here. Also, could he be a guest of the Palace, as I have no abode anymore? Speaking of such, may I stay in the palace too?

'Please do, Eric. The more information we have, I think, the better.'

'Marcus, I think before this is over, I will have to use that youth spell. I'm so stiff, I have aches on my aches. So, if you'll excuse me, Marcus, I'll get back to what I need to be doing.'

'Thank you, Earl Vantor!'

'My pleasure, Prince Marcus.'

Vantor walked from the Prince's quarters out into the inner keep.

He stood for a moment, then said to himself, 'I need to speak with Mother Superior of the Purple order, and then Zing Fan. My room,' he said and tapped his staff.

He appeared in his room in the inn. The fire had gone out, so a word of power lit the fire, and he sat in the chair, thinking to himself, 'The walk was too far; maybe that youth spell is really a necessity, rather than a want.'

'It's time for you to take your father's crown and become King now, son. With all that's going on, we will need a King.'

'No, Mother, I can't take the crown yet. I can do far more as the Prince now, and when this war comes, and it will come, Mother, I need to be battle planning the defence of the kingdom. I cannot be worrying about the mundane stuff around the realm. Once this war is over, I will take the crown. I'm sorry, Mother, I know this will not sit well with you, but the kingdom will need someone like you to keep it going and to survive. So, I am asking you, Mother, to remain our Queen for a little while longer.'

'For the sake of the kingdom and you, my son, of course, I will stay as Queen. So, Marcus, if I am still Queen,' she said with a big smile on her face, 'I, Queen of this Kingdom, so order you to supper this evening with Harry, Juliet, Edmond and his family. If you could make the arrangements. Thank you.'

'You're welcome, Your Majesty,' he said as he backed out of the room, bowing, with a large grin on his face.

Chapter 4

The following morning, both Princes and Princess Juliet met the Lord Marshal and the Queen in the anteroom. They sat around a small table.

'I have called this meeting as we are the head of this kingdom, and within a short time, we all know we may be at war. We need to start to allocate people to jobs, some jobs of power and some critical to the defence of the Palace. We need to have, I think, three levels of command.

'Level one: all of us, Queen Sienna, Admiral Taylos, Earl Vantor, Mother Superior of the Purple order, Commander Zarin and Lord Sandbite. Level two: as for one, plus the other leaders, including the civilian leaders. Level three will include all of levels one and two, and whoever else we may need there,' Prince Marcus said.

'The Palace is the last place we should have the meetings. What if the mist comes here and traps us all, pretty much like what's happened in the south? All the leaders gone in one swoop,' Edmond said.

'Good point, but where do you suggest?'

'I have an idea,' said Juliet. 'What about the old ruined church on the hill? I believe that the catacombs beneath the city spread out and that one of them goes to the church. Could we use that?'

'That's a great idea. Can you make sure we get the route cleared and marked, then set up underneath the church, so nobody knows we are there,' said Marcus. 'Also, Edmond, I need to look to hospitals and treatment of the injured and disposal of the dead. If you have anyone in mind, just let me know.'

'I think my wife will be interested. I will ask.'

'Mother and Edmond, can I count on you for the defence of the city, to organise meetings of city leaders, and all things therein? Prince Harry will return with some more spies, when or with whom we haven't decided yet, have we, Harry?'

'No, Marcus.'

'Myself, I will oversee the Army and Navy and the recruitment across the kingdom. The Sword Master, Zarin, will be responsible for all knights' training and recruitment. Lord Sandbite I want to set up and train a special spy force with Harry. I will go and speak to Sandy. We need him to take up his title and skills. He can move into the west wing,' Marcus said.

Juliet added, 'Brother, you know he has his grandson who lives with him? I met him. He was caught stealing in the orchard.'

'Will that be a problem?' the Queen asked Marcus.

'That should not be a problem, Mother. How old is he, old enough for squire school?'

'No, brother, I don't think so.'

'I'm sure we can find something, say, schooling with the monks. We need Sandy, and I mean to use his skills,' said Marcus with authority in his voice. 'Has anyone got anything else? No? Can we set a meeting for the day after celebrations for Midsummer's?'

'Edmond, can you arrange, please?' asked the Queen.

'I'm going to take a leisurely ride to Sandy's after mid-day meal, Mother, with your permission, and speak directly to him.'

'Thank you all,' the Queen said as she rose and walked away.

Gramps was putting them through sword and shield training: Taw, Josh, the twins and Dina.

'Dina, use your reach,' Gramps shouted. 'Jackus! Shield, shield,' just before Taw knocked it out of his hand. 'Earthie, you're dead again. Nice thrust, Dina.' Gramps looked up and saw three riders approaching the house.

'Carry on with what you're doing. Don't look at me; you'll get your head chopped off.'

The riders dismounted at the fence, and the lead rider handed his reins over to one of the others. They were dressed in plain black jackets, which crossed over the front and fastened in a row of black buttons down the right side of the chest, with a high collar and epaulettes all edged in red piping, black trousers with red piping down the outside leg and full riding boots. The lead rider wore a rapier on his left and a red sash; the other two had cavalry sabres. The leader walked to the gate. He had a large badge on his left breast and a hat with a red flash on it. As Grandfather walked to the gate to greet them, he looked up and recognised who it was had come to call.

'Your Majesty,' Gramps said, bowing. 'It is an honour and an unexpected one.'

'Thank you, Lord Sandbite. May we talk inside, Sandy, if that's convenient?'

'Of course we can, Your Majesty.'

'You two wait here,' the Prince said to his guards.

The group stopped their practice and stood by the woodshed.

Taw looked. 'That's Prince Marcus, and those are the Prince's special guards, the elite. What was the Prince talking to Gramps about?'

'Something's going on,' said Jackus. 'Maybe it's about us getting caught and being let off lightly by the Princess?'

'Don't say that. I don't want a flogging,' said Josh.

'So, Your Majesty.'

'Please, Sandy, call me Marcus when we are alone.'

'Very well. Marcus, would you like a drink? I have some nice cold mead.'

'Yes, that would be nice. Thank you. I know you're itching to know why I am here, Sandy, so I will tell you straight.'

'Your drink, Marcus.'

'Thank you.'

'The Cross,' Sandy said.

'The Cross,' echoed the Prince as they toasted. 'Well, you were at the meeting, so you know what we're facing or what's coming. No one outside of that meeting knows anything as yet, but that will change; word will spread. I will cut to the chase. I want you to be who you are, Lord Sandy Sandbite, commander and trainer of the Prince's elite special forces. I want you to move into the west wing, and I want two hundred Sandbite-trained soldiers in six months. You will have your pick across the kingdom from any garrison, including my own special guards. Weapons, training, whatever you need will be available. What do you say?'

'There are some things I need to think about, Marcus. Can I refuse?'

'You can, but I would consider it a great personal favour if you accepted.'

'There is my grandson, Taw, and when would all this start?'

'I would like you to begin straight away, but we can wait until after Midsummer's celebrations. As for your grandson, you and he would move into the west wing in the Palace. He can be schooled with the monks and maybe enter squire training early. Oh, and of course, you will be paid.'

'In that case, Your Majesty, I will come and train your elite force after Midsummer's.'

'Thank you, Sandy. Now, I must be off to attend to other duties.'

The Prince rose and started to walk towards the gate. 'Oh, just one other thing, Lord Sandbite!'

'Your Majesty?'

'As of tomorrow, you *will* wear your rank and dress in the uniform of the elite forces. I will send the tailor around to you on my return, and that's not a request.' He was saying as he rode off, 'No need to thank me, Lord Sandbite!'

The townspeople had started to gather around in little groups, looking at Grandfather and the meeting with the Prince.

'Thank you, Your Majesty,' shouted Gramps back at the Prince.

Gramps looked across at the children. 'Who said you could stop? Get on with it!'

'Yes, I've had a meeting with the Prince; the show is now over. Go back to your business,' shouted Gramps at the townspeople.

'Morning Greetings to you, Mother Superior Alice,' Earl Eric Vantor said in a formal voice as he was shown into a small room with just a table and two chairs.

'It is a long time since we last met, Earl Vantor, and my opinion of you has not changed in the slightest.'

'You haven't changed either, Alice. A bit older, like me, but still very beautiful and a tongue like a viper. But I haven't come here to trade niceties with you. The Prince and the kingdom have asked for your help. You are aware of what is happening in the Southern Kingdom?'

'Yes, we are aware, maybe a bit more than you, but what can we do for you and the Prince?'

'There are a number of children that have somehow managed to wander in and out of the red mist without dying. However, it seems that their minds are affected or completely gone; we don't know. We need to get one of these children and see whether we can help them by repairing the damage. Before it is too late. Then they may be able to tell us what is going on inside the red mist.'

'So you want me and my sisters to probe the child's mind? You do realise it takes a strong adult to be unaffected by the mind-probing? It is very aggressive to attempt to use it on a child. And to bring the horrors that they have seen flooding back to them; it could easily kill a child.'

'I do, and the Prince is aware how dangerous it could be, but the child is brain-dead as it is. Unless you can do something, the child will recover or die, and either way, the odds are the same, brain-dead or just dead.'

'I will seek the Prince's advice and come back to you.'

'So, what of you, Alice? Have you been here since we parted after the War?'

'Yes, I have, but that is of no concern of yours.'

'I see,' said Vantor. 'If the Prince wants this to happen, I will come for you, Alice, but I can only take four with me on the journey there.'

'Good day to you, Earl Vantor,' she said, and she left the room, leaving Vantor on his own with a bitter taste in his mouth.

Why had she refused to go travelling with him around the world? They had been young and had plenty of time for raising a family. Now they were old and had no family, but he'd seen the world.

'Harry, something is puzzling me. There are four sites that are covered by the red mist, correct?'

'Yes, Marcus.'

'So, does that mean we are dealing with four dragons or just one? If, indeed, we are dealing with a dragon at all. But it's imperative that we find out. We need to know, but how, Harry? How do we find this out? Is there really a dragon, Harry?'

'I think it may be as you said. We will have to use the children. We really don't like it, but we have no other way. We will need the information before the next meeting on the Monaday after the Midsummer's celebrations.'

'Very well, Harry, I agree. Get hold of Earl Vantor and tell him to tell the Purple sisters to probe the child or children, as we may need. But only enough to provide the information, and remember, we need it now. We cannot plan anything until we know whether we face one dragon or four, or something else.'

The boy's mother, Martha, and her husband, Sid, had fled the city and the kingdom when Dominic, their son, had somehow wandered out of the red mist. They took him and ran with him and their meagre possessions for the border. There was nothing special about the family; the mother worked in a local bathhouse, and the father was a farmer's hand. They had sought refuge in a small town called Tarvin and were staying in a barn of a local farmer.

'Alice, it's me, Eric.'

'Yes, I know who it is. What do you want?'

'The Prince has authorised the use of the child, so I need you to see the child.'

'Eric, you will have to bring the child here so I can work on him with the help of the other sisters.'

'Understood. I will be there early evening with him.'

'We will be ready.'

Considering Vantor was a wizard, he really disliked vaporising from one place to another, but he had no choice. He had to get to Tarvin and back with the child today, as he had no idea how long it would take or even whether they would be able to get any information from the boy. He pictured the town of Tarvin, the dusty road heading north out of town. 'That'll do,' he thought. He spoke the words of power, tapped his staff and arrived on the road out of Tarvin. Good thing there was nobody about, as when he just appeared, people made the sign of the Cross and ran away.

'Ah, there's the inn a couple of hundred yards away. A quick ale and the queasiness will be gone, and then I can get directions to this farm.'

Vantor arrived at the farm. The boy was like a shadow, just sitting there. Not talking, eating, drinking, his parents doing all for him. Vantor explained to the parents he was taking the boy to the Mother Superior of the Purple order to help the boy recover. After a little persuading and a bag of gold, they agreed he could go with the wizard. If he should survive and be normal, he could return home; if not, then the gods be merciful.

'I hate it when you do that, Vantor. You could have called first! You know: "Hello, I'll be there in a minute." No. The High Wizard entry – bang, you're there.'

'I did say I'd see you this evening!'

'We will take the boy now. Call in the morning.'

'Thank you, Alice.'

'Don't thank me yet. We may just kill him.'

'Taw.'

'Yes, Gramps.'

'We need to talk about some things, and I need to tell you now. You already know I am a Lord of the Crown. Well, as of today, I have to wear my rank and the uniform of the Prince's elite special forces. After the Midsummer's celebrations, we will be moving into the west wing to live.'

'Live in the Palace, Gramps? Why?'

'I am taking up a new post for the Prince. I am going to command and train a new Prince's elite special force. You will be schooled by the monks who school the squires, and maybe they will get you into squire training earlier than in two years. There is stuff happening at the moment that I can't tell you about. Trust me, boy, when I say you will know soon enough.'

Chapter 5

Dominic sat huddled into a tiny corner. The cave was very dark and cold. He had come as far back as he could. He could no longer see the entrance; in fact, he could not see anything at all. He knew it was there, just waiting, watching. It could see the tiniest thing, hear the slightest sound, then its huge claws would pick him up and he would be chewed as a little treat. That's what children are – little treats. The screams, the terrifying screams as it watched them, children torn limb from limb, its giant tongue licking them as they screamed in terror. But now the silence was back: the rest before meals. The silence and the dark, the screams and the claws. Don't move; it will see you. The silence and the dark, be still.

There, a speck of light. No, he was seeing things; it's gone. There, a tiny speck of light, there? No! The silence and the dark will keep me safe.

'D o m i n i c,' a voice said. 'D o m i n i c.'

There, the light again, a whisper in the cave.

'Dominic,' it said. 'Dominic, you're safe. Come to the light.'

No, it's a trick. The silence and the dark, the silence and the dark, it wants you to move.

'Dominic, you are safe now. Come to the light, come to the light,' a woman's voice said, not the gravelly tones of a dragon.

Am I awake? Am I dreaming? I am dead and waiting to face judgement.

'Dominic, come to the light. You are safe,' the voice said again.

I don't want to move; it will find me, silence and the dark.

'Can you hear me, Dominic? If you can, speak to me so I can find you. Can you hear me?'

'*Yes*! I can,' he heard himself say in a quick, snappy way.

Alice recoiled as the voice hit her.

'I've found him, sisters. He is deep within the fears of his mind. I'm going to try and push further. I need your strength, sisters. I'm going to try and appear to him and guide him out, but we can't break. If we do, he will be lost in his mind forever. Are we ready? Sister Shannon, I want you to visualise me as a White Nun of the Cross. Keep that thought.

'The rest, just please hold together and release your power to me. Can you hear me, Dominic? I'm coming to help you; you are safe now.'

He wanted to answer: 'But the dragon will come.'

'Can you see the light, Dominic? I'm coming to help you.'

'I can see the light, but you are very far away.' His voice was just a whisper.

'That's alright. I'm coming.'

'But the dragon will see and hear. Go away!' *The silence and the dark.*

'The dragon is no more. Dominic, look to the light. Do you know what a White Nun looks like?'

'Yes, I do, but...'

'Picture me, Dominic, the White Nun. Look, I am here, take my hand.'

Dominic looked up, and there in bright white was a Nun of the Cross, the long black cross on her skirt. He was safe.

'Take my hand. Come home with me. You have been in the dark too long.'

He reached out for her hand, and his world swam.

Dominic awoke in a room. It was lit by a small window allowing the sunshine in. He was in a bed with a grey blanket over him. He tried to sit up, but a voice said, 'It's alright, Dominic. Don't try to move just yet. I am Mother Superior Alice, and you are in my care. You are safe here. Eat some food, drink plenty of water, and rest if you can.'

'You are the voice of the White Nun,' he said.

'Yes, Dominic, I am. Rest now.'

'Eric, can you hear me?'

'Yes, Alice.'

'The boy is back and resting. One thing, the dragon of gold is very much real.'

'Thank you, Alice. I will let the Prince know.'

Lord Sandbite and Taw walked from their home down the street towards the blacksmith's for his horse. The townsfolk were looking at him strangely.

'Good morning, Sandy... Er, your lordship?'

They were unsure about what to say.

Gramps just said, 'I'm still Sandy, but you'll have to call me My Lord from now on – when I'm in uniform, that is.'

'Morning, Henry,' said Gramps.

'Morning, Sandy. My, don't we look smart!'

'Don't say anything. It's the Prince's idea, as I'm now back in his service. Alright if I collect the old horse and if Taw stays with you? I'm off into the Palace.'

'Of course, Sandy. Taw, you will find them in the barn, I think.'

'Thank you, Henry. I will see you later,' Gramps said and set off towards the Palace.

Prince Marcus, Earl Vantor and a squad of six royal guards rode out of the Palace just as Lord Sandbite arrived.

'Good of the morning, Lord Sandy. I trust that you are well?'

'I am, Your Majesty,' he said, looking down at his uniform with a face of disapproval.

'Don't worry, Sandy, you'll get used to it,' said the Prince with a grin. 'We are travelling to see Mother Superior at the Convent of the Purple order. It seems that she and her sisters have got through to the boy, Dominic, who wandered out of the mist. Why don't you join us, Sandy? It could prove to be very interesting.'

'As Your Majesty commands,' Sandy said. He wheeled his horse around, and the troop set off at a canter.

Suddenly, Earl Vantor pulled up his horse and almost fell off. He dismounted and sat on the ground. Everybody pulled up and came back around to him. The Prince and Sandy dismounted.

'Are you alright, Eric?' said Sandy.

'Just give me a second; I've just had a major shock.'

'Would you like some water, sir?' asked one of the soldiers.

'Yes, please.' Vantor took some water and drank deeply. 'That's better, thank you.'

'What is it, Eric?' said Marcus.

'You are aware that my brothers are investigating the sites covered in red mist. The first covered was Darkas, the city, in particular the Palace. Well, that was their last to visit before heading home.'

'Yes, and?'

'Well, it's gone.'

'What do you mean, gone?'

'I've been sent a vision by my brothers. No red mist, and the Palace, thousands of people, animals, everything is gone apart from piles of rubble. Where once a grand palace and hundreds of homes and businesses were, they are no more. Nearly a half-mile round, a vast flat area of rubble. My brother, Luke, sent it as a vision to me. I'm sorry, Your Majesty, it was just a real shock.'

'We need to move quickly. Are you alright to ride, Eric?'

'Yes, I'm better now, Your Majesty.'

'Can you send a reply to your brothers?'

'Yes.'

'Can they transport like you?'

'Yes, both of them can, Your Majesty.'

'Good. Can you tell them to meet us at the Purple Convent?'

'It is done.'

'Good. Let's make all haste to the convent.'

Dina, Josh and Taw were in the barn stacking the bales of hay for the winter when the twins showed up.

'Ha! Ha! Taw's working for a change,' and they started to laugh.

'Very funny,' he said.

'Make sure you stack them right. We don't want them falling down in the winter and getting wet,' shouted Henry.

'Come on, you two. Give us a hand, then we can go do something else,' said Dina.

'Oh, alright. Come on, Earthie. Let's help them.'

It wasn't long before they had finished and half of the barn was full; the second lot would be there at the end of summer.

'Mid-day,' said Taw. 'Let's go down to the baker's and get a batch with creamy cheese on.'

'Good idea,' said Josh. 'I'm hungry.'

'Where are we going to meet up in the morning?' Jackus said. 'We will have to be there when it's still dark if we have to be at the Palace at first light. What about the inn, the Cross Axes?'

'Yeah.'

'I'm coming too,' said Dina.

'Why? You did not get caught,' said Earthie.

'I would have done if Father had not got me putting out the washing. Besides, the Games Master won't complain. An extra basher, and he doesn't have to pay them, either.'

They got their mid-day meal from the baker's and went over to the large willow tree to eat it.

'Taw, what's going on with your grandfather?' Dina asked. 'He's now wearing the uniform of the Prince's royal elite and has the title of Lord.'

'I can't tell you yet. I promised Gramps not to say anything. What I can tell you is that he is forming and taking command of an elite special forces group of soldiers for the Prince. Gramps has been a lord for a long time, but he never told me about it or ever used it when he came back from the war. That's all I can tell you.'

Dominic sat on a long bench at a long table. He thought this must be where the sisters ate their meals. This was the first time out of his room. He'd been told he was going to meet some people who wanted to talk to him, and then he could go home to his family once he'd done so. Dominic wanted to get up and walk around and look out of the windows, but they were so high he would never reach them.

The doors creaked at the end of the room, and some people came walking in, the White Nun, an old man with a black walking staff and a young man, well-dressed and carrying a sword.

'Don't be alarmed, Dominic,' said the White Nun, and they sat down opposite him, with her in the middle. 'This is Prince Marcus, and this is Earl Vantor of the Astel Kingdom. They just want to ask you some questions. Don't be afraid; it's alright.'

Dominic sat at first frozen in his chair. A prince and an earl wanted to talk to him?

'We just want to ask, do you remember how you got into the red mist?' Vantor asked.

'Er, I don't, Majesty, sir, I... can't think, no.'

'Perhaps if we had something to drink, it would make things easier, don't you think, Mother Superior?' said the Prince.

'Of course, Your Majesty,' she said. 'Eric, do you think our guest here is relaxed enough? He looks a little tired.'

'Do you feel a little tired?' Vantor asked the boy.

Dominic looked at Vantor. 'I am tired.'

'Do you feel sleepy? Close your eyes; you are asleep. When I say: "Awake," you will awake and feel good and answer my questions. "Awake." He is ready, Marcus. We don't have long.'

The Prince and Vantor questioned the boy as much as they could. Some useful information, but still not enough.

'He will walk to his bed, and when he awakes, he'll remember very little of this. I will ask Luke or David to take him home. They should be here by now.'

'So the mist just swirls up like a wall, trapping all inside. Anyone trying to walk through dies. People running everywhere screaming, but nowhere to go. Then the most interesting bit: what the boy described could only be a dragon, a huge, gold creature breathing this red mist. So, we know that's true, but we don't know if there is only one, and that's a real problem. We also have no idea how he got out, how he walked through the red mist. For the first time, Eric, I'm concerned we won't be able to fight this dragon, and all will be lost.'

'There is always a way, Your Majesty.'

'This is a good one, Eric. Even you've got to admit to this one. A gold, silent dragon flies in; nobody sees or hears it. It breathes red mist all around, trapping people inside, then lands and devours everything inside, then leaves. But four places were attacked, not all at once but close together. So, are there four of them? How can we fight four? More importantly, where has the one from the Palace gone? And where will it strike next? Sorry, old friend, we end up with more questions than answers again.'

'Good day to you, Sister,' Luke said as he stood at the doors to the convent. 'We are to meet with Prince Marcus and Earl Vantor here this morning.'

'Please wait here,' and she shut the door. A moment later, another sister opened the door.

'Good morning, gentlemen, and who are you?'

'I am Luke Vantor, and this is David Vantor. Earl Eric Vantor is our brother.'

'Please come in and follow me.'

Down the poorly lit corridor they went and into a little room.

Eric stood. 'Your Majesty, these are my brothers, Luke and David.'

'Nice to meet you both,' said Prince Marcus. 'It is strange; I thought you would be older.'

'We look good for one hundred and fifteen and one hundred and sixteen, but then again, Your Majesty, we cheat and use the youth spell, unlike our brother here.'

'Ah, that will explain it then. You've met Lord Sandbite, I take it?'

'Yes, Your Majesty.' They walked out into the courtyard of the convent.

'Did you get much information, Your Majesty?' Sandy asked.

'Yes, some but not enough. That seems to be the order of the day, not enough. Luke, you sent Eric a vision of what was left of the Southern Palace. Can you describe it to me?'

'I can do better, Your Majesty. With your permission, I can show you.'

'You can? How?'

'Just close your eyes and prepare yourself.'

The Prince closed his eyes and felt a hand grip his forehead.

'Ready?'

Pow! There it was; he was looking at it. Luke removed his hand, and the Prince opened his eyes.

'Merciful be the gods in heaven,' said the Prince. 'It is like a burnt desert of rubble.'

'Prince Marcus, Luke and David will take Dominic home. I will need to go and see the brothers of the Green order. We will all be present for the meeting on Monaday after the celebrations. If Your Majesty could refrain from doing anything until I return. Thank you, Your Majesty,' Eric Vantor said.

Chapter 6

The Games Master looked as you would expect him to look: big, burly, long-haired and bearded. He stood on the cart and shouted:

'Welcome to the Prince's Hunt, and you are the bashers. Some of you have done it before; others have not. So, I want you to pair up new and old, as we don't want anyone getting shot by mistake by one of those lords. We start at the red tape at Mills Hill path, with a line stretching out across the two fields, keeping an eye on each side of you. Listen to me for the pace, and if I say, "Stop!" then stop. We set off at the sound of three trumpets. Everybody understand?'

The twins, Josh, Dina and Taw all shouted with the rest. They spread out across the countryside and were waiting to start. Dina and Taw were at the top end with a fellow called Billy. Dina knew him and told Taw he was known as a poacher but had not been caught.

'He poaches the prince's deer. If they catch him, they will chop off his hand; second time, his head.'

Taw was just about to say something when the first trumpet blast sounded, followed by two more blasts.

'Let's go! Start making a noise and walking,' someone was shouting behind them.

The Prince was with other lords, high rankings and visitors of the realm when the trumpets sounded the start, but Marcus's mind was not on the hunt. He set off with the others for the start, but he was still pondering about the meeting with the boy, the wizards and the vision and postponing the meeting for three days, until Earl Vantor would be back. But questions remained: how did the boy get out? Something about the red mist, children walking in and out. How? Were they ill? No. Because they were children? No, because they were a treat for the dragon, so why could they go in and out of the mist? We are missing something, the children and the red mist. It is imperative we find out how this is possible, but how? We can't just send children in and expect them to walk out again, can we? Marcus had so many questions in his head.

'Your Majesty, a deer to your right.' The Prince shot, but the deer was well gone.

'I'm sorry, gentlemen, my mind is at present not on the hunt, and it should be. Would you gentlemen like to carry on and excuse me from this morning's hunt? I will join you later in the day.'

A chorus of 'Your Majesty' was heard as the Prince turned his horse and set off in the direction of the Palace.

The Prince found a path and continued to trot along, still asking questions in his mind about the boy, when a stag jumped out from the left and disappeared into the bushes on the right. It startled his horse, which reared up, throwing the Prince backwards, and he landed heavily on the ground. His head throbbed as if it had been hit on an anvil; his left side also hurt like hell. He managed to stand up; his vision was blurry. If he could just get to his horse... He managed to walk a few paces, his hip and left side burning with pain, and he couldn't see clearly.

'Ah, there's my horse, over there.' He turned towards it, but he could not see, and there was no pain. The Prince fell unconscious to the floor.

The day's bashing went really slowly, through the fields and brush and finally into the outer edge of the forest. Rumour had it that the Prince had left late morning and had not returned, so what a waste of time it had been.

'The Prince's Hunt with no Prince,' Taw laughed.

So did Dina. She said, 'Anything decent worth hunting is well gone by now. Just some scrawny birds, and there was only one decent shot out of all of them.'

There was a long blast on the trumpet, which signalled the end of the hunt and bashing for them.

The Games Master called them all together. 'Right,' he said, 'those on punishment, give your names to my yard boy, Richard, there, payments to me, and anybody else, go home. Thank you all for not getting yourselves killed today.'

They walked over to give their names to the yard boy and were surprised to see about twelve others lining up to give their names also. They were the last in line to give their names. While they were waiting, Josh asked if they were all going to the Queen's tournaments the next day. All of them said yes, saying they would be up early, as jobs needed to be done before they could set off.

They had been walking and chatting for about half an hour and dusk was approaching when they heard the sound of lots of horses ahead. Soon enough, a whole company, about one hundred men, came cantering towards them, Prince Harry and Lord Sandbite at the front. The column of soldiers halted.

'Hello, Gramps. What's the matter? Sorry, Your Majesty,' said Taw as he noticed it was Prince Harry.

'Your Majesty, this is Taw, my grandson, his friends Dina, Joshua, and Earthie and Jackus, the twins. You were bashing today, were you not?' said Gramps.

'Yes, it was our punishment, Gramps, but you know this,' said Taw.

'Well, what you might not know is that Prince Marcus is missing. It was only discovered about thirty minutes ago when the stable hand found his horse in the courtyard. We know he left the hunt just before the mid-day meal, which means he's been missing for several hours. We'd better be off.' The Prince signalled, and they continued down the path.

Taw turned to Dina. 'You're the best tracker I know. Could we not find him?'

'I don't know. It will be dark in a couple of hours.'

'We could at least try for an hour,' said Joshua.

'Alright then,' said Dina.

'We will split up,' said Jackus.

'We? No, we will not split up. That way, we will all end up lost. Gather round,' said Dina. 'Just before mid-day meal, where were we?'

'We were on the open ground heading towards the forest,' said Taw.

'They would have been a lot slower in the forest the further they got in, so I reckon he was not far from Bellies Troth, so we should start there. It will take us about fifteen minutes if we cut across through Thickets Strip.'

'We'll get ripped to bits trying to get through there,' said Josh.

'Ah,' said Dina, 'but there are holes along it where boars, foxes and even badgers crawl through. We're filthy anyway, and it will save us thirty minutes not going all the way to the bottom and back up.'

Plan made, they set off to rescue a prince, if they ever found him.

Vantor appeared in the woods just short of the inn where his brothers were staying. He walked down and into the inn; it was an average place. He took a look around. There were Luke and David, sitting at a table.

He walked over and sat down. 'I got your message. Why is this so important?'

'I have ordered us some ale and some supper,' said David. 'We will tell all soon, but let's eat and drink first.'

After they left the inn, David said, 'We took the boy home, and we thought we would take a look around by the harbour and maybe find some information. We did. We can confirm that it is only one dragon, a very ancient one, like from the time of the gods. It is huge and has colossal magical power. It flies silently at speed and breathes a red mist. Once awakened, it marks off territories with red mist, then comes back and devours the buildings, like the Palace.'

'So, it is one dragon. How do we destroy it or send it back from whence it came?' asked Eric.

'Ah,' said Luke. 'We may be able to help there, too. We were in another inn about a day away from Mons Harbour, and a few local fishermen were chatting. They were a little suspicious of us at first, but we got to talking, and an old boy told us of this old tale. A huge fire mountain on the other side of the Great Sea exploded with a great blast, shooting boulders, flames and liquid fire out of it. The smoke went all the way up to the gods. Such was the blast from the mountain that the earth heaved and moved. This caused the sea to rise up into a massive wall of water, and it set off across the ocean. The wall of water hit an island and washed over it. When the water went down, the island was completely gone; all that was left was a red mist. That was four months ago.'

'Now that is an interesting tale. It actually fits with some of the books I've been reading. It stated that the four gods of the elements, Earth, Air, Fire and Water, imprisoned a gold dragon of immense power in a mountain. So if we presume this is that very dragon that's now escaped, how do we stop it devouring the world when there are no gods anymore? We need confirmation for the Prince, but how do we get it and where from? I can't go to him with tales from drunken sailors and stories of dragons.

'The Book of Histories in the Great Library refers to Jerome's Jewel. It states, "The jewel that was red will turn to blue when next the red mist plagues the earth." So, we need to know what Jerome's Jewel is, where it is now and whether it has turned blue. We need answers, brothers, and by the day after Midsummer's, Monaday. I am going to the Great Library to see if they have anything in their crypt as theirs, I believe, dates back to the Roman Era. If one of you goes to the witches and tries to find out anything about this jewel, the other can try some other towns and villages for information. We will meet up again the Sunaday evening in the Cross Axes. Good luck to you and the Cross.'

'The Cross,' and each of them vanished.

Dina said, 'We're looking for a set of hoofprints that have gone off on their own towards the Palace, which is roughly that way.'

'It's starting to get dark,' Josh said to his sister.

'We'll carry on for another fifteen minutes or so, then we will set off home.'

'Over here! Hoofprints going through the brush,' said Jackus.

They all came and looked.

'This looks more like it,' said Dina. 'Let's follow these. Keep looking either side to see if he has fallen.' They followed the tracks, but it was getting darker now.

'Here, here's a bow,' said Joshua.

'Ok, look around for anything else. This is the Prince's,' said Dina. 'It's beautiful and worth a fortune.'

'Prince Marcus!' they shouted as they wandered along. 'Prince Marcus,' but no reply.

'I've found him,' shouted Taw. 'He's here.'

The Prince was face down with blood on the back of his head. Dina and Taw checked to see whether he was alive.

'He's got a very nasty cut on his head, and he's very cold,' said Dina. 'Earthie, Jackus, build us a fire. Josh, help us.'

They turned the Prince over and propped up his back, and Dina set about bandaging his head. They placed spare clothing over him, and the fire was going.

'What do we do?' said Josh. 'It's too dark to go and get help, and we can't move him while he is unconscious.'

'We need some sort of shelter. Twins, get to it. Josh, help too. Taw, can you remember your way back to Thickets Strip?'

'Yes, I think so, but in the dark?'

'My head hurts,' said the Prince, raising his hand towards his head.

'Don't touch, Your Majesty. You have a nasty cut to your head. I have bandaged it for you, but I can't stitch it. Here, sip this. It will do you some good. Are you hurt anywhere else, Your Majesty?' Dina asked.

'I think my left side and hip. But who are you?'

'Sorry, Your Majesty. I am Dina. These are Taw, Earthie and Jackus, the twins, and my brother Joshua. You were thrown off your horse and have been missing all day. Everyone's been out looking for you.'

'How come then you found me?'

'We were bashing, and it had finished. Dina can track anything,' said Taw.

'Even princes, it would seem.'

'Well, yes, Your Majesty. It wasn't that hard, really. Taw, if you take a torch and make your way to Thickets Strip and then down to Bellies Troth, do you think you can find the main track to the Palace from there? And there may still be some soldiers out looking,' said Dina.

'Yes, but I will have to go around the Strip. I'd never make it through in the dark, so it will take me some time.'

'We will be alright here, so go and get help.'

'Taw, when you find help, tell them to bring my coach, as I don't think I can ride a horse just yet.'

'Yes, Your Majesty. Oh, you might want to put some torches out on the track in about an hour so I can find you.'

'Yes, Taw.'

He set off, but it was a slow pace, and the ground in the dark was difficult, but he plodded on until he got to the strip. 'Not that far now,' he said to himself, plodding on towards Bellies Troth. 'That's the main track to the Palace. That's great. I'm so tired.' He carried on walking for some way, then saw torches in the distance coming toward him. They were obviously mounted soldiers.

The Prince sat talking to the group, and he laughed when they told him the story of being caught in the orchard, supposedly for stealing fruit, when all they wanted was to watch the knights training and ended up with a day's bashing. Now it had turned out to be the longest day of all.

'So, Dina, you're a good tracker and, so I've heard, a jolly good shot too, and you all seem to be quite a good team when you're together.'

Taw stood in the middle of the track as the horses approached, waving his arms.

Two columns of soldiers stopped, and a sergeant said, 'What do you want, boy, standing in the middle of the track like that?'

'We have found the Prince,' said Taw.

The sergeant looked at Taw. Scruffy, dirty, unwashed street urchin. 'Get out of the way, boy, before I have you flogged, and if I see you again, it will be a clout around the ear. Now, be off with you. Forward!' he shouted.

Taw reached out and grabbed the reins on his horse.

'My name is Taw Sandbite. I am the grandson of Lord Sandy Sandbite. Do you know the name, Sergeant?' asked Taw, with all the steel in his voice he could muster.

'I. Er... I do.'

'Then believe me when I say that my friends and I have found Prince Marcus. You need to send word back to the Palace to bring the Prince's coach to Bellies Troth. We are not sure if the Prince can ride. The rest will need to follow me to mark the route from Bellies Troth and then on to where the Prince is.'

'If you're telling us lies, boy, I will make sure you hang,' said the sergeant.

Taw said, 'In that case, we leave the Prince there, and they will hang you instead when they find him, and find you left him there!'

'Well then, we'd better see, but be warned, boy! You four there, ride with all speed to the Palace and inform Prince Harry and the Lord

Marshal. Ask them to meet us at Bellies Troth with the Prince's coach. Go now. You climb up here with us, and let's get to Bellies Troth.'

'Sergeant, we need to line the route from Bellies Troth with soldiers with torches, so they can find us.'

'One soldier, every ten yards with a torch, from here,' shouted the sergeant.

It was not long until they saw the fire.

'Over there,' said Taw.

They pulled up and dismounted.

'I'm back, Dina, with help,' said Taw.

'That seemed quick,' said the Prince. 'Well done, you.'

'Your Majesty,' said the sergeant, 'how are you? Real glad we found you.'

'Thanks to these young people, I am alive, I think. Let's see if I can stand and walk.' The Prince stood, but he was clearly in pain. 'At least the dizziness has gone,' he said with a smile.

The sergeant and a soldier helped the Prince over towards the horse.

'Let me sit down,' said the Prince. 'There is no way I will be able to get on the horse, never mind ride it.'

'The coach will not be able to get up here either,' said Taw. 'We need to find a way to get His Majesty further down towards the path.'

'Wait, I've got it!' said Dina. 'We could use the wheel chair.'

'Wheel chair?' said the Prince.

'Your Majesty, it is four strong poles, interlocked into a square in the middle. You sit on the square, and four people take a pole each and carry you. We use it for moving broken wheels at my father's forge. Taw, Earthie, grab four decent branches,' which they did and fastened them into a chair.

'Well, I never,' said the Prince and laughed with the astonished sergeant.

They carried him through the brush towards Bellies Troth and the path.

When they got to the path, the soldiers took over carrying the Prince, with them walking behind. A line of torches approached them, and Prince Harry and the Lord Marshal pulled up to a halt, with the coach behind them and a troop of soldiers.

'Nice to see you, Harry,' said Marcus.

'Your Majesty,' said the Lord Marshal. 'Glad to see you alive.'

'Thank you both. Now lend me a hand and get me into the coach. The children will travel with me in the coach,' Prince Marcus said. 'Come on, in you get.'

Once they were all in, they set off towards the Palace, glad the day was over.

Chapter 7

The Dragon of Desolation is the Mother of all Dragons. She can never die, for she is immortal. She is the birth of all dragons under the stars of the heavens and is made of pure, unadulterated magic. Earth, Air, Fire and Water, combined with the Blue Jewel of Dragonite, for the blue flames are her only weakness. Charged with these five elements together, she will sleep the sleep of aeons. But if ever just two of the four elements combine in force, they will awaken the sleeping dragon. The end of her eternal slumber. She is free and will devour the earth in red mist. May the gods have mercy on all our souls.

May the gods have mercy! The fishermen were right. The Dragon has been released, and the gods are no more. The four elements in force combined with the blue flame jewel are their only hope, and even if they had all of them, they would not know what to do with them. "May the gods have mercy on us" is the best they can hope for.

Earl Vantor sat down. It was one of only a few times in his life when he had completely no idea of what to do. The force of the mountain exploding and a giant wave of water had unleashed a terrible foe onto the earth. It would move where it wanted to, devouring all in its path, and they had no idea how to stop it or put it back to sleep.

'I feel so tired and stiff, back is creaking, and the fingers are getting the stiffness that old age brings,' Vantor told himself. 'Once more, I am going to need to be stronger. A doddery old man will not cope with what we need to do if we are to survive.'

He stood, took his staff in his hand and started the chant. Mixing it with words of power, he repeated, 'The rhythm of life.' The stone in the staff began to glow, pale at first and gradually brighter, until a bright purple filled the room.

He felt its power course through his body. A sudden jolt and the light was gone. He looked down at his hands. Gone were the wrinkles and the liver spots. Young, smooth, powerful hands were now his. The aching back, gone, the tiredness gone, all the other tiny aches and pains, gone. He was thirty again and in the prime of his life.

The coach pulled up to the inner keep.

'Thank you all very much. You have saved my life, and I will not forget it. So, tomorrow morning, you and your families will be my guests of honour at the Queen's Tournament. Dina, also as a special treat, you will shoot your bow in the Archery Tournament. I know you're two years short, but I am the Prince, and I command it. Until the morrow, I bid you all farewell, and again thank you. The coach will take you home, and it will also collect you in the morning,' said the Prince.

The coach set off.

'Wow, what a day! Can't wait to tell Father. He will be so proud of us,' Joshua said to Dina.

'And me, to shoot my bow. Fantastic!'

'Yes,' said Jackus. 'Mother and Father will be well pleased. Honoured guests of the Prince in the Royal Enclosure. Wow!' and they all started laughing.

Prince Marcus was getting his head seen to by the physician.

'You did a good job on this, sire, but I'll have to put some threads in it to close it up. You were lucky the children found you and bandaged your head because you would have bled to death overnight.'

'Yes, I was lucky; they are good children and make a good team together... Wait a minute!'

'Sire?'

'No, not you. A good team? I need to speak with Harry and Lords Marshall and Sandbite first thing in the morning, but now I need to sleep.'

'Sandy, I'm glad you've come this morning. I wanted to chat to you about something important and gauge your reaction. We know that a dragon is loose in the South Kingdom and devouring everything it covers. We have had a few reports now that some children are able to walk in and out of the red mist without any injury, albeit their minds are lost. We have also seen that the Purple witches can bring them back.'

'Yes, Your Majesty, I am aware of this. And?'

'Yesterday, I was involved in an accident, and I am quite lucky to be alive.'

'I know this also, as my grandson was one of them involved, Your Majesty.'

'Sandy, just call me Marcus when we are alone. Your grandson, Taw, went off in the dark to find help. Dina, the girl, bandaged my head and looked after me with her brother and the twins, the two ginger boys.'

'They are all friends from the local town, Marcus. This you know. What are you getting at, Marcus?'

'I can't believe I am going to say this, but the children make a hell of a team together. They are resourceful, intelligent and, I dare say, physically and mentally fit. Without any formal or specialised training, I would put them up against a team of soldiers, not to fight, but to gain intelligence. So – still can't believe I'm saying this – what if we trained them? Your sort of specialised training and then sending them where we can't send adults? I would put you in charge of training and make Harry their captain. We could add one or two others to their team and maybe have two teams. Well, Sandy? What do you think?'

'I am uncertain. Sounds a really good idea, but they are children, and you would be asking them to take on a very dangerous mission. And their parents? Are they just going to allow you? You may be the Prince, but can you, if needs must, send them?'

71

'Before that, we need to ask the question. So, do we ask the parents first, or do we ask the children?' Marcus said.

'As for my grandson, I would say to ask him first. It is his decision. If he agrees, then he agrees. The others, I would say the same; ask the children first, then we can persuade or deal with the parents as the matter arises. That was in line with what Harry said. But,' Sandy added, 'what happens if the child can't walk through and is killed like the adults?'

'The answer, Sandy, is that won't happen. They just seem to bounce off, so they'll either get in, or they won't. I admit it is extremely dangerous, but we have no choice. I need to speak to Eric Vantor about possible spells or something to try and protect them. There is nothing set in stone as yet. There's training; things could change; anything could happen before, or if, we send them, Sandy.'

'I understand, Marcus, and as for Taw, my grandson, I think he is responsible enough, so as I said, I would let him make the decision, then reassure him, if need be. About asking the other parents first? No, Marcus, that would be a mistake. Ask the children first; be honest and tell them enough of what's happening. They are almost grown up now, so yes, ask them first. As for the parents, you could, if necessary, get the Queen to make the children wards of court, then the parents would have no choice. It would be the Queen's decision to let the children go.'

'Harsh, Sandy, even for you!'

'Marcus, have you given thought to what the children will get from it or what they might want? That we could discuss, but it would have to be worth it.'

'One step at a time, Sandy. Today, the children and their parents, including you, are my honoured guests at the Queen's Tournament. So, when the coach arrives, can you meet them and escort the parents to the enclosure? I will ask Harry to send the children to the throne room, under the pretence of just wanting a quick word before we start the day's festivities. If they all agree, then I will speak to the parents at the end of the day.'

Chapter 8

General Karim was a seasoned soldier and had served the royal family since joining as a young officer many years ago. If someone had told him that one day he would be heading into the Astel Kingdom to ask for help, he would have cut them down where they stood. Now though, here he was, with ten thousand mounted troops crossing into the Astel Kingdom to do just that. It galled him. He was leaving fifty-four thousand assorted other troops at the border. With that number, he could completely invade and take over Astel. Princess Shulla (her formal title was 'Her Divine Majesty Empress Shulla, Uncrowned') was very insistent.

'We are going for help, General, and not for war. If you cannot obey my orders, then I will have your head and replace you, do you understand?'

He, a decorated general for many a year, being told what to do by a spoilt, sixteen-year-old princess! 'Yes,' he said.

It would take them another two, maybe three, days before they came in sight of Astel Palace. The Princess had sent an envoy, Captain Aziz, and twenty of her Saracen personal mounted guards ahead with a formal greeting to the Queen and an announcement of their arrival. They would reach the Palace tomorrow evening if all went well. For now, some forty miles into the northern kingdom, they had not seen a single troop.

Although they had passed a few towns and villages, they had avoided them on instructions.

'Make camp,' ordered the General. 'Full defences, just in case. We don't want to be attacked in the night if someone does not know we are here on friendly terms.'

Taw, Dina, Joshua and the twins arrived in the inner keep in the Prince's coach with their parents, all dressed up in their fine clothes.

Sandy, Lord Sandbite, greeted them all.

'Good morning, everybody,' he said, and they replied. 'Prince Marcus has requested that the children be shown into the throne room as he wants to speak with them. They will join us in the Royal Enclosure later. I am to escort you now into the enclosure, if you'll follow me. Soldier, the children are ready for you to escort them into the throne room where Prince Marcus is awaiting them.'

'Thank you, Lord Sandbite. Follow me,' the soldier said, and the children set off behind the soldier.

Their parents set off with Gramps, who winked at Taw as he left.

Prince Marcus said, 'Please help yourselves to water if you wish. Harry and I have taken this opportunity, firstly, to thank you so very much for helping last evening and saving my life. The second is more complicated. I take it you all know what a secret is?

'What we are about to tell you is a secret and must not be disclosed or shared with anybody who is not involved, and you will get to know who is involved. This includes your parents. Excluding you, Taw. Your grandfather knows. If we find that our trust has been broken, or the information disclosed to anyone, let's just say that it will not be pleasant. The Crown is putting together a unique squad of special soldiers, made up of young adults, for a very dangerous mission. So dangerous that some may not come back. They will be highly trained by the best in the kingdom. They will live at a secret location where they will train, eat, sleep and be put through the worst training possible to make them the best.

Details of the mission are top secret and only told to you if you make the grade and go. We believe you are quite a good team as it is, but we will make you the best. We are asking for volunteers, as it is lives on the line. We will then ask or inform your parents of the decisions you've made. So volunteers to join the Prince's Elite Troop (PET, for short). Your decisions must be with Prince Harry by the mid-day meal. Are there any questions?'

'How long is it for, and when do we start?' said Taw.

'Training will start on Monaday as time is short, and as for how long, I have not thought – until the job is done, or you resign.

'Prince Harry will look after you today and answer any questions you have, but be aware of who can hear you. I will speak to your parents at the end of the day, depending on your answers. Be warned, all of you; this is no school or play area. It will be tough, and it is, as I said, very dangerous. Remember, also, this is secret, and please give your answers to Prince Harry. Now I must escort Mother and Princess Juliet to open the Tournament. Harry, can you escort them to it? Goodbye for now,' said Prince Marcus.

The Royal Tournament was opened by Her Majesty the Queen, with Princess Juliet and Princes Marcus and Harry.

The Queen gave a short speech: 'Good luck to all,' and included a thank you to the children for rescuing Prince Marcus.

Dina and Taw had already made their minds up, even before they had left the throne room. Jackus and Earthie took a little longer, but Josh was not sure at all. He was smaller, skinnier and not really good at anything compared to the others. He would let them down or worse now, get them killed, remembering how, going to watch the knights, he had got them all caught. Prince Harry was not too unlike themselves. He was more like an older brother than a Prince. Taw liked him, and he saw the way Dina looked at him and guessed she liked him too.

Taw and Dina asked most of the questions when they could, such as when they'd see their families and whether they'd get paid, and he answered them as best he could without giving away anything about the mission.

'Father, can you pass me my bow and quiver? I'm shooting in the tournament soon.'

Henry passed her the bow first.

'That's a very nice bow you have there,' said Prince Harry. 'May I have a look?'

'Yes,' said Dina.

'She found it in Astel Forest when she was about ten. The bow was all caked in mud and had no string. She spent nearly a week cleaning it, especially the carvings on the front, and it wasn't until she was waxing it that they really stood out. She loves it to bits and is a damn good shot with it, too,' said Henry with a proud smile.

Prince Harry handed the bow back to Dina and wished her good luck.

The final of the jousting had finished, and Princess Juliet presented the winner with an ornate dagger, which he graciously accepted. The quarter-finals of the archery were now being set up in front of the royal and main stands, in preparation for them to commence after the mid-day meal break. Josh was still not sure. He so wanted to, so he talked to his sister and Taw.

After speaking to both of them, he felt a lot better. He did not want to be left behind and certainly did not want to let them down by not going, either. The decision made, Joshua approached Prince Harry. 'Prince Harry?'

'Yes, Josh?'

'We have all decided that we will volunteer to serve the Crown and go on this mission.'

'Thank you all. I will inform Prince Marcus.'

The crowd and the Royals looked on as Dina lined up as one of the last eight for the quarter-finals. She had easily won her way through the rounds.

'Three arrows at thirty paces. Only gold will do,' shouted the marshal.

Her opponent was to shoot first. One, gold. Two, gold. Three, on the line. Dina stepped up. One, gold. Two, gold. Three, gold and winner. Dina jumped for joy. She was in the semi-finals, and Henry and the rest of them congratulated her.

Prince Harry was talking to Gramps and the Lord Marshal, something about Dina's bow, but Taw could not hear them properly.

There was a single trumpet sound, and everyone looked up. There, walking down towards the stands, were two columns of mounted Southern Kingdom soldiers, flanked by royal knights. The Queen and the royal family stood, the soldiers halted in front of them and all dismounted.

One man stepped forward. He formally bowed to the royal family.

'Your Majesties,' he said, 'forgive my ill manners for interrupting on your festive day. I am Captain Aziz of Her Royal Majesty Empress Shulla (Uncrowned)'s Mounted Saracens. I have been sent here as her envoy to greet you in the words of peace. Her Majesty wishes your help and assistance. She travels towards you now, with a small escort of ten thousand mounted Saracens, and hopes to be here tomorrow.'

'Thank you, Captain,' said the Queen. 'Will you kindly approach?'

The Queen and Prince Marcus stepped down and came walking towards him.

'I am Prince Marcus. Captain Aziz, was it?'

'Yes, Your Majesty.'

'I am sure you are tired and hungry after your journey. My captain here, Captain Craig, will take you and your men to the Palace where you and your men will be fed and looked after until the day here is done and we can talk. Is that satisfactory to you, Captain?'

'Yes, thank you, Your Majesty.' He bowed again and went to his horse and mounted.

They all turned around and set off back towards the Palace. The Queen and the Royals, with the Lord Marshal and Sandy, had a quick discussion.

'On her way here, with ten thousand troops. It could be an invasion,' said Marcus.

'Then why send an envoy, if they are invading?' said the Queen. 'No, I think it's the Princess. She is now the ruling monarch and does not know what to do or who to trust.'

'At least we now know they are on their way here,' said Sandy.

'Yes, that is a problem.'

'Why? We know they are not invading,' said Princess Juliet.

'No, maybe not, but we still have to house ten thousand troops and possibly feed them and their horses,' Marcus stated.

Princess Juliet said, 'I never thought of that.'

'Also,' said Marcus, 'If they run into one of our roaming garrisons, we could have a war on our hands. We need to send an escort to meet them, bring the royal party here, and take the rest to an area we can house them. We can think of the housing later; firstly, we need to send that escort.'

'I will go,' said Princess Juliet. 'Who better to chat to her? If I leave now, we could be there before nightfall.'

'Yes,' said Marcus. 'You will take one hundred mounted knights with you. Make sure you travel with the Princess and that the knights are at the head.'

'Is that alright with you, Mother?' asked Juliet.

'Yes, I think that's a very good idea, Juliet. You two are about the same age, I think.'

'Off you go, then. The knights will meet you in the keep,' said Marcus.

The semi-finals were drawn up. Again, three arrows in the gold but at forty paces. However, Dina had been drawn against the current champion, Draken, who had won for the last three years. This time, she was to fire first. One, gold. Two, gold. And three, gold. The crowd cheered, and even Draken smiled at her, then he took up his place. One, gold. Two, gold. And three, gold.

'Another two arrows,' shouted the marshal, as was the custom.

Draken shot first this time. One, gold. Two, gold. Dina stepped up. She pulled back on the bow. Her arm was starting to ache; she had never fired so many arrows before and was not pulling back far enough to reach the distance they were now shooting. One, gold. Again, she pulled back her arm. Twitching now with the effort, she let the arrow go. Two, gold, and the crowd erupted in cheers. The other semi-final had finished, and a man called Flynn had won three arrows to two and was in the final against Dina or Draken.

'Target back five paces,' ordered the marshal. 'Two more arrows each.' Again, they faced each other, two gold, and two gold.

'Your Majesty?' The marshal looked at the Prince.

'We will have a final of three. Each will fire three arrows, one at a time at fifty paces; first to miss is out.'

The crowd roared with excitement. The archers drew feathers to see who would shoot first. Draken was first, then Flynn, then Dina. Draken took up position and fired.

'Gold,' shouted the marshal.

Flynn stepped up next, aimed and fired.

'Miss,' shouted the marshal.

Flynn hung his head; failed at the last. Why did he pick the lighter arrow when he knew it might drift in the wind? Dina, last to fire, aimed and fired.

'Gold,' the marshal shouted again, with the crowd roaring.

Draken took up his bow, still a little annoyed that a spit of a girl was here in the final with him.

'Don't let it get to you,' he said to himself. 'She'll beat you. Concentrate.' He took aim, slowly releasing his breath, and fired.

'Gold,' shouted the marshal, and the crowd cheered.

Dina stepped up; she had chosen her arrow. She took aim, slowly releasing her breath, and the arrow sang towards the target.

'Gold,' and the crowd shouted and cheered Dina. The crowd was thrilled, and the noise was nearly deafening.

'One more arrow each,' said the marshal.

Draken said to Dina, 'That is some of the very best shooting I have ever seen for a child. Who taught you?'

'No one, really. I taught myself and got some tips off Sandy, Lord Sandbite.'

'It seems to have worked. We both know we can hit the target at this range. What about increasing it another five paces, and another five after each arrow, and make the gold half size? First to miss, the other wins.'

'Yes,' said Dina. 'Sounds good, because we may be here all day.'

The target was moved back five paces, and the gold reduced by half.

The crowd was silent as Draken stepped up and fired.

'Gold,' the marshal shouted, and again the crowd roared.

Dina stepped up, the silence broken only by the birds. She took aim and fired.

'Gold,' shouted the marshal again.

The crowd were loving this exciting final, the seasoned archer against the little girl. Who would have guessed? Back another five, to sixty paces. Dina had never shot so far. Draken stepped up, took aim and fired.

'Line,' shouted the marshal.

The crowd murmured and were quiet. "Line" meant that the arrow was between the gold and the outer colour.

Silence crept in as Dina stepped up. She held her bow up, slowly released her breath, and fired. 'Had she won?' she thought, as the arrow flew towards the target. To be honest, her arm was nearly dead, and she really did not want to shoot anymore.

'Miss,' shouted the marshal.

There was a big aahhh from the crowd, then lots of cheers and shouting.

Draken approached Dina. 'I thought you had me beat then, young lady. That takes some doing, to shoot like that all day, and you just a slip of a girl. I think maybe next year the kingdom will have a new champion,' and he shook her hand.

The trumpet sounded, and the royal party stood. The Queen thanked both archers for a fabulous final and presented Draken with a golden arrow, making it known that next year it would be open to all.

Chapter 9

Vantor had been in the Great Library for nearly two days straight, researching all he could find. There were a few bits here and there about dragons but nothing of importance or help. There must be something, but nothing. He sat down, feeling tired.

'Need some food and sleep. Glad I'm thirty again,' he said, chuckling to himself. 'Wait a minute! The Green monks – they have scripts going back to the Templar Knights. Sometimes you're so stupid. I think a bath, some food and a sleep are overdue, then off to the monks, and I'll ask my brothers to join me.'

Once refreshed, he set off towards the monks. He knew he would have to travel the normal way, but he wanted some fresh air, and the walk would do him some good. He could think while he was walking and decided that he would try by himself first without contacting his brothers. Eventually, he arrived at the gates to the courtyard and made his way to the Abbott, who was very helpful. The only place he was likely to find anything on dragons and stuff would be down in the lower crypt. Vantor found the spiral stone steps that had been well-worn aeons ago. Now, large cobwebs and dust had settled there. He lit the torches on the way until he came to a big, long room.

A word of power lit the room's torches. Lined on either side were stone caskets, some three or five high. At the end lay four far more ornate ones. Across the room to the right was a small square doorway with no door. Vantor walked in, and again, a word of power lit the room. All around the room were shelves, and on the shelves were scrolls, thousands of them piled on top of each other. Some were rotten and could not be read, as to touch them would turn them to dust. Some were very delicate, others sealed in metal tubes.

There were four tall desks, all facing into each other, forming a hollow square. This is where the scribes would have written the scrolls, and then they would have placed them on the shelves. Interestingly, though, there was a very ornate wooden chair in the middle, just away from the desks. Vantor looked at it.

It was almost a throne. It was beautifully carved, with a high back, big armrests, and huge claws carved into the ends of them. This must have been the Abbot's or, at the very least, the scribe overseer's. He might ask if he could have this when it was all over, but for now, back to work.

'I will need to call David and Luke. This is just too much.'

The brothers arrived some time later. Vantor had already made a start, trying to fathom out whether there was an order to the scrolls, but this seemed not to be the case.

'This is fantastic,' said David. 'If we had the time, I'd love to come down here and study and sort through this.'

'But sadly, we don't,' said Vantor.

'So, how far have you got?' asked Luke.

'Just to this first row here, and only halfway down.'

'Even with three of us, it will take far more time than we have,' said David.

'Yes, I agree,' said Vantor. 'Any ideas?'

'Actually, I might have.' David closed his eyes and started a whisper of a chant. With his palms turned upward, he began to chant more loudly and slowly raised his hands and lowered them. Scrolls all around the room began to move. For a few seconds, he did this, then raised his hands higher. Some scrolls around the room rose above the others.

He held his hands there and said, 'Grab the ones in the air.'

Eric and Luke quickly got the scrolls, and David released the spell. All the rest fell back, but they had the scrolls that had been raised.

'What did you do?' said Eric.

'I just cast a spell for all scrolls mentioning dragons to rise. Quite simple, really, but I was surprised it worked.'

'Who knocked over the chair?' said Eric.

'I don't think any one of us was near it, and I didn't hear it fall.'

'Neither did I,' said Luke.

Eric walked over to the chair, which was lying on its back. The base seemed solid, but Luke said, 'That's not a solid seat. It opens up.'

Eric stood the chair up and lifted the seating board to reveal a compartment. Inside were what looked like some old rags. Eric reached in and pulled them out. There was something tied and bound up in leather.

Quickly, he untied the bindings to reveal a book. This was no ordinary book. It was covered in rich, soft leather of black and gold. He tried to open it, but it would not open; it was stuck.

'Wait,' said David. 'There is something impressed in the leather at the bottom.'

'It is in a foreign language of some sort,' said Eric.

'No, it is the language of the ancient ones. Let me see!' said David.

David whispered an enchantment in a high, squeaky voice, then Eric opened the book. The pages inside were edged in gold. It was beautiful: full-colour drawings, Old Testament lettering, pages bordered in gold. But wait, they could not read it. The language was in the ancient tongue and script. Eric looked inside the front cover, and there, spread across both pages in full colour, was a drawing of a gold dragon breathing red mist.

The Tournament finished with the mounted knights bashing each other with a sack of straw. The winner was the last one on horseback. It was not a serious competition; most of them had been drinking and just fell off. Others cheated and pulled their mates off. It was a good, humorous finale to the day, and the crowd enjoyed it. The trumpets sounded, and all looked towards the Royal Enclosure. The Queen and the others stood. The Queen gave a speech and congratulated all who had taken part and the winners. Then, as customary, she wished them good fortune in the year to come and an enjoyable tomorrow. The crowd clapped and shouted approval as again the trumpets sounded three blasts to signal the end of the Queen's Tournament. The Queen, escorted by both Princes, left the tournament and headed towards the inner keep.

Taw, Dina and the rest of the crowd followed the royal party at a short distance. The children and their parents were shown into the anteroom by Gramps. They had been told that the Prince wanted to speak to them all. The children knew why, but the adults did not.

'Please take a seat,' said Gramps, as he too sat. 'The Prince won't be long.'

Just then, Marcus walked in.

'Please remain seated, everyone. I need to make this quite short and to the point. I have other guests to see, so forgive my bluntness. In essence, your children, young adults, I should say, have been asked and accepted into the Prince's Elite Troop and are now subject to the military. They work for and are paid by the Crown.'

There was chatter around the table. The Prince put his hand up. He did not want to be interrupted.

'They will be part of a very special force led by Prince Harry. They will live and train in a special training area. Do not ask them about what they are doing or about their missions because, as of yet, they do not know. You will see them once a week, for an afternoon, and they will start first light Monaday. I have made available funds for you to hire people to carry out the tasks they would have done in your business if they had remained with you. They were all asked first, and they agreed.'

The Prince looked around the table. 'Are there any questions?' he asked. The parents all looked stunned. They looked around at each other.

'No questions?' the Prince said. 'Thank you all very much for coming. Enjoy your Harvest day tomorrow. Troop, I'll see you soon,' and he left.

Prince Marcus made his way to the knights' quarters where he met Captain Aziz.

'Your Majesty,' he said and stood up.

'Please, relax,' said Marcus and sat down with him and some other knights.

'So, Captain, can you tell me why your Queen needs our help?'

'She is not our Queen as yet. She has not been crowned, but she is the only one of royal blood. Our Emperor was murdered in the night, by what we do not know, but he was thrown around the room and cut to pieces, with nobody in there. Then a great red mist appeared over the Palace and city. Three other parts of the kingdom, also, four if you include the island. When the mist was gone, there was nothing at all left behind, as we found on the island. The Princess wants and needs your help to defend her kingdom against whatever it is, as she and her generals don't know what to do. One general is unhappy about this, but the Princess insisted.'

'What sort of forces are left in your kingdom, and are they still loyal to the kingdom and the Princess?' asked Marcus.

'We have ten thousand mounted soldiers with us under the command of General Karim, the one I just told you of. There are another fifty thousand at the border, made up of soldiers, large bowmen and archers. They are commanded by High General Tulla.'

'I know the General,' said Marcus. 'Jazz, yes, Jazz Tulla.'

'You are correct, Prince Marcus, Your Majesty.'

'Your ten thousand men will be billeted outside the city as we do not have room for them in the city.'

'Do not worry, kindly Prince. They bring everything they need with them. They just need an area big enough and a water supply.'

'That's good, then. My captain will show you where to set up tomorrow, ready for your people. Captain Stone, if they use the area north of the city, next to the river Astel, along towards Goblet Harbour.'

'Yes, Your Majesty.'

'We could have been asked,' Henry said. 'Why were we not? After all, they are our children.'

'What would you have said? "No, Prince Marcus,"? You heard the Prince. There is something special about our children; that's why he picked them. Or was it because they saved his life?' said Sadie.

'They are all very brave. It is not a choice the Prince had. I cannot tell you why yet, but you will know soon enough,' said Sandy. 'I shall show you out now,' he said, 'if you all follow me out into the courtyard in the inner keep.'

They were all talking as they left the Palace, walking home, when Henry said to Sandy, 'I bet you had something to do with all this, Lord Sandbite?'

'No, Henry. In fact, I was totally unaware until after mid-day meal,' he lied. 'If you have a problem with it, then go and speak to Prince Marcus. I'm sure he will listen to you, but I think Dina and Joshua may not, nor thank you.'

'You're right. I'm sorry, Sandy; it's all just a bit of a shock, both of them serving the Crown.'

'No, forgive me, Henry. In fact, why don't we all stop at the Cross Axes Inn for supper? I'll pay, and I'll claim it back from the Treasury.'

They all laughed and set off towards the inn.

'Hello the Camp!' shouted Sir Dale.

'Who wishes to enter?' came the reply.

'Princess Juliet and her escort, the knights of the Kingdom of Astel.'

'Quickly, get the General,' the soldier said to his friend.

'One moment, Sir Knight,' shouted a voice. 'Open the gate,' said the voice to the soldier.

He didn't have to look, for he knew that voice all too well.

'Greetings to you, Sir Knight. I am General Karim, Escort to Her Royal Highness Princess Shulla of the Southern Kingdom. Please follow me, Sir Knight. I will take you to Her Majesty.' With that, he turned his horse and started to lead the way. He halted before a large multi-coloured tent and dismounted.

The knights formed two ranks in front of the tent until two came forward, and they too dismounted.

'General, may I present Princess Juliet,' said Captain Dale, the Knight escort.

'Your Majesty,' General Karim said and bowed. 'This way, please.'

As he turned, his way was blocked by six monstrous, half-naked guards with huge Saracen swords. The guards parted and allowed them access. The tent was huge. It had one massive central space, then lots of openings all around it, going off to other tents.

From outside the tent, General Karim announced: 'Sir Knight and Her Royal Highness Princess Juliet of Astel Kingdom.'

Princess Shulla stood and walked over to greet her counterpart, Princess Juliet.

'Princess Shulla, I am Juliet, and this is Sir Dale.'

'Welcome to my humble abode, Juliet and Sir Knight. I am Shulla. Please do sit, Juliet. I am sorry, Juliet, but your man is not allowed in my tent as I am not married or crowned Queen as yet. It is one of our customs. As you can see, I have ten female bodyguards inside, six eunuchs at the entrance. Your Sir Knight and his comrades will be well looked after by my general.'

'Sir Dale, do you mind?'

'Not at all, if it is what Your Majesty wishes.'

'I do. Thank you, Sir Dale.'

He saluted, about-turned and walked out of the tent to where the General waited.

'I am not permitted to enter. For me to go in when I know not to will lose me my head,' the General said. 'Now, Sir Knight, what do they call you?'

'My name is Freddy. What about you?'

'I am Rajh to my friends. Come, your men are being looked after; now to look after you, our guest. Food, wine and some lovely women to keep you warm. Come, let's go to my tent.'

The Princesses sat and chatted halfway through the night. They talked about the problem of the dragon and the red mist, and the fact that they needed to talk to Marcus, and soon. Then, once business was done, they were like schoolgirls, chatting about anything and everything. To say they got on is an understatement.

Chapter 10

The celebrations for Harvest day were well underway. People were dancing, singing and generally making merry in the streets. Nobody noticed when Vantor and his brothers arrived back.

'We must make our way to the inner keep and bring Marcus up to speed with what... Wait a minute! What's going on here? All the main streets are lined with soldiers,' said Eric Vantor.

'Is this part of the celebrations?' asked David.

'No,' said Eric. 'This is something else. Look, royal knights and someone behind them. It's Princess Juliet, and who's that with her?'

'That is Princess Shulla from the Southern Kingdom, and General Karim,' said Luke. 'They are escorted by royal knights and Saracens.'

Inside the inner keep, the soldiers fanned out, allowing the Royal Princess to come forward. The Astel Royal family were waiting on the dais, the Queen and both Princes. The trumpets sounded and Princess Shulla and her party dismounted; they both bowed before the Queen.

'I am very pleased to finally meet you, Your Majesty, Queen of Astel. I am the Royal Princess Shulla and rightful heir to the Emperor's crown of the Southern Kingdom.'

'Welcome, Princess Shulla, to our home. Please come and accept our hospitality.'

'Thank you, Your Majesty.'

They walked up the steps together and proceeded into the inner keep, followed by the city's dignitaries.

Vantor and his brother followed on until they got to the inner keep where a guard stopped them. 'Who are you three likely to be?' he asked.

'I am Earl Vantor, and these are my brothers. We need to speak with the Prince.'

'You do now, do you? Well, I happen to know Earl Vantor, and he looks nothing like you. He's about eighty years old, with a white beard and hair, and he smells, so get off with you before I call the sergeant and throw you in jail for the night.'

'Oh, let us in, you idiot. It is me.'

The soldier drew his sword, and so did his companion.

'I told you once, Mr...'

Vantor said, 'I've not got time for this,' and there, it was done.

The soldiers' swords were now wooden.

'If you don't get out of my way, you'll be a toad next – for the rest of your life.' Vantor barged through while the soldiers were still looking at their swords.

The formal meeting was now done, and they were taking their places for dinner. Vantor and his brothers were not invited, so they left with the rest of the guests. Prince Marcus saw the brothers and wondered where Eric was, and whether he had returned.

Josh, Taw, Dina and the twins were enjoying the day's fun and games in the town, laughing at the antics and at people who were drunk. They sat on the grassy area near the central area of actives. Taw was chatting to Dina about the knights' jousting and what a shame it was that Prince Marcus was unable to take part. Then he said, 'Dina, I've never known you to miss anything.'

'Yes, well, I'd been shooting all day, and my arm was tired. I was squinting a little, too. That's after aiming all day, too.'

'No, Dina, I know you better, and I don't believe you. The marshal shouted, "Miss." That means you missed the target completely. Not even he missed; he got Line. So, I don't believe you.'

'Alright, Taw. Listen, don't say a word. Yes, I missed because I wanted to. I did not want to be the Prince's champion archer at all. I wanted to go on the mission. If I was the champion, I would not get to go on the mission.'

'Wow, Dina, so you would have beaten him! Don't worry, I won't say a word, but you could have had a golden arrow!'

'Shut up now, Taw!'

He smiled at her and she at him.

'Hey, Josh. Want to go on the merry-go? Dina and I are going.'

Aden and John Smith, the royal cousins, arrived back from the Southern Kingdom while the banquet was on. They made their way to the kitchen in the inner keep and managed to get some food. The cook said they could stay in the kitchen workers' rooms overnight. They thanked her and set off for a night's sleep. They would be able to sort things out tomorrow with Marcus.

Back in Rollstream, the children had all decided that they would again meet at the Cross Axes at dawn and make their way to the Palace. Dina and Josh had packed clothes and stuff into a hog. Dina, of course, had her bow and arrows. Taw had packed a few things, mainly clothes, as had the twins, but the twins' parents were all over them, their mother crying.

'My little boys! Going off to war!' was all she could say, and no matter how many times they told her they were not going to war, the more she said it.

'Tell her we are only going training. Come on, let's go,' said Taw.

Dina and Josh gave their dad a hug and said goodbye. He, too, had a tear in his eye as he walked away. They all set off towards the Palace, the twins' mum still crying.

Earl Vantor and his brothers sat going through the book page by page, studying each carefully. There was not a lot in the first part that they could understand. It was, as far as they could tell, a story of the dragon killing and eating ordinary folk, but children were special, very special. Some were considered by the dragon a very rare delicacy. Others she could not eat, and some she was even afraid of.

'This is very interesting,' said Luke. 'What is the difference? Afraid of? Delicacy? How does the dragon know?'

'I would say smell,' said David, 'or can she see something else in them, maybe what they really are?'

'No, we know it's not boy or girl, tall or short, fat or thin, hair or eye colour, so what? Let's read on! The dragon sleeps for aeons. She's immortal and can't be killed, so the mighty gods put her to sleep. That's what we need to do,' said Eric.

'Ha, ha, ha,' said David. 'Eric here thinks we are gods and we can put her to sleep.'

'Wait a minute, what did you just say? What if some of the gods were children who put her to sleep? She would be afraid of a god. Maybe she can sense something in the children, but again, what? Fear? If you remember the boy, Dominic, he said, "The screaming and the quiet." The "screaming" came from the ones being eaten. The few whose minds had shut down were not afraid, so it left them,' exclaimed Eric.

'By the Cross, I think you're right! That would explain it – and is that the same for adults?' said David.

'No, I don't think so, as she would know that brave men will try to fight, but a child, no, it just dies.

'We need to start writing all this stuff down, or we will forget a vital clue. North, South, East and West, the four points of the compass, and each relates to the four elements, Earth, Air, Water and Fire. All seem to be connected somehow, but how? Perhaps we should take one at a time and examine it for what it is,' said Eric Vantor.

'Good morning,' said Prince Harry. 'Good morning, Your Majesty,' was the reply from them all.

'This is Captain Kelly. He will be your main instructor. He has been specially selected to train you and put you through your paces. I will meet up with you later. Captain Kelly, please carry on.'

'Yes, Your Majesty. So, can any of you scabby troggs ride a horse?'

They all could, thanks to Taw's Gramps.

'Good, follow me and keep up.'

He set off at pace to the stables outside by the royal forges, then stopped.

'Come on, come on, I've not got all day. Sorry bunch! Select a horse. They will be yours from now on; everything they need, you will do. Get the horses ready for travelling.'

'Wonder where we're going?' asked Earthie.

'Did I say you could talk?'

'No.'

'Then shut your mouth. You will do what I tell you, when I tell you, and we will get by fine, understand?'

In silence, they all selected a horse, saddled it and kitted it out. They mounted and were ready to leave the courtyard.

Prince Marcus came and stood in front of them.

He said, 'Welcome to the military. When you get to where you are going, you will be given a uniform. You will wear it. Your bed, food and anything else will be provided.

'You will not be allowed to leave the camp or speak to anyone about your training or why you are there. There will be another group the same as you. You will not talk to them, either, or have anything to do with them. Do I make myself clear?'

'Yes, Your Majesty,' they all replied.

'Your training will be hard, fast and tough. We will try to break you, to make you tougher than you ever thought possible, to push you beyond anything. If you survive the training, there will not be a man who can defeat you. So good luck to you all. I will visit during your training.'

'Form two ranks!' shouted the captain.

Two riders came forward from the rear and formed up behind them.

'Look to your front, you miserable, ugly-looking troggs. Now we are all finally here; we wait for the other group.'

The other group walked up, mounted on their horses. They were led by a captain, but that's all anyone could see.

'Look to your front. No talking and stay in line. Follow me outside of the city and stay in line. Do I make myself clear?' he yelled.

'Yes, Captain,' they shouted.

They set off at a trot in their pairs. Taw was next to the captain, then Earthie and Jackus, Dina and Josh, but who were the two behind them, Taw wanted to know. They rode through the Palace and out onto the roadway. Here they picked up the pace and began to canter.

They rode in silence for about four hours.

Earthie was thinking, 'I'm hungry, and my legs and bum have gone to sleep. Must be close to mid-day by now.'

Just over the brow of a hill, they saw a village next to a lake.

'That's Lady Lake,' thought Dina and a couple of others. They appeared to be approaching the town of Stoney.

The captain called a halt. 'I need not remind you. We are on the Prince's business, and that is all you will say to anyone. We are stopping at the garrison for mid-day meal. We will then set off again after a short break.'

They walked their horses into the garrison; other soldiers were looking at them and talking, but nobody said anything to them.

'Follow me,' the captain said as they walked through the town until they reached a stable.

They dismounted, and the captain said, 'Over there, you will find a meal ready for you and a drink. Get it inside you, then come and sort your horses.'

'Yes, Captain,' was the reply.

As they walked towards the mess area, Taw turned around to look at the two at the back. One was a girl, the other a man/boy. They both had cloths over their faces and heads to protect them from the dust, so he could not see who they were. They collected their food, and Taw stayed back a bit to join the newcomers.

As they sat, Taw said, 'Is that you, Sam? It is you, Sam!'

'Shhh! Keep your voice down,' said one of the newcomers.

'I'll wait until we are all sat down, then I'll introduce you,' said Taw.

The other girl sat next to Dina, and she said something. Dina's face changed. She was going to say something, but the girl stopped her.

'Later,' she said.

They ate their meal and moved back out to the stables to sort their horses out. The captains were not about, so Taw said, 'Everybody, this is Sam Baxter, who I fought with in the training compound at the Palace.'

He introduced them all until he came to the girl, whom he didn't know. Her face was still covered. 'I'm sorry, but I don't know your name yet.'

'That's alright, Taw Sandbite. I know of you,' she said.

Taw looked puzzled. 'Who are you?' asked Taw.

Dina said, 'Come in closer, everyone. Do not draw attention to us all or shout out, but this is Princess Juliet. Nobody is to know who she is. She is just another one of us and here to do the training.'

Juliet removed the dust cover. 'Just so you can see me as I am,' she said with a smile. 'I am no different from you. I will be treated the same as you and be part of your team. Nice to meet you all.' She then replaced the dust cover.

Taw thought she looked prettier like that than when she was dressed as the Princess.

'Let's mount up!' shouted the captain, and they set off once more. The captain allowed them to whisper this time. As they slowly made their way south, Juliet and Dina now rode together and seemed to be getting on.

The room started to fill: Vantor, his brothers, the Lord Marshal, the Sword Master, Lord Sandbite, Sienna, Alice of the Purple order, the Admiral, the Smith brothers.

Prince Marcus announced, 'Her Majesty the Queen and Princess Shulla.'

They all bowed.

'Please be seated, everyone, and for those who don't know, this is Princess Shulla of the Southern Kingdom. She has come to us for our help in defeating the dragon. Before we start: Earl Vantor, you are looking extremely well for someone who was just a short time ago old and quite feeble. Would you kindly secure the room? Thank you,' said Marcus with a smile, and everyone smiled too.

'With pleasure,' Eric Vantor said and uttered the words of power.

'Welcome, everyone. A lot has happened since we last met. We have some new people here, too: Princess Shulla, Aron and John Smith, Mother Superior of the Purple order, and Captain Aziz. I have talked at length over our problem with the dragon with Princess Shulla. Lords Archer and Sandbite and I agree that military might has no effect on the dragon, but it might distract it.

'At best, we can use the military to evacuate any city or town at a moment's notice, should the dragon attack, and try to protect what we can. We will also need to protect them from shadows, sheets and Dragmen. To do this, according to Queen Sienna and Mother Superior, every sword, spear, knife, axe, arrow and anything metal we fight with must be rubbed with silver every day.

'Lord Marshal and Lord Sandbite, you will take an escort of twenty knights each, report to the Treasury and collect one silver piece for every soldier in the kingdom. You then will cover every garrison in the kingdom and issue them to the commanders. They, in turn, are to issue them to the soldiers to use every day on their weapons. They are not allowed to spend it, as the charm needs to be refreshed every day. So every morning, every soldier will produce his coin to his captain. Failure is punishable with four dozen lashes; second time, they will be hanged. There are no excuses, from the general down to the newest soldier.

'Each general or commander of a garrison or town is to prepare for and plan for evacuation, when and if it happens. There will be no time for any possessions; it will be get out or die. From their homes, tented areas are to be prepared near the towns and cities with stockades and camouflaged to protect the people. There are not to be erected yet, but stores and plans must be in place, thirty days from now,' said Marcus.

'Before I hand over to Earl Vantor – Eric – Princess Shulla will be returning to her kingdom with one thousand knights to assist her in establishing law and order again in her cities and towns with her own commanders. General Karim will be taken and executed tomorrow by Captain Aziz for treason against Princess Shulla. We will take no part in this, apart from lining the route, as per normal, and hanging our own sentenced prisoners afterwards. I will hand over to a thirty-something young Earl Vantor now. Thank you.'

'Thank you, Prince Marcus. I do feel much better. My brothers, Luke and David, and I have been very busy. We have examined every site. There is no warning when the red mist will appear. However, when it does, it starts from above and drops down, forming a line. As the dragon flies around it, it encloses all within the mist; how big or small is entirely the dragon's choice. Once it is down and the circle formed, it has an option; it either leaves it and comes back sometime later, or it sets down and begins to feast.

'If we can evacuate outside the mist as it is being laid by the dragon, we will save many lives. We all know that when it has finished, there is nothing, nothing but a circle of rubble left behind. At this moment, we do not know where the dragon is. It can return to one of the sites covered already or pick a new one.

'We suspect it may be in the mountains of Rajh. We also discovered an old book in the crypt of the Templar Knights. This is it,' Vantor said as he placed it on the table – a heavy leather-bound book of black and gold.

'It is written in a language long since forgotten. However, some of the script is in Latin. It is beautifully illustrated and ornate. This was many years in the making, and here is a picture of what we think the dragon looks like. We have also found out that it is immortal: it cannot die, and we can't kill it, either. All we can do is return it to what it was, put it back to sleep, but we don't know how. There is information about a beautiful red jewel in the shape of a tear, and by my reading, it turns blue when the dragon is close. This we must find, as it will give us a chance if the dragon is near, once it leaves the mountains.'

'Thank you, Earl Vantor. Queen Sienna and Mother Superior, I will need you both to work together in protecting the people from the sheets, shadows or Dragmen, whatever foul things they be. I want all the people in this room protected, apart from the Vantors. They can do their own. Also, there are two groups of children who will need protecting. They will also need training in both your skills. This is a must. Can you do this?'

'I think we can. The hardest bit will be protecting the general public, as they are so spread out, but I'm sure Alice and I can plan something,' said Queen Sienna.

'We have, as you just heard, recruited two groups of children, two very special groups. They will be very highly trained in combat, mental abilities, spells and enchantments. They are going on a secret mission, only known to a select few, and we think, just maybe, we have a chance of surviving.

'Has anyone anything to add to the meeting?' asked Marcus. 'No? Are there any questions? Please remember, this is still secret for now, so please keep it so. Thank you. Your Majesty, would you like to say anything?'

The Queen stood. 'This is our kingdom and these are our people. It is our duty to protect them, so let's see that we do. Thank you all. Earl, would you lift the spell? Thank you.'

Chapter 11

The new troop was heading towards a village called Lockshoe, but some distance from it, they turned and entered a forest. They followed the trail for some time, then again, they turned off down a more obscure track.

After a couple of minutes, they came to a clearing; in front of them was a huge wooden fortress, tall trees spiked at the top bound together, two taller towers at the corners and a huge set of gates in the middle.

A sentry shouted down, 'Halt. State your business, or die.'

The captain said, 'If that's you up there, Prattle, I'll "die" you when I get my hands on you.'

'Yes, sir, Captain. It's me, alright. Open the gate for the Captain and his people.'

The gates opened, and they rode in. The place was a hollow square, with everything around the walls. They headed towards the stables and dismounted.

'Welcome to your new home. Corporal Spike, reporting as ordered, Captain.'

'This sorry lot are your new recruits. Sort them out, and we will begin at first light tomorrow.'

'Yes, sir. Line up, line up, you shambles!' he shouted. 'Hello, my lovelies. My name is Corporal Spike, and I am your basic instructor. I am here to break you, rip you apart, and put you back together, to rebuild you into some sort of soldier. Well, it won't be easy, you will not quit, you will hate me, but the further you go, the more you will learn.'

Jackus said under his breath, 'I'm scared.'

'Who said that?' the corporal screamed. 'Who said it? On your faces! Now! Now, lie on the floor, arms out in front, palms down. I'll teach you to speak when not asked to. Faces in the dirt!'

He walked along all their hands and then back again. Nobody said anything this time.

'On your feet! To the left, boys with no dicks; on the right, boys with dicks. On your beds, you'll find your uniforms which you will wear from now on. They are bright yellow, so we don't miss anyone, with black work boots. There will be another group here later. You will not talk to them under any circumstances. Your presence here is secret, as you know, and anyone who breaches the Prince's trust, well, let's just say, it's not nice. Now get away and be here first light, ready to go.'

They ran to their rooms where their beds were lined up, with yellow uniform and black boots on each bed.

As the sun dawned on a new day, the route to the inner keep was lined by knights and Saracens. Up on the gallows stood Captain Aziz, with a huge Saracen's sword.

A large wooden block had been placed at the front between the nooses on the upper rail, waiting for its guest to arrive. On the royal dais stood Princess Shulla, flanked by two Saracen personal guards, Prince Marcus and two knights. The General had been woken by the Queen's knights, stating that his presence was required by his Princess and he was to come immediately. He knew something was amiss when they got to the inner keep door. The knights stopped, and he was escorted by four of his own Saracens. They halted in front of the royal dais.

'What is the meaning of this?' he demanded. 'I am a general. I do not get summoned like a commoner.'

'General Karim,' said Princess Shulla, 'do you know why you have been brought here?'

'No, I do not.' He saw Captain Aziz on the gallows, waiting, and a deep fear set in. 'I demand you stop this nonsense at once. You're acting the child again. If you stop it now, you will not be punished.'

'No, General. Your attempt to recruit loyal soldiers of my father has failed. Your attempt to rule over me has also failed.'

'But Your Majesty, I have served your father all my life, and I promised him I would look after you like my own daughter.'

'Yes, General – where is your own daughter? She is dead, driven to suicide by your forcing her to marry someone to further your ambition. She despised you.'

'No, that's not true.' His voice was shrill.

'Where is your wife, General? Also dead. Because of you. She refused to seduce someone for you. They were found dead together, but if they were alive, they would never have even met, but that was a mystery. Finally, your attempt to murder me "by accident" on the return trip home has sealed your fate. You could have been happy as a general, even the next High General, but now you're not even that.

'You have been found guilty of treason against your Sovereign and your people. Therefore, you will lose your head by public execution so all will know what punishment treason carries. Guards!'

'You can't do this, you silly little girl! This is not a game! I am a general! Arrest her!' he screamed.

Four Saracens grabbed him, his tunic was removed, and he was dragged towards the gallows, still shouting and screaming, 'You little bitch, you can't do this!'

He was forced to kneel down, and his head was held in place with a leather strap. He still tried to shout. Princess Shulla nodded her head. Captain Aziz swung the curved sword, and there was silence.

The Princess looked at Marcus.

He said, 'It had to be done. You were not safe while he was alive.'

'I know. But I'd never have known if it was not for your Mother Superior Alice reading his thoughts of my accident on the way home.'

'Your Majesty, the task is complete,' said Captain Aziz.

'No, not quite, Captain. Please kneel.'

The captain did so, with all the other Saracens looking on. 'Captain Aziz, your loyalty has been unquestioned since my father passed. It is my pleasure to promote you to General of my personal guard. Arise, General!'

All the Saracens cheered and waved swords in the air.

'Now, General, take me away from here. Thank you, Prince Marcus,' she said.

Once they had moved away, the captain of the guard came into the courtyard with the six prisoners who were to be hanged, and one by one, they were.

The Queen and Prince Marcus met with Princess Shulla in the throne room.

'It is time for me to return to my kingdom and try to rebuild it and fight a dragon. But before that, I will be crowned Empress in Manch City a week from now. I would be most pleased if you could all be there for my coronation. Even if you can't all be there, will you please attend, Prince Marcus?'

'I will be there.'

'I can't thank you enough for all your help. The thousand knights, and coming to my aid.'

'You're most welcome,' said the Queen.

Princess Shulla turned and walked from the throne room. A thousand knights waited in the Palace, and ten thousand Saracens waited outside to escort her home.

'Your training is going to get steadily harder from now on. Today, how to stay alive. All of you, into the lake to see if you can swim. Go!'

'At least the water is warm,' said Earthie.

Dina and Jackus were swimming happily, as were the rest of them.

'Good, you can all swim. Archers!'

Twenty archers stepped forward.

'Ready! Fire!'

The arrows were fired at them across the water.

'Down!' someone shouted, and they ducked under the water. Earthie and Jackus just sat on the bottom. The rest were bobbing up and down as the archers fired. Earthie grabbed Dina, and she thought he was trying to kiss her. He was, but to give her breath. Jackus did the same to Juliet. When they realized what the twins were doing, the others soon sat at the bottom of the lake, looking at each other, astonished they were breathing underwater with the twins' help.

The archers and Corporal Spike stood looking. No sign of any of them. Where were they? Had they all drowned? All of them?

'That's great. "Sorry, Prince Marcus, but I've killed them all in the second week." I'll be hanged, for sure.'

Earthie signalled to Jackus to take a look, so he headed to the surface. He saw the corporal walking up and down, with no sign of the archers. He signalled the others to head for shore. They walked along the bottom until they emerged from the water.

The corporal stood half in shock. 'Are you wizards or something?' he shouted. 'Get over here and line up! I want to know exactly what went on there.'

Earthie said, 'I can explain. My brother and I have always been able to go underwater and not drown.'

Dina said, 'I thought you were having a joke when you talked about going fishing.'

'Quiet, you!'

'So, what we did was to give our breath to them. We found out by accident once, when this man was drowning.'

'That's enough! Get yourselves back and dried. Be ready after midday meal for spell training.'

'That was amazing,' said the others as they walked back.

Juliet said, 'I thought he was trying to kiss me in the water!'

'So did I,' said Dina as they laughed together and made their way back to get changed.

The Prince was right; they were very special. It soon became routine: physical training, with Dina and Sam competing for first. As for the others, Taw was first with weapons; unarmed was Josh; twins with spells and stuff.

A couple more weeks had passed, and they were waiting in the classroom for a new teacher. Whoosh!

'Good morning, I am Earl Eric Vantor. Advanced training of the mind, spells, enchantments and incantations are what I am here for.'

Juliet and Taw excelled at these studies, while the twins were just behind them. Juliet could see things that Taw could not until she showed him, but he, in return, was able to do spells and enchantments better. Vantor spent more time with them over the next couple of weeks.

Juliet and Taw went to Vantor's study, as usual, one evening. He was engrossed in reading a huge book and did not see them enter.

'Wow!' said Juliet, 'that's a beautiful book!'

He looked up. 'Ah.'

'She is like a goddess, with all those swirls around her. Who is she?'

'She is the goddess of Air.'

'What's the funny writing around it?'

'I don't know.'

'Now ... ah'choo!'

'Bless you, Juliet!'

'Thank you. I can read that,' said Juliet. '"Though I stand before thee, Dragon, I am the Vessel of..." It's gone; I can't read it anymore.'

'What?' said Vantor. 'Why can't you read it?'

'I don't know.'

'Try!'

'I am!'

'What did you do?'

'She sneezed,' said Taw.

'Yes. Sneeze again!'

'I can't.'

'Try!'

'I am trying! Phew! It's no good. No, wait. I can read it again.'

'What does it say?'

'"I am the Vessel of Air, and you must obey it..." It's gone again.'

'Wait!' said Taw. 'Blow on it, Juliet.'

She did so. 'Yes. "You must obey its call. Sleep, I bid you! Sleep the Dragon's sleep...." That's it.'

'That's great! Can you blow on it again and read the whole thing, so I can write it down?'

'Yes, Earl Vantor. Ready?'

'"Though I stand before thee, Dragon, I am the Vessel of Air. You are commanded by the four elements to obey my call. Sleep, I command you. Sleep the Dragon's Sleep." Is this important, Earl?'

'Yes, very. Let me turn the page. Can you read this one?'

'"This is a Man of Fire...." No, it's not working.'

'Just as I thought. That means that only the bearer can read their own element. I'm sorry, but this evening is cancelled. I need to go out.' He wrapped the book and vanished.

Princess Shulla was travelling back towards her kingdom with General Aziz, the knights and the ten thousand Saracens. They reached the border where High General Tulla greeted them. After a short break, when the High General had caught up with what was happening, they set off for Manch City and the coronation. Fifty-two thousand, plus another twenty-one, had joined them, plus another ten thousand and a thousand knights;

just short of a hundred thousand were now on the move. David Vantor and six sisters of the Purple order travelled within the Princess's escort. The ten witches of Black were nowhere to be seen, but they were there protecting, as were the others.

Chapter 12

Earl Vantor and his brother, Luke, had been busy trying to decrypt part of the book, with help from the Abbot of the Green order.

'There are four swords that are linked to the elements, but only the Chosen can wield the swords. We know Juliet unlocked the Air, and it's only her. We cannot; we have tried. So three remain. Many little pieces; it's like a jigsaw. Without all the pieces, it's almost an impossibility to make any sense of it all, but we must. Four swords, four elements, the Chosen, the Jewel. We know the jewel is called Dragonite. We know Juliet is Air, one of the Chosen. We know what has to be said by Air. Logic is needed. We need four swords, three more Chosen, the Dragonite, the verses of the other three elements.'

Vantor was getting frustrated. Each day the same questions, with no answers. Might as well drown himself in the lake… The lake!

Vantor vanished and appeared in the camp, giving two soldiers' horses a startle. 'Where are they training?' said Vantor.

'Just outside, skinning rabbits, I think,' said the soldier.

Vantor walked out of the fort side gate, and they were there.

'Corporal, I need to talk to the twins, Earthie and Jackus, for a moment.'

Vantor sat down on the grass with the boys and opened the book on the Water page. 'Can you read this?' he asked.

They both looked and looked puzzled. 'No, it's in a language we don't understand.'

'Damn,' Vantor said. 'I was sure, with that underwater trick you did.'

'Wait a minute,' said Earthie. He went over and grabbed his water bottle.

'You are not pouring that over this book!' Vantor shouted.

'No, sir. I'll pour it over my hand while I try to read it.'

'Good idea. Let's try.'

Earthie began to pour the water. '"Though I stand before thee, Dragon, I am the Vessel of Water. You are commanded by the four elements to obey my call. Sleep, I command you, sleep the Dragon's sleep."'

'Brilliant! Well done. So two have we found, and the other two verses must be the same, but for Fire and Earth. Thank you, boys. Go back to your studies,' and he was gone.

Vantor met up with Prince Marcus and explained they now had two of the Chosen ones who could command the elements.

'But we still have the other two to find, and this Jewel and also the four elemental swords, so not much, really. But it's slow work with the book, and I fear we will not make it in time. At present, we think the dragon is in the Rajh mountains because there are no reports of any attacks.

'The main problem, as you know, is that it could strike anywhere. There is a steady stream of people leaving both Mons Harbour and Taddy City, making for Manch City. Both roads meet up at Lake Blue. The problem is reports of raiders and bandits, and in between these, we could have shadows, sheets or Dragmen, and we would not know about it, Marcus,' said Eric.

'Can you, Eric, get word to your brother David, to inform Princess Shulla and General Aziz? If so, they can send some forces to protect them.'

'Yes, Marcus. There. It is done.'

'Dina, I want you to shoot with Taw's bow today, and he can use yours. In fact, I want you all to swap weapons. Today will be a test day. You will be up against the other group. The group who make it to the fire watch tower will win. If you are caught, or any member of your group is caught, you know what happens. You have ten minutes to get ready, then a twenty-minute start before we start to hunt. Your group leaves by the side gate, the others by the front gate.'

They knew if they were caught, they would be blindfolded, beaten, half-drowned, or subjected to some other nasty trick, or worse, the mind games. It was no good just running; you had to be clever, too. They worked in pairs, covering each other's tracks, doubling back, hiding in trees, avoiding direct routes. Taw and Juliet were paired today. They were following and covering tracks. Taw liked working with Juliet; she was nowhere near as feeble as he'd thought she would be, being a Princess. She had put Sam on his backside the second day of training, with a thunderous backhand swing, taking him off his feet. He lay there for a minute while trying to catch his breath; everyone laughed.

'Taw, concentrate; they're coming. Over here.'

Taw lay flat on his back in the stream, with no time to move. She quickly lay on top of him, as it was the only place deep enough to hide both of them. They lay very still, listening, waiting and hoping they did not find them. Taw looked at Juliet, her eyes, her mouth; she was beautiful. She was looking at him, too. There was something there. He thought about kissing her, then someone whispered, 'Over here.'

Juliet peeked a view and saw someone running a few yards the other way.

'Quickly. Now,' and she pulled Taw up and took off the other way.

They caught up with Earthie and Sam.

'The others are up further,' said Sam. 'We think they caught one of the other team. We are making our way round by that crooked rock, and we'll stay there for a while. That's what Dina said, anyway.'

Dina, Jackus and Josh were in the front. Twice Dina had used Taw's bow. Both times she just about hit the target, but at least they would have something to eat later. She was not happy; she wanted her own bow back.

'Quiet,' Dina said. 'Down.'

'That you, Dina?' came a whisper.

'That you, Taw?'

'Yes.'

'Good. Give me back my bow. Thanks.'

'I could not even pull the string on yours,' replied Taw.

'We all here now?' Dina asked.

'Yes.'

'Let's go, then. Follow me,' Dina said, and they set off. 'There, about one hundred yards on the right, but there are two soldiers just before it. We need to distract them.'

'I'll go,' said Sam. 'I'm one of the fastest. Wait for me to get them after me.' Sam distracted them, so they came looking for him, but he had already passed them. As they ran to him, he ran towards them and then ducked out of sight. The soldiers passed him and kept running into the woods. The group walked out by the fire watchtower.

'Well done, you seven. You have won. So, you can now have your mid-day meal. Dina, why have you got your own bow back?'

'I found Taw's a bit difficult to use. Just not used to it, I think.'

'So, you two think you can do what you want, do you?'

'No, Corporal,' she answered.

'Corporal Spike.'

He turned and saw that Prince Harry had walked up.

'Hello, Prince Harry. I was just about to rip into these two for swapping weapons back.'

'I'll take it from here. I need to speak to Dina. Dina, come with me and bring your bow with you.'

They walked a little away from the group. Dina was worried. Was he going to take her bow? The others were looking on.

'Sit down,' Harry said to her, so she did, and so did Harry. 'Pass me your bow. This is a very special bow, Dina, a very old one. It belongs, or did belong, to Queen Sienna's mother, the Black Witch Queen Gomorrah, a fierce witch warrior queen who ruled for nearly three hundred years. She was killed in a battle many years ago, two or three hundred, according to Sienna, Queen of the Black witches now. Oh, don't worry, she does not want her mother's bow back. It has chosen you now, Dina; it's yours until you die. I need to show you something. Remove the string.'

Dina did as she was asked.

'Now, I want you to take up the bow, aim as if you had an arrow, and fire at that tree.'

'That's strange. It feels as if there is a string and arrow.' She shot.

A black arrow hit where she was aiming, then disappeared. Dina dropped the bow.

'Don't be afraid of it, Dina. It is yours, and if you're ever out of arrows in a battle, you won't be. But put the string on and use arrows, because people don't like bows without strings. Keep this to yourself, and well done, Dina.'

Chapter 13

Princess Shulla called a halt to the huge column, nearly one hundred thousand soldiers and probably another twenty thousand carrying baggage and stuff. They set up camp about fifty miles out from Manch City. The Princess called a meeting of her senior people, the High General Tulla, Generals Aziz and Anrak, David and the sisters of Purple. She had asked David to repeat the message from Prince Marcus about the south and what was happening there. A plan of action was set, and the Princess, with the High General, gave out orders.

'General Anrak will take forty thousand mounted soldiers and surround the Blue Lake. Once a force has been established, he will send out patrols to Mons Harbour and Tandy City and patrol them. Any bandits, robbers, deserters, or anyone committing crimes against the people are to be executed. No excuses; their heads are to line the roads. This will show all that law is still enforced here. A fortification will need to be built, large enough to hold at least three hundred thousand soldiers, south of the lake.

'If you find any military, beware, as they could well outnumber you. If you still believe that they be worthy, it is up to your judgement whether they rejoin. I will give you a letter of absolute command over all military and governance in the south until I rescind it after my coronation. However, your main task in all this is to protect my people. Do you fully understand your orders, General?'

'Yes, Your Majesty.'

'Then go, General, and may the sun shine on you.'

'Your Majesty,' said David, 'two of the Purple sisters will go with them.'

'As you wish, David. High General Tulla, would you be so good as to take an advance of a few thousand soldiers into Manch City? There, find suitable accommodation for a new Palace and a home for us. It might be prudent also to see what military are there.'

'If it pleases Your Majesty, I'd like to take about fifteen thousand, just to be on the cautious side, as that number will be enough to make them think twice.'

'We will arrive in Manch City in the morning. Thank you,' said Princess Shulla.

'Your Majesty, if I may. Two of the sisters will go with him, too, to the city.'

'Yes, of course, David. General, the sisters are most useful at knowing whether someone is lying or trying to deceive. Use them on anyone you suspect, especially the military or any governance that might be there.'

'Thank you, Your Majesty. I will set off now and be there before dusk.'

'May the sun shine on you.'

General Tulla walked out and thought of his task ahead. It would be nice if the city turned out to greet the new Empress-to-be, but only time would tell.

Further down south, General Anrak arrived at Blue Lake in just under three hours and already could see a stream of people. The people all started to run away as they approached but settled back when they were not attacked. The General sent half his force around the other side of the lake, with orders to drop off one hundred men every half-mile and meet at the southern tip with four thousand men, placing his trusted colonel in charge. The General did the same on the near side of the lake and met the rest at the southern tip.

'I want a full-size fortress with turrets, drawbridge, the works, here. I want a thousand men on it now. I want patrols of five hundred men patrolling each road to the Harbour and Tanny City. All criminals and deserters are to be brought here, then executed. They will line the routes with their heads. Any military are to be sent to me.'

By the same time the next day, the fortress was well underway. Over one thousand criminals had been executed and lined the routes. A detachment of soldiers from Tanny City arrived in the late evening when they heard the military were back and that the Princess was ruling.

Captain Lordus reported to the General. 'I have been trying to keep some sort of law and order inside what is left of the city,' he said, 'but there are strange things and even stranger people. What war does to them I don't know. I have twenty-five thousand mounted Saracens, and eight thousand bowmen, who I believe are still loyal, General.'

'I want all your commanders to report to me, Captain.'

'Yes, sir.'

When he left and started shouting orders for the commanders, the General asked the Purple sisters to nod towards anyone not telling the truth. They reported in groups of twenty. In the fourth group, one of the sisters grabbed her other sister's arm.

She said to her, 'A Dragman. Back row.'

It sensed them and tried to run, but it was surrounded by soldiers. It screeched a terrible cry, then stopped as its head fell to the ground.

'What was that?' said the General.

'A Dragman. It steals the body of a living man.'

'How are we going to know them and find them? There are thousands of soldiers.'

'They do not eat or drink,' said David. 'Have men you trust keep a watch.'

Only one more was found, but it was enough to know they were about. But who or what was controlling them? Twenty thousand extra soldiers were sent on to Manch City, and the others were redeployed, supporting those around the lake, the fort or patrolling.

'Josh, what are you doing? Leave the fire alone.'

'I'm just getting it right, like the forge at home. If the coals are right, it will cook mid-day meal better. Look out, Sam.'

'Sorry, Josh.'

But Josh was crouched down and fell face-first into the fire, putting his hands down on the coals to stop himself. Juliet screamed. The others just looked. It was as if time stopped, and Josh was in the fire, face down. Sam had tried to squeeze through a gap between Josh and a tree but accidentally pushed Josh forward into the fire.

Strange that Josh did not cry out or jump up screaming, as anyone else would. Dina grabbed Josh back out of the fire; the others were all still in shock. Josh stood up. They all looked at him, and looked again. His face was black, and so were his hands.

'Don't touch,' said Dina as she poured water over him.

'Are you alright, Josh?' Juliet asked.

'Yes,' he said, as he tried to wipe the black off.

Dina gave him a cloth to wash it off.

'Ah, that's better,' he said.

Dina was helping. 'Do your ears,' she said. 'You know you have no eyebrows, and the front of your hair is burnt. But Josh, you're not burnt. We saw you go into the fire.'

'Yeah, I know. I was working with Dad at the forge once when a piece of orange coal fell out, and I caught it. It did not burn me, don't know why, but Dad said to keep it to ourselves. Look on it as a good omen. I did not knock over the mid-day meal.'

They all started to laugh.

Their corporal had seen it all from a distance. 'Yes, Prince Marcus, they are special, and I am learning more and more.'

'Prince Marcus, there is a funnily dressed gentleman at the gate demanding to see Earl Vantor, although he did not call him that at first. He called him the clever fool, man of the tricks. We tried to stop him at first, and he just threw ten soldiers around like toys. Seven are unconscious. He is now surrounded by eight knights with lances.'

'Did this person give his name?' asked Marcus, as they were walking towards the courtyard and heading to the Palace outer gate.

'Fa wa waa. Something like that.'

When they got to the gate, the man was sitting on the floor, waiting. The knights had been unhorsed, and they sat far away from the man.

'What's going on here?' demanded the Prince.

The little man stood up and bowed to Prince Marcus.

'Honourable Prince Marcus, I am Master Zing Fan Tu Wah. I am here because your Earl Vantor asked me to come about big gold dragon.'

Marcus bowed in return. 'Welcome. We did not expect you so soon, Master. Was there a problem out here?'

'No, Prince, no problem, but soldiers need much training, they do.'

'Please come with me, Master. Is that what we call you?'

'You, Prince, call me Zing Fan; all other call me Master.'

'Very well.

We will show you where you can freshen up, eat and rest after your long journey, and when you're ready, Vantor will be here.'

'I may like it here, Prince.'

Marcus went back to the gate and spoke to the knights. 'What happened here?' he said.

'We were coming back in and heard a rumpus at the gate, so we investigated. The little man moved like nothing I or we have seen. We surrounded him and had our lances pointed at him. Next thing, he grabbed one and was jumping from one horse to another, kicking and punching. We were all on the floor before we could draw our weapons. Then he said, "You have made one mistake already; do not be so stupid to make it two," then he sat down waiting.'

'Interesting,' said Marcus. "I would love him to teach that to me and the children, especially them.'

News of the Princess still being alive was travelling quickly across the Southern Kingdom, and military units started to report in the new capital, Manch City. The General had marched into the city. The military there was about half its normal strength. They were doing nothing, just milling about. The General in charge of the city had been murdered about a week ago, but nobody was interested or concerned. The captain who greeted the General was half drunk and undressed, unshaven and filthy.

'Captain Adulda at your service, my sweet General. Welcome to Manch Shitty; wine's not bad, whores are ugly, and they're free because there's no pay and...'

'Arrest him!' screamed the General. 'Round them all up. I am going to the Council building.'

The General looked at the Council building as he approached. It was a huge stone-built building, almost like a palace; there were beautiful ornate gardens at the front with great big black and gold iron gates and fences. The General halted at the gates. 'This will make a fine new palace,' he thought.

'Good afternoon, General. Sergeant Singh here. May I ask your intentions, sir?'

The General looked. The soldier was standing to attention and saluting him.

'Nice to see you, General Tulla,' said the sergeant. The General saluted back.

'I am in charge of Her Majesty Princess Shulla's armies, and I am taking this building on her behalf as her new Palace. Any objections, Sergeant?'

'No, sir,' and he opened the gates.

The General rode in with the army behind. 'Secure this place!' he commanded, and the soldiers rode off.

General Tulla dismounted near the sergeant. 'What is your name, sergeant?'

'It is Singh, sir. Sergeant Singh, sir.'

'Well, Sergeant Singh, you are no longer a sergeant. I am promoting you to captain. Are you in charge here?'

'Yes, sir. I have a platoon of forty men, well-armed, and a bunch of tough lads. We decided to protect this place and its staff here, as that was our duty when all went to Hell. The officers deserted or went into town and never came back, so I took charge.'

'Well done. Now, walk with me and show me around.'

'Yes, sir. One hundred and eighty-two military prisoners have been arrested, General, most for being drunk, one hundred and nine of them. The rest, seventy-three, more serious: rape, robbery, murder, a whole host of things.'

'I want the drunks all demoted to soldiers and out in the city on work details, cleaning this city for Her Majesty's arrival tomorrow. The others are to be executed and their heads on spikes to line the roads into the city.'

It did not take long to get the building sorted and ready for Her Majesty. Four abreast they rode. Two Astel knights in the middle and a Saracen knight either side, they approached Manch City, the long column of knights escorting the Princess, soon to be Empress, into the Kingdom. The citizens had turned out in their thousands trying to get a glimpse of their new Empress, bunting everywhere, crowds cheering as her carriage neared the new Palace. The knights separated, two going left and two right, to complete a huge full circle in the forecourt of the new Palace, and her carriage stopped at the steps. The trumpets sounded, and a great roar went up from the crowd.

Her Majesty stepped down, walked a couple of steps up, then turned and waved to the crowd. Again, roars and clapping from the people. David and the two sisters joined Her Majesty and walked up the steps and into the new Palace.

'Welcome, Your Majesty,' said General Tulla.

'Thank you, General,' she said. 'Now, first things first. I want every single member of staff in here, lined up. Now, please.'

'As you command, Your Majesty. Make it happen!' shouted the General, and soldiers started to run about, getting people into the grand foyer. The four of them took their places on the raised platform at the rear of the foyer. David stood next to Her Majesty, the sisters on the other side of David, away from Her Majesty, with General Aziz on her other side.

'They are all here, Your Majesty,' reported the General.

'Good.'

Princess Shulla walked down towards the people who were lined up.

'I am Princess Shulla, and soon to be Her Royal Highness the Empress, so I just wanted to meet you all quickly, so I know your faces. I will walk along, and all I want you to do is to tell me your name and what you do. My aides, David and General Aziz, will accompany me.'

What they could not see was that there were two Saracen guards behind them, with swords drawn. She set off along the line of people.

'Abus, Head of House, Your Majesty,' and so it continued down the line.

About halfway through, Patricia, one of the sisters, nodded her head. There was a swoosh, and a head tumbled to the floor. The staff were screaming and looking very scared until General Aziz shouted:

'Stand still, and be quiet! Tell Her Majesty your name and what you do.' Again Her Majesty set off down the line of now frightened staff. A woman tried to run towards the doors. She never made it. She fell, with an arrow sticking out the back of her skull and two in her back. They were trying to deal with this when another woman shouted that she was about to faint and collapsed on the floor, but this was not the case. A Dragman rose from the body. With dagger drawn, it raced towards Princess Shulla. A flash, and a loud bang, a howl and the smell of burning. It was over.

'That was close,' said Princess Shulla.

'A bit too close,' said David.

'I am so glad you are here, David, otherwise I would be dead by now.'

The woman was now being held by two guards.

'What of the woman, David?' asked Princess Shulla.

'Let me look, Your Majesty.' David examined the woman.

She was disorientated, unsteady on her feet and asking why she was in the hall. 'I was in the west wing, making the rooms,' she stated.

'She does not know anything. She was taken over by the Dragman. We need to get everyone a piece of silver to wear or carry as soon as we can, Your Majesty,' said David.

They continued along the line with no further incidents.

'General Aziz, I want everyone in the Palace to wear a circlet of silver around their necks at all time. If it is not there, they lose their head. Can we see to that now?'

'Yes, Your Majesty.'

'General, that includes guards. Anyone found without one, on the spot, head off. I'm sorry, David, but this must include yourself and the two sisters.'

'That is both acceptable and understandable. Sister Patricia and Sister Grace will take turns. One of them will always be by your side. This is a must, Your Majesty, until we discover who is controlling the Dragmen.'

Chapter 14

'Here comes the Princess now. Wait! When she gets to you, stab her in the heart! I'm ready. She comes now. What's happened? Where are you? Speak! Quickly, move to the next one. There, by the Princess's foot. What is that? No, it can't be! A head and a body next to it. How do they know?' asked Baroness Verna of the Red witches to herself. 'When the Princess gets two or three away, you run at her. Wait, where are you going? Stop. Stop. NO. I fear it's too late; I think she is dead.'

'Dragman, can you hear me?'

'Yes,' came the reply.

'Don't bother with the mortal body; attack as soon as you think it is best. Now is.'

Arrgghhh. Baroness Verna sat down. She was exhausted, and the Princess was still alive. They have a magician, a wizard, but where from? He must have come from Astel Kingdom. She pondered it for a moment.

'They also have telepathic sisters, but how many? This is going to make things a lot more difficult. I need to inform my mistress, the Dragon.'

'David,' said Sister Patricia, 'I thought that the sisters of Black were watching for Dragmen and sheets?'

'Yes, they are, but these were already in place, so the transform or energy surge was done previously and therefore was unable to be detected. But now, if someone were to attempt to take over a person as a shadow, they would know immediately and resolve the issue.'

'Eric, Luke, can you hear me?'

'Yes, David, we are here.'

'We have encountered two Dragmen here and one sheet among the Palace staff. We have dealt with them, but I sense something, something I can't put my finger on just yet. It's not the Dragon controlling them. I know that. It is like us, but more powerful. A lot of power is used. I think it is to make them obey. That's it. It is primitive, with a lot more power, to force them to obey. It's definitely human and not the Dragon controlling them.'

'Thank you, David. Keep us informed, and we plan to be there in three days for the coronation with Prince Marcus. The Cross.'

'The Cross to you all, too.'

'Master Zing Fan, very good to see you,' said Eric Vantor, as he bowed. 'You made very good time getting here.'

'Greetings, man of tricks, magicer,' the little man said, as he also bowed. 'We had good wind, and fast travel on very fast boat and very bumpy. Not good for many green people, no food or drink, lots for Zing Fan.'

They both laughed together.

'Come with me, and I'll show you the book we have found.'

They walked into Vantor's study: lots of papers, scrolls all stuck to the walls, all clues. Eric lifted the book upon the table.

'Big book, Eric.'

'Yes,' said Eric, 'for a very big dragon.'

They studied the book for some time. Eric showed him some of the stuff they had found and what they had managed to work out.

Zing Fan said, 'Eric, I think there something wrong with this border around the pages. It is not just pretty design. It looks like writing between these patterned lines.'

'Yes, it does; you're right, Zing Fan, but yet it makes no sense.'

'When I find me lost, Eric, best to start again at beginning.'

'We'll start at page one again,' said Eric grinning.

'No, magician, take me to where find book.'

'Good, now flick the leg. That's it! Ughh!'

The soldier went down, and as he hit the floor, Lord Sandbite said, 'Good, nice use of the elbow. Keep it up. Nicely done, Joshua.'

Gramps had arrived with four of his elite soldiers three days ago and was training the group in unarmed combat. They would have never guessed that Gramps was more deadly without a weapon. The speed and force and precision of his blows were deadly; they all agreed that they would never like to fight him properly, ever.

As the days went by, the group were getting better and better at it, but by far the best was little Josh. He had taken everyone down, including his big sister, Dina. She did not like it much, but it happened anyway.

They had stopped for mid-day meal and were eating in the small mess hall. The group were at one end, on one side, the other group at the top end, on the opposite side. In the middle, there were about twenty-five soldiers spread from side to side of the room. At their right side were the instructors and seniors, with Gramps among them, chatting away. Some of the soldiers joined them, and they were laughing and joking after their meal.

It was time to be outside and continue training, and they were all set when Gramps said, 'Take him.'

Two of the elite guard grabbed Corporal Spike and held him.

The group just stood looking. This must be some sort of training? It did not turn out that way.

Earl Vantor and a funny little guy in an orange suit thing came out of the mess hall. The wizard Vantor was holding his hand up at the corporal, speaking words of an enchantment. He was talking in a funny voice. The corporal's face was all twisted and contorted. He was starting to scream.

It looked as if there were two corporals. It hissed and spat.

'I'll tell you nothing!' it screamed again.

Vantor was moving his hand and saying more words; the screaming continued.

'Nothing, I'll tell you!' Then a silence. Corporal Spike was on the floor, but Vantor held a human shape in the grip of his magic hand, wriggling and twisting. Then, in a flash, it was gone. The group just stood there, looking in amazement.

Vantor's voice broke the silence. 'You have seen your first Dragman. Fortunately, I was here to hold it; otherwise, it would have tried to kill all of you. I want you all to place these circlets of silver around your necks now; they will protect you from being taken over.'

'What about Corporal Spike? Is he still alive?' asked Juliet.

'No. There is a problem if they have been too long a shadow. Then the original brain dies, and once separated, the body can't survive without the brain and dies.

'This is Zing Fan, or should I say, Master Zing Fan. It is so very good to see you after such a long time. You were not Master then, but I bow to you, Master Zing Fan,' said Gramps.

Everyone looked on in astonishment.

'My young friend and disciple, Sandy Sandbite! It is good to see you, old friend. How are you?'

'I am good, Master, thank you. I am teaching these young ones the basics of our skills.'

'I hope, Sandbite, you train these better than your knights. They need much training.'

'Master, maybe you could assist a little later, and perhaps I could also hone my skills.'

'Lord Sandbite, can you tell us what is happening? There seems to be a lot of strange stuff going on,' said Dina.

'Before this gets going, Lord Sandbite, Master Zing Fan and I need to go. We will catch up later.'

With that, Earl Vantor and the little Master vanished.

'Let's go into the small mess and take some seats,' said Gramps.

Once they were all sitting around, he started to tell the group about the Southern Kingdom and the awakening of the dragon.

'The red mist surrounds four locations that they know of, but we need to know what the red mist does to people and, more importantly, what it can or can't do to children, and about the return of shadows or sheets, now called Dragmen, and possibly who may be controlling them. Which brings me to where you young soldiers fit in all this. You were all selected by Prince Marcus himself, after you rescued him in the forest. He was impressed by how you all worked together as a team without any training.

'He thought how good you could be with the right training, especially considering how the red mist works with the young, and you have proved him right. We would put you up against any team of soldiers, even now. Your mission will be to infiltrate the red mist, possibly where the dragon lies, to gain vital intelligence and report it back to us. Now you know what your mission is to be, what do you think?'

'We are dead,' said Earthie.

'No, not if all that we know at this time is correct. You will still need more training, though, from Earl Vantor and hopefully Master Zing Fan.'

'Do you know when we will go on this mission?' asked Josh.

'We don't know yet; we are actually waiting on the dragon. We think it has left the Palace and Darkas and gone to the Rajh Mountains. We must be sure it has gone, and even more importantly, we need to know where it will go next.'

'So, what about Corporal Spike, that Dragman thing? How can we tell who is a Dragman? Are there any signs we need to look for?' asked Sam. 'There was something not quite right with him when we came back, but I could not identify it. Some of the things he said were a little strange for him.'

'I asked about him at mid-day meal. Remember me chatting to the other soldiers? Well, it turns out he never ate with the others; in fact, he never ate. Remember that! It is one of the only ways to tell. It is mid-afternoon now, and we've had an eventful day, so you can have the rest of the day off to relax and think about what I have told you. Remember, this is highly secret. We start training again tomorrow as normal.'

Earl Vantor and Master Zing Fan arrived at the Green monks' monastery and headed down to the crypt. 'This is the chair we found the book in. It was concealed in the base. We believe it was written at these four desks.'

'Why four desks to write one book?'

'We believe that four Templar Knight monks wrote the book.'

'No, magician, not true. The book is far older. They left clues translated, if you like. Look at this desk; what is this lid thing at the top?'

'We thought it was for candles to write in the dark down here.'

'Yet, magician, there are no wax marks or dribbles from the candles. Are there any on the floor? It was to hold something, like a candlestick thing. Bring book, magician, place on desk. I have it. There is a lid; open it. It held a mirror and a lens.'

'What, Master? A mirrored lens?'

'Yes, look between the lines on the border of the pages; it is upside-down and backwards; now, using a mirror and lenses, we can translate it.'

'Finally, a break,' said Vantor. 'On the page here, it shows four swords, North, South, East and West. But it has no meaning or instructions, as the next line we can't read, Master.'

'Ah, magician, we need to move desks.'

Eric moved to the next desk and looked at the book. 'Yes, I can read the next line. Each sword is marked with a symbol. Wait! I'll move to the next desk: "Fire, Water, Air and Earth".'

Prince Marcus's arrival at the training fort took all by surprise. The new training sergeant, Sergeant McNally, went by the book. He had them practising unarmed combat all morning, then in the afternoon mental resistance and enchantments with Gramps and Luke Vantor. Working in pairs, they were trying to make their partner do something, whilst the other resisted in this mental battle. It was amusing as the girls seemed to be a little stronger at this than the boys. Taw was trying his best to beat off Juliet, but he was on his knees. 'You will lie on the floor,' commanded Juliet. As best he could, he tried to resist, but it was not working; one hand was down on the floor. Juliet said, 'Got you.' Taw collapsed onto the floor, and Juliet released him from the mental onslaught.

'Thank you, Juliet. I thought you liked me,' said Taw.

'Just think if she did not like you,' said Luke Vantor.

Prince Marcus was watching, and Sam was faring no better with Dina. He was slowly losing until the laughter broke out when Taw fell to the ground and broke Dina's concentration on Sam.

'I have stopped off here to invite you to accompany me to Princess Shulla's coronation in Manch City, two days from now. You will be fitted for new uniforms of the Prince's Elite Troop – PET for short. It will be navy with gold piping. Also, get instructed in court etiquette and learn to dance, just in case.' The big smile on his face betrayed the seriousness of the situation.

'Earl Vantor will be travelling with us too, as he will continue your training. This will be the first part of a mission, so it is very important you pay attention.

'You will be in the presence of high dignitaries from various countries for a few days while we are there. You are aware of Dragmen and how to find them. Do not attempt to tackle them on your own. If you find one, report it immediately to one of us. Your main mission whilst you are there will be to gather as much intelligence as you can, not on the Southern Kingdom but on those who escaped the red-misted cities. How, when, why, what they saw, what they did, what they heard.

'As far as everyone will be aware, you are all court courtiers, and you are there to assist and direct guests around. Master Zing Fan will also train you in more advanced unarmed combat. Part two of your mission can wait until we finish this part. I think that is all I have to tell you for now,' said Prince Marcus. 'Does anyone have any questions?'

'Prince Marcus,' said Juliet, 'I will be known by some people, so I can't possibly be a court courtier.'

'Quite right, little sister. You will be yourself, Princess Juliet, and Dina will be your handmaiden. Mother has sent suitable clothing for you, and her handmaiden has also put clothes in for Dina. I take it that is acceptable, little sister,' he said, with a big grin on his face.

Chapter 15

'Princess Shulla, Your Majesty, there is a captain from Darkas. He has requested permission to enter.'

'Why, General Aziz? Is he someone special?'

'He says he has a gift for you but will only give it once he confirms to himself that you are who you say you are.'

'Do I have his head removed for speaking like that to me? Could he be a Dragman?'

'No, we checked.'

'What about just taking the so-called gift?'

'Your Majesty, he says it is not here, and if he does not send a signal in the next ten minutes, it will be destroyed, as per his orders.'

'Whose orders?'

'He refused to say, Your Majesty.'

'Very well, General. Show the captain in.'

The visitor was escorted into the throne room surrounded by four guards, and there were a least another ten or twelve female guards around the room. They stopped about five yards from the dais, and the captain bowed.

'I am so sorry, Your Majesty. Please forgive my bad manners and my ultimatum. But I must follow my orders and be sure. I'm sorry again, Your Majesty, but I will need to see the back of your left leg before I can release it.'

'I will take your head if you dare so speak to Her Majesty again,' said General Aziz, as he drew his sword.

'If it pleases Your Majesty, I am begging with my life and the life of my men. I swore an oath to pass it only to Her Imperial Majesty, and her alone. I was so ordered to see the back of your left leg, to confirm, before I release it or destroy it.'

'What is "it", Captain?'

'Again, Majesty, I can't say until it is proven to me, or I die.'

'There would be only one reason why this request would be made, and very few people know of this; in fact, I think only family. It is the S-shaped scar that is there. Is that correct, Captain?'

'Yes, Your Majesty, but also how it occurred.'

'Very well, Captain, your men's heads and your own hang on the outcome.'

'Yes, I understand, Your Majesty.'

'General Aziz, bring him forward so that he may see, but see your sword is resting at his throat should he decide to do anything. Can you see, Captain? Can you see the scar?'

'Yes, Your Majesty. So how did it happen?'

'I was four years old, Captain, and playing in Father's meeting room. I found a pretty box on a table and opened it. Inside was a beautiful jewelled curved dagger. I decided I wanted to play with it and took it out of its sheath, but as I did so, Father came in, so I tried to hide it behind me. It fell, and as it did, it sliced my leg, giving me a unique scar.'

'Thank you, Your Majesty. That is indeed correct. May I be permitted to signal?'

'You can tell the General your signal, Captain, and he will see it is done.'

'It is a flaming arrow sent into the sky.'

'Release him, General, but keep the guards close. So, Captain, tell me now what you know and how you know.'

'All were running for their lives in the city. We were trying to prevent stealing and looting as people went crazy leaving the city. We stopped two servants we knew from the Palace, who had a wheelbarrow. One of them was your old teacher. We searched the barrow and found jewellery and a crown. We think it is your mother's. There was also a big red ruby set in a gold hand. We were going to execute them, but she told us that the Queen had given them to her when your father, the Emperor, had been killed.

'She swore an oath to get them to you, and she was to say, "My little chicken legs, run for your life. You will need the Dragonite. Run, run little chicken legs." Before she was to hand it over, she was to ask about the scar on your leg. Only with the correct answer was she to hand it over to you. She trusted them to me to get them to you, and again I swore I would follow your mother's orders, Your Majesty.

'We have been hiding out and dodging patrols, as we were unsure of who was who, and who could be trusted. We found the two servants some days later. They had been slaughtered near a village not far from the city. So, I beg your forgiveness for my men and myself, Your Majesty.'

'Rise, Captain. You have done well. You and your men are to be congratulated on fulfilling your oath and orders. I am promoting you to colonel. As for your men, we could do with some good loyal soldiers, couldn't we, General?' she said with a smile on her face. She then started to laugh a little.

'Your Majesty?' The general looked at her.

She chuckled again and said, 'Chicken legs, General, chicken legs. That's what my nan called me. Only my mother, the Queen, would know that, General.'

'The package is here, Your Majesty,' said the newly promoted colonel.

'Bring it forward,' he commanded.

The Princess stepped down and walked towards the bundle of clothes he was now holding. He placed them on the floor and opened up the clothing.

Firstly, he took out a crown and handed it over to the Princess.

'It is my mother's crown. I shall wear it on my coronation,' she said, as a tear welled in her eyes.

Next, there was some expensive jewellery, diamonds, rubies, necklaces, rings and bracelets. Then he brought out a large red ruby, set in a solid gold slender hand, curled around the base and one side. It was beautiful. It was an apple-sized ruby but with a sapphire edging of blue. On top was a small beautiful diamond, held in place by one of the fingers with a long nail on it.

'What was so important about this jewel? Apart from its being exquisite, Mother knew something, enough to get it out of the city. What did she say? "You will need the Dragonite." General, find me the magician, David, and send him to me immediately. I think this may mean more to him. Thank you all. General, clear the room, please.'

Princess Shulla reached down to take hold of the jewel. It was warm to the touch, so she wrapped it in a silk scarf.

'Collect the rest,' she said to her handmaid, 'and follow me. General, we will need a strong box to keep these in. Can you arrange, please?'

'Yes, Your Majesty.'

'You all look very smart.'

They were dressed in navy blue jackets, which fastened diagonally from the left shoulder, with two rows of gold buttons following the fastener, a high round collar and epaulettes. Two circles of gold on each sleeve just above the wrist, all edged in gold. Navy trousers with twin gold stripes down the outside of each leg, a gold waistband with a black sword attachment, but no sword, and black boots. Princess Juliet and Dina were absent, doing their own dressing. On the right breast was a gold crown about two inches square, with *Royal* on top and *Elite* below.

'Prince's Elite Troop,' Prince Marcus said. 'Now, all line up.'

They were all looking at each other; how very smart they looked.

'Alright, get them off now and pack them neatly into your kit. You will now be known as the Troop and not the group. Well done. We will be leaving tomorrow when Prince Marcus and Earl Vantor are ready.'

Earl Vantor and Master Zing Fan had been studying the book in between training the group. Good progress had been made on both accounts. The book was more difficult.

There was another vital element missing, which prevented it from making any sense. It was impossible to either decipher or translate it correctly. They had been in and out of the crypt numerous times, and used the desks, in turn, to correctly decipher the book. Zing Fan was out in the other room where the tombs lined the walls; then he turned to look at the four at the top. Just four, one-high, going across the room. He walked to the first. They were very old. He cleared the heavy dust off the top. There seemed to be something engraved into the tomb.

'I wonder if it has a date,' thought Zing Fan.

He took a piece of cloth and started to brush off the dirt, so he could read:

'"I am one of four; I am not Fire nor Wind nor even Water. I am what I am, whilst history repeats itself. Time cometh to pass; the sword of my past will be again joined with my brothers for our tomorrows."'

What a strange inscription on a tomb.

'Magician, come look, look at this.' Zing Fan had taken to calling Eric Vantor magician. It seemed to amuse Zing Fan and annoy Eric.

Eric ignored him.

'Magician, magician, come – you look.'

Eric came in. 'What is so important about a bunch of tombs, Master? Dead don't talk.'

'Ah, you have eyes, but you do not see. All is of fours, is it not? If one opens one's eyes, they will see. There are four elements, four desks. Look around; what do you see, magician?'

'A bunch of tombs either side, stacked four or more high, four more across the room at the top. All in fours: four elements, four desks. Wait! Four Templar Knights, and four tombs.'

'Come, read first inscription on top, magician.'

Eric read the inscription, then moved to the second tomb, cleaned it off and read:

'"I am two of four; I am not Wind nor Water nor Earth. I am what I am."' Eric then went to the third: "I am three of four; I am not Water nor Earth nor Fire. I am what I am."'

He moved to the last one and cleaned it off, and began to read:

'"I am four of four; I am not Earth nor Fire nor Wind. I am what I am."

'They are all the same except for the obvious differences. The four Templar Knights? They were the ones who worked on the book and translated the scripts for the first time. We need to open these tombs,' said Eric. 'I think the swords of the elements are contained within each one.'

'No, magician, bad omen; we leave dead. Not good to disturb dead sleeping heroes, magician.'

'We must, Master. Reading the script, it says, "I am one of four," so the first is Earth, then Fire and so on. We will need the swords if we are ever to put the dragon back to sleep. We will need tools and more help to remove the tops, so we will return tomorrow and hopefully retrieve the swords. But now I am tired and hungry, and we must remember I am required at the Princess's coronation the day after tomorrow.'

'Very well, magician, you may be correct in your assumption about the swords.'

'Come, Master. Tomorrow is a new day.'

Chapter 16

Restless was her sleep; why? She half woke; something had changed, something was different, something was there. She had been there a short time, resting in the cradle of the mountains. The hunger was stirring again, and it took many of those little things to keep her magic flowing. Only the man-things could provide the right supply of food for life magic. Not much meat or substance; the small ones were the best supply of magic, but again, it took so many. It would suffice for now, but more would be needed if she was ever to leave this world. There it was again: she could feel it, calling; something was loose, but from where?

Time for food again, and she took to the air; higher she went, soaring above the clouds, stretching her huge wings. It was good to be awake again and flying, except for the hunger. Why was I asleep for so long? I can't remember, remember... ah, the child goddess. These thermals are wonderful. I'll circle for a while, and it will be time to eat; there it is again, calling.

Marcus arrived in Manch City with a small escort of one hundred mounted knights. Josh said, 'I thought they would all be in dress uniform.'

'No, Josh,' said Dina. 'We are not in our best while we travel; otherwise, we would be filthy for the coronation.'

They were led into stables where they all dismounted and started seeing to the horses. Once they were done, Prince Marcus called them together.

'Hello, Juliet,' he said to his sister. 'You look well.'

'Hello, Marcus. Good to see you. How is Mother?'

'She is good, keeping herself busy with the kingdom's merchants and bankers and also seeing to the defence of the city. I have been kept informed of your progress. It's been said that as a team, you are awesome, and some of you have special skills, which I'd love to see, but another time perhaps. Tomorrow, we will move further into the city and meet up with the other knights in the evening. The following day, the knights will line the route with the Saracen knights.

'Juliet, you and Dina, as your handmaid, will accompany me into the Palace, as we have royal accommodation. The rest of you will also go into the Palace and be around the throne room and Palace in full dress uniform, as we discussed. Juliet, Dina and I will be on the dais with Princess Shulla. Remember, you can't listen if you're talking. Eyes and ears open, mouth closed, and get among the guests after the ceremony. We don't know whether any Dragmen will attempt to gain entry or not, but we must expect they will.

'Earl and David Vantor and the sisters will be around. There are eight ways into the throne room, so we can't watch them all. If a Dragman is spotted, do not take it on, on your own. Once they have ditched the body, there is no substance to them. They are just smoke, but they can deliver a death blow through your heart. Alert everyone as soon as possible.

'The day following the coronation, you will all leave with Prince Harry on the second part of your mission. Do not ask anything about it, as you know I can't tell you at this time, but Harry will when it is time.'

'Eric, can you hear me? It's David.'

'Yes, brother, what it is?'

'I think we may have found the stone. Is there a description of it?'

'All we know is that it is a large oval-shaped ruby and will turn blue when the dragon is near, awake or even present. It may be that the jewel just turns blue.'

'This is a large red ruby, tinged with blue, held by a gold slender woman's hand.'

'We cannot afford to leave it out if we are unsure. Get it covered in something protective and keep it in the dark. We don't know whether the dragon is aware of it or senses it, but either way, we need to be sure and safe. I will be there with you tomorrow, brother. The Cross,' said Eric and was gone.

'There it is again, distant, faint,' said the Dragon to herself, 'but where is it coming from and what power does it possess? I need to find out!'

'Baroness, hear my voice!' commanded the Dragon. 'I command you, send forth thy soldiers to see what calls to me from afar and bring it to thy mistress. Kill all who oppose me and my divine right to rule this puny world. Do you understand me, Baroness?'

'Yes, My Lady. It will be as you command. Soldiers of the holy one, open your minds; seek out what calls to thy mistress. Let no one stand in your way. Go now; go with speed.'

Across the Southern Kingdom, fifty soldiers, five monks and ten others set out to find it.

'Sisters of the Holy One, go forth! We need more soldiers soon for our mistress; send as many as you can back here,' said the Baroness.

The Dragon was pleased with herself. She had found a plaything.

'The Baroness has been useful since I awakened,' she thought. She had heard her call out for her people. It had not been hard to twist her primitive mind and will and persuade her that she, the Dragon of Dragons, was indeed her liege.

Time for some much-needed food, there by the sea. Time to be unseen again and renew the walls. The Dragon, now invisible to all below, silently flew in and began the red mist again as she had countless times before. Soon, though, they would know she was there, as the red mist wall began to grow, travelling in a huge circle around Mons Harbour; the tiny creatures were yelping and running around, but it was too late now. The circle was complete.

Silently she drifted in and landed, but the landing was anything but quiet, as buildings collapsed and crashed to the floor under her massive size.

'Now for some food, or should I spoil myself and have some of those delicious smaller two-legged things that scream so high?'

The Dragon began to look around, and the screaming began.

'Luke, it is Eric. Are you there? Can you hear me?'

'Yes, Eric. What can I do for you?'

'I need you to go to the monks' monastery and down into the crypt. In the crypt, there are the four tombs of the Templar Knights. You will need tools and help to open them, as we believe that the four swords of the elements are contained inside. Once you have them, take them under escort to the Palace and down into the catacombs. The Lord Marshal will secure them, and the sisters will watch over them. Once I have finished down here in the Southern Kingdom, we will return to the meeting place in the catacombs.'

'Very well, brother. I will see to it.'

The knights lined the route to the new Palace with a mixture of Astel and Saracen soldiers inside and out, as requested by Princess Shulla – the gesture showing that the two kingdoms were at peace.

Prince Harry stood and said to his new troop, 'Today is the day of all days for you all. Sergeant.'

The sergeant came forward holding a bunch of swords.

'Step forward each of you, one at a time,' and in turn, they were presented with one of the swords, after taking a knee and swearing allegiance to the Crown and country.

'You are all now commissioned into Prince Marcus's Elite Troop. If you look at your swords, you will see they have been designed with a crown and PET under it. Your official rank is Regent Knight, which is your court rank. Juliet is already a Princess, so she still carries that rank, but when in this role, she is the same as the rest of you. Dina will be Lady Regent Knight, and as such, at present, she is the only one.'

'So, Captain Harry, where do we fit into the rank scale? It would be interesting to know,' said Taw.

'In this role, you are higher than a knight, a captain, or a baron; almost level with an Earl. But as I said, you carry a court rank of Regent Knight, basically Queen or King's Knight, second only to the monarchy. Are we about ready then, Troop? You all look so smart in your blue and gold uniforms. Well done, and I'm proud of you all. Remember, we are on a mission and not a jolly day out, so if we are ready, let's go.'

The troop walked out towards the new Palace of Princess Shulla, as smart and as proud as they could be.

'Hello, Eric,' said David. 'I have managed to persuade the Princess to keep the jewel locked away for the time being. However, it will be on display during the coronation, as a sign of her divine power and right to rule over her people, as her ancestors have passed the stone down for hundreds of years.'

'Yes, David. Can we go and see it, please?'

'Yes, come with me. We will ask the Princess.'

Princess Shulla was sitting with Prince Marcus, the High General and General Aziz. They were going through plans for the day and security issues when Eric and David came in. Princess Shulla was pleased that they were all there for her coronation. She thought she would have been dead had it not been for them.

'Thank you all,' she said. 'I am so happy and thrilled you are all here for my coronation and that I am alive, and we have plans to keep me that way.'

'Greetings, Your Majesty,' said Eric and David as they approached.

'Before we all depart and get ready, is it possible for me to see the ruling jewel, Your Majesty?'

'By all means, Earl Vantor. Is there a problem?'

'We don't know yet, Your Majesty,' said Eric.

She signalled, and two soldiers brought over the solid chest made of wood with steel bands around it, placed it on the floor, bowed and then left. Princess Shulla produced a key and unlocked the chest. She opened the lid and took out the jewel.

'Well, I have never seen it like that, red with blue,' said Princess Shulla.

Eric and David looked at each other and Prince Marcus.

'This is warm,' said Princess Shulla. 'Feel it.'

Eric did and agreed. 'What did you mean, Princess, when you said you had never seen it like this?'

'It has always been a big red ruby, without sapphire blue edging on the cutting lines.

'There it is again. Find it, find it now, it calls to me.'

The Dragon pulsed with her mind.

'Find it; send my creatures forth to seek it and destroy whoever stands in their way.'

David and Eric jumped when they felt the dragon's pulse. It was so powerful they staggered. Marcus and the Princess looked on as David and Eric almost fell.

'Quickly, put it back! Do it now, now! Our lives are at stake!' Eric shouted.

The Princess placed it back into the chest, closed the lid and locked it.

'What on earth is going on?' she said.

'The dragon is aware of the stone. They are connected in some way. It calls to the dragon, and it has sent someone or some creatures to find it. The stone can be heard by the dragon when it is out in the open,' said Eric.

'We will have to be even more careful then, today, if we have things searching for the jewel. Tomorrow, we will try and unravel what we do next,' Marcus told the Princess and Eric.

'Shulla, I would request that you do not take the jewel out for display, or we could have the dragon here today, and we are nowhere near ready to fight a dragon, are we, Eric?'

'No, Marcus.'

'I will do as you say, Marcus, although some of my people will be unhappy that it is not on display, indicating my right to rule.'

'At the moment, I don't think anyone will question it. We can always show it after we have killed the dragon or put it to sleep again.'

Meanwhile, four huge creatures, black, beetle-like and as tall as two men, had awakened from their sleep and were answering the call of their mistress, the Dragon.

Chapter 17

'Prince Harry, we have now issued every soldier with a piece of silver, and six Dragmen were found and executed,' said General Aziz. 'However, we have another problem. There are many high nobles attending the coronation today. We cannot ensure they are not Dragmen, and it will be most difficult with some of the other royal families.'

'General,' said Harry, 'as part of Her Majesty's coronation and the new friendships and alliance with the Astel Kingdom, each person entering the throne room will be given a silver coin from the Astel Kingdom as a gift of peace. Anyone refusing will most likely be a Dragman, so let's try and capture them then. We don't want to make a scene of it outside the throne room, so anyone who even starts to refuse, knock them unconscious and take them away.'

'That is a brilliant idea, Prince. I will see to it.'

'Ah, hello, Marcus,' said Eric. 'I had almost forgotten to tell you that the dragon is now at Mons Harbour.'

'No, it can't be, Eric! When did this happen?'

'We believe it was a few hours ago,' said Eric. 'Zing Fan and Luke are in the catacombs under the city. They are moving the swords of the elements to there, as it will be where we will control everything, prior to setting out to destroy the dragon.'

'I need to talk to Prince Harry now. Eric, excuse me,' Marcus said and walked off to find Harry. He had two hours before the start of the coronation.

'So many people in the city,' thought Marcus. 'If the dragon were to attack here, it would be colossal. The jewel? Oh, my God, it calls to the dragon. We need to get it out of the city now. First things first, find Harry. Where would he be? Sorting the troop out.'

Quickly he ran from the Palace to the hotel the troop were staying in. In the main room, they were just leaving, all dressed in their new uniforms.

'Wait,' said Marcus. 'Harry, I need to talk now, over here.'

The two troops just stopped and looked at each other and then at both Princes. Marcus had never been like this. He was always calm and very calculating.

After a few brief words, Marcus turned to the troops and said, 'Good luck to you all. I very much hope I see you again. The Crown and kingdom are proud of you.'

Then he saluted and was gone.

'Change of plan,' said Harry. 'Troop one will be setting out on part two of our mission. Troop two will remain here. Troop one, saddle up, ready to travel within the hour, normal civilian clothes, weapons hidden but accessible. Go now! Troop two, you will be under the command of Prince Marcus. Proceed as per your orders. Attend the coronation thirty minutes before the start. Ensure you have your silver with you. Good luck to you all as well, Troop two,' and Harry went off towards his troop.

Prince Marcus returned to the Palace and found Eric Vantor. 'Eric, we need to get that jewel out of the city. If the dragon gets a location on it, it will attack here. The outcome of an attack would be too great a loss.'

'Gods, Marcus, you are right. I can't go to Her Majesty now. You will have to go. How will we get it out of the city?' asked Eric.

'We need two more chests, so we can put one inside the other, and then into the other, then fill the outer one with silver. Eric, if you can't go and see the Princess, go and arrange two hundred knights from each kingdom, and then escort the jewel to Astel Kingdom catacombs. I will go and speak to Princess Shulla and get her to release the stone to us and sort the chests.'

Number One Troop were mounted up and ready to move out when Captain Harry arrived.

'We all here?' he asked.

'Yes, Captain.'

'Let's go easy on the way out of the city; then we can open the pace a bit.' As they passed through the people, it was clear that the coronation celebrations were well underway.

Zing Fan was busy running things through his head. 'This is getting complicated,' he muttered to himself. 'Always go back to beginning if lost. Need, we do, four people of elemental power to wield the four swords of the elements. So –' He wrote it down on a piece of parchment. 'We also be needing the four points of the stars, North, South, East and West. So. We have eight; how do we use them against the dragon?' he asked himself. 'I have it; the four all match together.' He drew a circle. 'Think I might have just got big, big clue.'

On the circle, he put the dragon in the middle, then matched North with Wind, South with Fire, East with Water and West with Earth. 'That must do something, and where jewel? Also, how we surround it when we can't even see the dragon? More questions I can't answer. My head hurts,' said the little man. 'Time to go to bed.' He climbed up into the monastery to find daylight was just breaking. 'Ah!' he said. 'I'll still sleep,' he muttered to himself.

Princess Shulla was in her private chambers when Prince Marcus approached with General Aziz.

'We will not be allowed in, Prince. It is forbidden.'

'Then the Princess will have to come out to see us, General.'

'But that, Prince, is also forbidden.'

'Either way, it has to be. The fate of this city and indeed the safety of the Princess rests upon it.'

Four burly Saracen guards barred their way. They informed the two they would be allowed no further.

'Please inform Her Majesty that I, Prince Marcus, must speak to her this very minute. The kingdom and her people are in grave danger.'

'We do not take orders from jumped-up foreign princes.'

'You will take orders from me. I am General Aziz, and you will pass the message on to Her Majesty.'

'No, we will not, General,' and they drew their swords.

Marcus said, 'Where are their silver bands?'

At that, the guards advanced on Marcus and the General.

'Guards, guards!' shouted the General, as he and Marcus drew their swords.

Alarm bells started to ring across the city.

'What's that for?' said Marcus, as he engaged one of the guards.

'It's the city bells warning of invasion or attack.'

'But by who? Is it the dragon?'

On the far outskirts of the city, four large creatures had appeared and were moving quickly towards the city.

Chapter 18

Captain Harry and his merry troop had been travelling for about two hours when Harry called a halt and told them to walk the horses a little way before they had their break. The roads had been busy with people making their way to Manch City for the coronation of the new Empress. They were just north of Lake Blue, and it was a lot quieter now, except for the Saracen patrols. They had already been stopped twice, but a letter authorised, signed and displaying the royal seal, stating that they were on royal business, was enough to allow them passage.

As they sat and ate their mid-day meal, Taw said, 'Captain, may I ask where we are heading?'

'Yes, Taw, I was just about to brief you all. Close in, everyone. We are heading south. Once we get to Lake Blue, we will follow it down on this side, then cross west and on to Mons Harbour. You need to know that Mons Harbour is occupied by the dragon. As far as we know, there will be very few people about, apart from those inside the red mist wall.

'Our job is to scout from the start to the end, to see whether we can find a way in, out or through. Nobody is to venture inside for any reason at all. If you think you have found a way, come and tell me. Gather any other information you can, but be careful. There are or will be some less scrupulous people about. Kill if you have to, maim if you can. Remember, there could also be Dragmen here. We will find a place to set up tonight and secure it, as it will be late in the evening when we get there.

'Dina and Sam, your job will be to see to the horses. Taw and Josh, security and booby traps. Twins, get some food on. Then we will make a watch system for through the night, sleep, breakfast and ready for the day ahead. Mount up. Let's try and arrive a little early to be organised.'

Eric Vantor was walking down the corridor and heard the shout of 'Guards, guards' and then the clash of swords. He hurried towards the sounds of conflict. As he turned the corner, he could see both Prince Marcus and the General fighting with four guards. He held up his hands in front of himself and started reciting words of magic. The four guards slowed, then stood static. The General was amazed and looked at Marcus.

'Quickly,' said Marcus. 'Disarm them.'

As they did so, about ten guards showed up.

'Quickly, tie these men up,' instructed the General.

The guards tied them up where they stood.

Eric asked, 'Are we ready now? They may reject their bodies and attack as Dragmen. Stand back, everyone. I will release the hold, but if they try to leave their bodies, I'll have no choice but to kill them.'

'Do it,' said Marcus.

Eric Vantor lowered his hands slowly, and the statue effect began to wear off, but one started to turn to smoke. The magician said two words, and there was a flash of light; four bodies hit the floor, dead. There was a smell of burning in the air.

'Quickly, the Princess.'

They opened the doors and found a harem of women, gasping and ready to fight as they entered.

'Where is Princess Shulla?' Marcus asked.

Then two sisters walked through the next door.

'What's going on?' said one of the sisters.

'Is the Princess alright?' Markus asked.

'Princess Shulla is perfectly fine. She is bathing. What seems to be the issue?'

'Clear the room,' the General said. 'Four of you, on guard outside the door. The rest get rid of those bodies.'

Meanwhile, Prince Marcus explained what had happened and about the jewel.

'I will ask now, Prince Marcus,' and the sister walked off.

A few minutes later, she came back.

'Yes, Prince Marcus, take the jewel, but once the dragon is gone, she would like it to be returned.'

'Tell her thank you, sister. Eric, I want to send David with it instead of you. Is that alright?'

'Yes, I would have said if you had not.'

'General, shall we get this done?' said Marcus.

'Yes, and attend our Empress's coronation.'

Captain Harry and the group reached the outskirts of Mons Harbour. The big red wall of mist was just visible. There were very few people, all moving away from the city. As they reached the outer city wall, they were met by a group of Saracen soldiers.

'Nobody is allowed to pass,' one of them stated as he stepped in front of Harry.

The group stopped and waited. Taw had noticed there were at least six bowmen on the wall and three or four just inside. Harry took out the letter and passed it to the soldier.

The soldier read it, then laughed. 'You think just because you have a letter written by some sheepherder, you can pass? I don't think so, boy! Only passes here today are of a gold type. If you get my meaning?'

'Oh,' said Harry, 'why didn't you say so? I'll have to dismount to get it.'

The soldier looked pleased with himself. Harry fumbled at the saddlebag. Taw had given a warning to the others to be ready, and hands were slowly moving onto weapons. The soldier came around and stood next to Harry; then Harry moved quickly. He held the soldier with a knife to his throat, facing the city. The group had dismounted and were all now armed behind their horses.

Harry said to the soldier very quietly, 'Who's in charge here?'

'I am,' he said.

'Not good enough,' said Harry, and a slight trickle of blood ran along the knife.

'The officer,' the soldier said.

'The officer, where is he?'

'Asleep in the big hotel there.'

'You there, inside the gate. Go and get the officer now!'

'I bloody told you, Gerick. I wanted nothing to do with this.'

A few minutes later, a Saracen knight arrived at the gate.

'Good evening to you, sir,' he said to Harry. 'I am Captain Urisa, in charge here at Mons Harbour.'

'Good evening,' said Harry and released the soldier, who fell to his knees.

'The letter,' the Captain said, and the soldier passed it to him. 'The royal seal? May I ask your name, sir?' said the Captain.

'Yes, I am His Royal Highness Prince Harry from Astel Kingdom on a very special and secret mission on behalf of your new Empress Shulla.'

'Your Majesty, my sincere apologies. Please come with me. Guards, execute him.'

The man, Gerick, was screaming as the group followed the captain through the gates of the outer city.

With the jewel secure in the chests, two knights from Astel and two Saracens got into the protected carriage with two hundred of each kingdom's knights to escort it to Astel. They got off at top speed to get clear of the city. Their instructions were non-stop ride, walk, ride; spare horses for the carriage, six at a time, but the jewel must reach Astel and be kept safe. They missed the attack from the creatures, which were surrounded outside the city and butchered by two regiments of mounted Saracens.

The ceremony was a long, drawn-out affair. Prince Marcus stood behind the now Empress Shulla, as did the High General Gunar, General Aziz, the two sisters and some other high dignitaries. What took so long was not the actual ceremony but all the heads of the various tribes from across their kingdom coming forward, kneeling, presenting gifts and swearing allegiance to their new Empress.

Once this part was completed, they retired into another room. Shulla sought out Marcus, and then she asked all to leave. She sat, and Marcus joined her.

'I'm so glad that's over,' she said. 'I now feel the full weight of what this job means. I'm not sure that I'm going to be any good at it! Marcus, what do I do?'

'It will be hard, Shulla. Never trust anyone fully. You'll have to be strong. I can maybe arrange an advisor to you, but you'd have to do this in private, as if your people think you're being ruled by an Astel, they will kill you.'

'May I be permitted to keep the two sisters, as I feel so much safer whilst they are around me? They know when there is evil or bad intent around and who is lying to me!'

'At this time, Shulla, they will stay until the situation with the dragon is resolved. Once the dragon business is concluded, we shall meet officially and maybe make a better treaty and be of more assistance to you.'

'Thank you, Marcus. I know you will take the crown, too. Two young people ruling such a vast area! We should attend the banquet,' she said with a smile.

They set off back into the other room to chat to the other guests whilst waiting for the banquet to start.

Prince Harry and his group walked through the city but stayed close to the outer wall until they came to an inn called The Lizard.

The Captain stopped and said, 'Your Majesty, you and your group will be safe here at this inn. The innkeeper is still here but is going in two days. By then, you'll need to find your own accommodation. I have no orders here, but within two days, we will withdraw, too. It will be a free-for-all here then, Your Majesty, if you follow what I'm saying.'

'Yes,' said Harry. 'Thank you, Captain, for your help.'

'I will just introduce you to Ravi, the innkeeper, and then I'll be on my way.'

'Just one thing, Captain,' said Harry. 'I am *Captain* Harry, if you don't mind, or Harry to you, do you understand?'

He nodded, and just then, Ravi opened the door, as he had heard voices.

'Ravi, this is Captain Harry and his group. They'll stay with you until you leave. Send the bill to me, and I'll see it's paid when we reach Manch City.'

'Come in, come in,' said Ravi. 'Take a seat and I'll sort you out.'

They walked into the inn; it was dimly lit, but a nice fire was going. There were about eight tables in the middle, with chairs around them. Along the back wall was a long table with a bench seat against the wall, with two or three candles lit on it. They made their way to this long table.

Earthie and Taw were settling the horses into the stables at the rear of the inn. Once they had done, they joined the rest of them.

The door opened, and Ravi and a woman came in from the kitchen.

Ravi said, 'Sorry for the wait, but my wife here, Malla, was sorting your rooms. I myself have put some food on to cook. It will take about an hour, if that's acceptable? Would you like to see your rooms? If you'll follow me.'

'Are there no other guests staying here?' asked Josh.

'No, young sir. Nobody left who wants to pay since dragon came. We are waiting for wife's sister and family, then we go too.'

The rooms were pleasant enough, two to a room, with Harry and Taw sharing. They came down and sat around the large table. Ravi put some wine jugs and goblets on the table.

'The bread may be a little hard as it was baked this morning,' he said. 'We'll have fresh tomorrow, but that's it, too, as Aaron the baker leaves tomorrow.'

Ravi's food was tasty, a nice round of steak each with potatoes, mushrooms and onions, and a rich gravy to pour over the top.

'Food's not been a problem here, but it will be soon. If you're planning on staying longer, you could do me a favour and look after the place, then secure it when you leave. I'd be much obliged,' said Ravi. 'And, of course, help yourself to what food is left, but as I said, it won't last long.'

'Thank you for your hospitality and your kindness,' said Harry. 'We will do that, thank you.'

Just after they had eaten, two men walked into the inn. As Ravi approached them, they turned and walked away.

'Well, I never,' he said. 'That's the third time today two people have walked in, not said a word, then just walked out. I don't much like that,' said Ravi. 'Is something amiss, or smell bad or something?'

'No,' said Harry. 'Right, listen up, you lot. Ravi, this includes you if you want to stay alive. Secure every window and door, upstairs and down. Bring your stuff down here, your mattresses too. Mr Ravi, you and your wife will need to do the same. I believe they are Dragmen and will return. Off you all go now and bring everything down here.'

Chapter 19

Prince Marcus and Eric took the shortcut home once they had left the city. Eric met up with Luke and Zing Fan. Marcus went to find his mother, the Queen, and bring her news on the last few days' events. Eric Vantor, his brother and Zing Fan were discussing how things were progressing. They were in the crypt, trying to put all the pieces of the puzzle together.

'So far, the swords of the occupants are positioned in line with the four compass points; however, they must be held by a person of that element. We have two,' said Eric.

'Who and where are the other two?' asked Luke.

'Good question,' stated Zing Fan.

'Each must be guided by a magician or a person of power, but both have their own words to say at the same time, as well,' replied Luke.

'The others too, you are quite right,' said Zing Fan. 'However, we have an even bigger problem. How get dragon to stay in one place long enough for us to get around it before it eats or fries us? Two big problems,' said Zing Fan with a smile.

Dina and Taw had got one of the middle guard times; everyone was staying downstairs in the main inn room. Tables and chairs had been stacked against the doors and windows. Other furniture had been used to block off the stairs. Taw had just made a cup of tisane for them both when a noise was heard from the front doors. Dina and Taw crept forward with swords in hand, ready, but it never came again. However, someone then tried hard to get into the back, kicking and running at it two or three times, but then gave up trying. Everybody was now awake, all with swords in hand, except for Ravi and his wife, who were huddled together looking scared.

'They won't try again,' said Harry. 'Everybody back to sleep. Well done, you two.'

Jackus could not go back to sleep and stayed with Taw and Dina till their watch finished; then he was on with Josh. Morning soon arrived, and all had breakfast made by Mrs Ravi. Then the group helped Ravi and his wife to get the horses ready. They were leaving; it was too much for them.

After the goodbyes, Harry called them all together.

'Time to make plans,' he said. 'This place has a cellar that will be our way in and out of here. This will be one of our safe houses, so we will today fortify this inn from inside. Booby traps set around the way in and out, all windows and doors secured with metal, nails, wood. Split into teams and go and find those things we need. Josh and Juliet, you're on food. Earthie and Jackus, tools, and stuff to fortify this place. Sam and Taw, weapons. Dina and I will scout further into the city towards the road, just to see if we can locate another safe house. Avoid trouble as much as possible. Most, if not everyone, will leave today. All be back before dusk. Nobody be late.'

Prince Marcus had informed the Queen of all that had occurred in the Southern Kingdom, and she was pleased.

'Maybe now that Empress Shulla rules the Southern Kingdom, we could become better allies and friends, Marcus,' said the Queen. 'If someone of note were to marry Shulla, like maybe your brother, Harry, that would secure the crowns in both our kingdoms, with you ruling the north and Harry the south.'

'Yes, Mother. Why not just get me to marry her, and I would rule both kingdoms? Solves the problem,' he said.

'Don't be like that, Marcus. Your brother would be ideal, but I fear she would have to marry a Saracen, or they'd chop her head off.'

'Yes, Mother, so let's leave all this matchmaking until we solve the problems we have. The dragon first, or we'll be dead.'

'Prince Marcus, the escort from the south has arrived. They are on their way in now.'

David came in with the four guards. Two had been injured.

'What's happened?' said Prince Marcus.

'Sorry, Your Majesty, no time. We must get this into the catacombs and shield it. Quickly, follow me,' said David.

Just then, Eric Vantor, Luke and Zing Fan entered the throne room.

'Stand still, everyone!' ordered Eric Vantor, his voice thunderous in the throne room. Everyone stood still, looking around at him. Suddenly, there was a bright flash of light and a loud noise. As twirls of mist cleared, there in the doorway was a Shadow Dragon, some six foot long, with wings and a tail, its eyes shining in contrast to its grey, smoky colour.

It said in a garbled tongue, *'I now know where you are.'*

The soldiers drew their swords, but Eric said, 'It will do you no good; it cannot be killed by a mortal sword.'

'True, wizard,' said the Dragon. *'I will come...'* but then it was choking, holding its throat. *'No!'* it screamed.

It was thrashing about, then gone.

Zing Fan was sitting down, legs crossed, hands pointed upwards in a prayer-like fashion. He opened his eyes and said, 'Never like Smokey Dragon, but not hard to kill.' He then promptly stood up and said, 'We must go quickly.'

They made their way down under the keep; down and down it went.

'Magician,' said Zing Fan, 'cast your spell of hiding now.'

With that, Eric obliged, and the spell was cast. Into a large, open room they came, with nine tunnels going off in different directions. In the centre was a basic table and six chairs, a small barrel of water, some goblets and, of course, on the table, the Dragon's book.

The four swords of the elements, and now finally, the Dragon stone, the Dragonite.

'They must all be kept in separate boxes, each protected by the five spells of concealment,' said Zing Fan.

'I placed the spells on the Dragonite after the second attack, but they knew where we were,' said David.

'Who attacked you?' said Marcus.

'They were like the living dead. They were already dead, but still alive and attacking us. Strange,' said David, 'very strange.'

Harry and Dina walked through the narrow streets of the city, keeping away from the main roads as lots of people were leaving the city. They did not seem to be in too much of a hurry, though.

When Harry asked, they just replied, 'The dragon is sleeping – can't you tell? There is no screaming.'

So that was it; it was safe to move when the screaming stopped.

Dina said, 'What about another inn as a safe house, with a cellar?'

'No, we need something like that.'

Harry pointed to a building on the end of a row. It was a night watch house. It had bars on the windows and doors, a front door at street level, but steel bar doors on the inside. Cellar doors front and back for access to the holding cells, again with steel bar doors on the inside. Best of all, it had an extra cellar door opening out into the alleyway, again steel doors inside. Quickly they made their way over to it. The streets were deserted now. They moved in the darkness and made it to the house. They entered via the rear cellar door, and once inside, they secured the door with two iron bolts.

'That should do,' said Harry. They looked around inside and made sure it was secure.

After returning to the inn and meeting up with the others, Harry told them about the night watch house they had found and secured.

'It is two streets below the Harbour Square. The next street is where the wall of red mist is,' said Harry. 'We will take a quick look, Dina and I. The rest of you, try and sort sleeping and cooking areas, and make sure no light shows.'

Dina led the way. They ducked in and out of doorways and down alleys until they reached the last corner. What confronted them was awesome. Both of them recoiled at the sight of the mist. It was as tall as two tall pine trees; it stood straight up and continued for as far as they could see. Dina walked up to the wall.

'Don't touch,' said Harry, 'it may kill you. We will start investigating tomorrow. Don't want to do anything now.'

Dina and Harry made their way back to the safe house and met with the others. Dina told the troop about the wall and how big it was as they ate supper and settled down for the night. Taw and Josh had drawn first watch for the night. As everyone went to sleep, Taw looked at Josh and thought how much he had grown in the last few months; in fact, they all had. Sam and Earthie were on watch when the screaming started; horrible screaming, some just cut off mid-scream. All the troop had woken at the sound. The screaming continued for the rest of the night and the morning, but the troop breakfasted and then set off in twos to investigate along the wall.

'I have it,' said Zing Fan. 'Magician, I think I solve big, big part of puzzle.'

'Now slow down, Zing Fan. What big part have you solved?'

'The jewel, we know it calls to the dragon; even when it is in the box, it calls to it. So that's what we use; we use the jewel to lure the dragon in. Once there, we can position the others around the dragon and trap it with the swords of the elements.'

'That sounds really good, but, and a big but, what is to stop the dragon eating us and or anyone else who is there?' said Eric. 'Someone will have to hold out the jewel in front of the dragon. Again, who is going to do that for the first time? Want to give it a try, Zing Fan?'

'Ha ha, magician make funny joke.'

'When I last held the stone, it was slightly warm to touch, but as it turns blue, it gets hotter. Soon it will be far too hot to touch or hold. That's why I have instructed the blacksmith to have three new boxes constructed, with lead and steel lining in each. The lead will help shield it, and the steel stops it from burning through. So, Zing Fan, do you still want to hold it?' said Eric with a big grin on his face.

'It is funny, magician, but book says someone must hold the stone in front of dragon. How then? Or who? We need new special person to find.'

Chapter 20

Harry, Taw, Juliet and Earthie were in one group; Dina, Sam, Josh and Jackus were in the other. They made their way to the second secure house next to the red mist by two separate routes, Harry leading one, Dina the other. They entered through the rear cellar door, avoiding the booby traps they had set up. Dina's group arrived first and entered, and shortly after, Harry arrived with his group. Harry gathered the troop around and started to outline his plan.

'Two will stay behind and guard the house; one will overlook the entrance, armed with a bow, and kill anyone who approaches. The other will be on standby at the door just in case anyone needs a quick withdrawal to safety.

'The rest will be in teams of two. They will set off ten minutes apart and be given an area of the wall to see whether there is a possible way in, or anyone coming out. Be mindful that there are Dragmen, but there are also other criminals and debauchers.

'Defend yourselves; kill if you need to. Any children must be approached cautiously, as we don't know whether they could be Dragmen. Check now you all have your silver with you. Check weapons. All good?

'Taw and Juliet, you will go first and have area A, left on the map. Dina and Jackus, you go ten minutes later; you have area C, right on the map. Josh, you're with me, and we go to area B in twenty minutes. Sam and Earthie, that leaves you two on watch here. Sam, you cover the door as you're stronger, and Earthie, the bow overlooking the entrance.

'Any questions from anyone?' asked Harry. 'No? Taw, Juliet, off you go.'

Ten minutes later, Dina and Jackus set off towards the left. Harry and Josh waited the ten minutes and were about to set off when Sam at the door said:

'Wait! There are three men outside, just up the street.'

'What are they doing?' asked Harry.

'Looks like they are having an argument about something. No, wait, two of them have just stabbed the other one; he has collapsed on the street. They are robbing him, going through his pockets. It's all over. They are walking off towards the outer city. It looks like the guy on the floor is dead.'

'Let's go now, Josh, and head right, then left up that alleyway,' Harry said.

Taw and Juliet had made their way down to what looked like the poorer area of Mons Harbour. The houses were in rows and very close together, all in drab old colours that had faded over the years. They were following one street down from the wall so as not to be seen. There was very little sound of screaming down this way.

As they got to the bottom of the harbour and the red mist wall, Juliet noticed something.

'Over there,' she said to Taw and pointed.

The building had collapsed under the red mist, but they could see a doorway that they thought would lead to a cellar.

'Taw, I wonder if the red mist can or does get underground?'

'What do you mean, Juliet?' Taw answered.

'If the red mist travels along the ground, but as here, it sits on top of the ground and stays on top, we could get to the other side by going underneath it; by going through the cellar.'

'That might be possible,' said Taw, 'but should we try? It could kill either of us or both. I think we should inform Harry and come back with the others and try.'

'Yes, I agree, Taw.'

They crossed back across the road and, keeping to the walls, slowly made their way towards the safe house. Juliet stopped at a corner and signalled to Taw. Two men were heading towards them; they were ducking in and out, but there was nowhere to hide.

Then one of the men shouted, 'Over there.'

Taw and Juliet started to run down the road. The men were following, and the shouting was alerting anyone else who was about. They reached another corner, and more men were coming. Only two ways to go and the wall behind them; there was nowhere to run to. They were trapped and now surrounded by twelve men. Taw and Juliet drew their swords as the men moved in.

'Drop your weapons,' said a voice from the group of men.

Taw and Juliet looked. Who was talking? A scruffy-looking man with dirty, long blond hair and beard stood with four other men with crossbows aimed at them.

'What have we here then, gentlemen? Drop your weapons, or you will die here where you stand, and we'll have your gold anyway. Now drop them!'

Taw and Juliet had no choice but to drop their swords. As soon as they did, the men grabbed them.

'This one's a fit young filly, boss; make me and the boys nice and happy like.'

'Shut up and search them. We'll find out who they are and why they are here,' said the leader. 'Tie 'em up and bring them with us.'

Taw and Juliet were searched and their hands tied behind their backs; then a noose was placed over their heads.

'Just in case ya thinks of runnin' off,' said another man. 'Yes, a nice young filly this one,' the man said as he stood in front of Juliet. Then he reached out his hand and grabbed Juliet's breast and gave a hard squeeze.

Juliet drew her head back and head-butted him square in the face and nose. His nose exploded in a torrent of blood, and a loud crack was heard as he staggered backwards, his nose broken. Then Juliet kicked him right between the legs, and he tumbled to the ground in agony. All the other men were laughing at him and calling to him as he staggered to his feet, aided by some of the others. He had just about regained his composure and walked over towards Juliet, saying, 'You'll regret that, bitch,' when, to Taw's amazement, she kicked him so hard again between the legs that he dropped to his knees, screaming in agony. The other men were nearly hysterical with laughter; even Taw had a grin on his face.

'Enough of this nonsense. Bring them,' said the leader, and they were led away.

Prince Marcus, Eric and Luke Vantor, and Zing Fan all met in the catacombs. The new boxes were ready, and they were going to move the jewel to its new home. Eric cast a spell of shielding inside the existing protection spell. They could not take any chances. The last thing they wanted or needed was for the dragon to attack the kingdom. Zing Fan opened the box containing the jewel.

Eric put his hand in but pulled it out again. 'The jewel is very warm. I can handle it and place it in the new chest, but as you will see, it is now half blue and giving off a blue glow.'

'Why is it changing, Eric?' said Marcus.

'Let's move it quickly first, then we can discuss it, if you don't mind, Your Majesty,' said Eric.

Eric took hold of the jewel. 'Ready, Zing Fan? Now.'

Zing Fan opened the lid of the smallest box, and Eric moved the stone from its box and placed it into the new one. Zing Fan shut the lid and slid the bolt across. Lifting the small box, he placed it in the next box and again slid the bolt across. Finally, he picked the box up and placed it in the third and last box. This time, two laps were pulled over and two padlocks fitted, all secure.

'Magician, why you glow blue?' asked Zing Fan.

The two others looked at Eric; he was indeed glowing blue. He had a blue aura all around him. The others stood back.

'This is very interesting,' said Marcus. 'Do we put you in a chest, too?' He smiled.

'Very funny, Your Majesty. I don't know. More to think on.'

'Maybe we have more to consider. Can dragon see or sense you?' Zing Fan asked.

'Good question, Zing Fan,' said Marcus. 'How long will it last? Is it permanent? One thing is certain: we will need to be cautious. Eric, you will have to remain here until we can figure this out. Zing Fan, would you remain with Eric while Luke and I try to find a solution?'

After a little discussion, Luke and Marcus returned to the kingdom keep. Luke could not help himself, on the way back, making fun of his blue brother, even suggesting he form a new order! The order of Blue monks, which he found highly amusing, as did Marcus.

'So you're brother and sister? And you were just leaving the city now? How convenient that you happens to be armed as well. Strange, really, as you both have Astel accents, too. Spies? No, too young. Thieves? No, too well-dressed. Just look at their boots, cost a month's wages, them would. We have a bit of a problem here, me boys; what ya all thinkin'?' the blond man said.

'Give me five minutes with the pretty one here, and she'll talk. She'll be screaming her little head off,' said one of the men.

'No, I doubt that. This one is a real fighter and made of steel.'

'Exactly what this is made of,' said Harry into his ear, as the cold steel of his sword touched the man's throat. 'Now be a good man and have them cut free before I start to cut.'

Just then, one of the men put a knife to Taw's throat and said, 'Now this is fun. What's you going to do –' He did not finish his sentence as an arrow struck him in the forehead. A split second later, another man behind Juliet fell forward with an arrow in his back.

'Now, everyone stand where they are,' ordered Harry. 'You there, with the red cap on, cut them free. Now.'

The man walked over and cut their hands free from behind their backs. Taw and Juliet stood and removed the nooses from around their necks.

They quickly retrieved their weapons and walked over to Harry.

'Now, gentlemen, we are going to leave, but nobody need move a muscle as we do so, for another five minutes. If you do, your reward will be an arrow. Do we all agree?' said Harry. 'Good,' and they turned and walked away.

Once they'd turned the corner, they ran into a shop, down the stairs, out the back across the street, through the alleyway, turned right along the back of the houses and into the safe house. Once in the safe house, Juliet and Taw said thank you to Harry.

'We were running out of options.'

Just then, Sam and Dina arrived. Dina said, 'I had to kill another one before we left, but we are good now.'

Harry shut the door and bolted it. 'Follow me,' he said.

They came to another door on the right and went into a small room.

'Light the torches,' said Sam.

'Where are we going?' said Taw.

'Down here, just follow us,' said Harry, as he climbed down a hole in the floor. They followed him down into a large tunnel.

'What is this place?' said Taw as he stood and looked about.

'We think it was built by the early Crusaders. Tunnels run everywhere under the city; they are like our catacombs. We found a partial map, but we don't know if it is all finished; some parts stretch out towards the other cities. That's enough for now,' said Harry. 'Let's get back to the first safe house. We can discuss it more there.'

Once they had arrived at the safe house, the troop got themselves sorted and sat down. Harry told them how Josh had spotted the men and was about to warn them about the men he had seen, but the men had spotted Juliet and Taw.

'I followed you and sent Josh for help. Josh returned, and we quickly devised a plan of rescue. I was to get the best part,' said Harry, laughing. 'I was to sneak up on the leader, with all the others about, and put my sword to his neck. God only knows what would have happened if I'd been seen. Anyway, we are all back safe now, so check equipment and get some food. We do nothing for the rest of the evening.'

'Harry, Taw and I think we found a way under the red mist through a cellar, but I think that your way may be better, brother,' said Juliet.

'We would still have to test it,' said Harry. 'Both that way and through the tunnels. If we could just observe what is happening on the other side, or rescue some of the children. We could do with one of the magicians here. We need to test the red mist before we try, but that's not going to be possible. So, two choices: one, I wonder whether we can pass underneath without dying, or two, try and get word to a magician.'

Zing Fan was puzzled. Eric was still glowing blue, with no sign of it growing or fading. Eric had tried two or three spells, but none had worked. Zing Fan still thought it was hilariously funny.

He was preparing an old ritual that he hoped would release Eric from his blue glow, and Zing Fan was going to make sure he would never forget.

'Eric, step into the star chart. Do not let your feet touch the lines. Eric, you must face north and hold arms out like a tree.'

'I...'

'Schuuu, no speak with mouth; you think only. I speak for two of us, magician. Must start soon; do not move or speak until I have finished.'

'How will I know, Zing Fan, when you have finished?'

'Silly blue magician, you not be blue anymore.'

With that, Zing Fan began to chant a strange tune, eerily like a hum and a whistle at the same time.

'Zing Fan, I can't stand. My arms too. Sooo heavy,' he pulsed to the little man, but the tune went on, not faltering one bit.

Higher the tune became; higher again it went. Eric was numb, but higher the tune went on. Eric looked at his hands. They were there, but not there; he could see through them. He was also not standing on the floor anymore; he was hovering about two feet up. Eric tried to say something, but his voice had gone, and so had he! He could no longer see any part of himself, no hands, no arms, no nothing. The blue haze hung in the air six feet off the ground, a round ball of shimmering blue, a beautiful, liquid, shining blue ball. All was dark, no sound, no movement, a black abyss of nothingness, just the blue ball. It was gone; just black remained.

'Eric, Eric, Eric, Earl Vantor! Magician, can you hear me? It's Zing Fan, you big blue torch.'

Eric became aware as his head was about to explode. It was like a bass drum throbbing, and he was lying on the ground on his side, Zing Fan leaning over him.

'Magician not blue anymore, friend. We have done it, but we have make more perils for us.'

Eric sat up, and Zing Fan gave him some water.

'So, Zing Fan, what happened, and how did we make thing worse than they already are?'

Harry sat everyone around that evening, discussing the day's events.

'We have two possible ways of getting through the red mist; one is through the cellar door at the end of the harbour, found by Juliet and Taw. The other is through the old Crusader tunnels or catacombs. Both are very high risk, very narrow at the cellar one, and nowhere to run or hide if caught. The tunnels are very wide; we don't know who knows about them or whether they are safe.

'We know the mist is there. When we can see, it is red, but what about if we can't see it, like in the tunnel or cellar? And if we can't see it, is it strong enough to kill us?'

'I will try first,' said Taw.

'No, you can't,' said Dina, followed by Sam and Juliet.

'Taw, you realize that if it is still there, even if you can't see it, it may kill you?' said Harry.

'Yes, I know, but it has to be done, so I will try tomorrow, and we will know then.'

Harry held up his hand to the others.

'It's decided. We know it has to be done, so we do it and get on with it.'

169

Chapter 21

Morning came fast, and in their pairs, they made their way to the second safe house.

'It is closer to the cellar door one from here, so I will try that one. There is a little cover in the rubble. What's your thinking on that?' said Dina with an icy edge to the tone of her voice.

'It is narrow and dark, and I don't think it is patrolled by anyone,' said Taw.

'Taw,' said Harry, 'I will stand next to you when you go through. When you get through, have a quick look around, and then come back and we can make a plan. Taw, Dina and Earthie will come with me to the cellar; the rest can remain here in the house, observing us just in case, until I return or send word. Ready, move.'

Dina led the way towards the lower part of the harbour where the house with the cellar door was. The streets were very quiet; no sounds at all, no birds, no seagulls, no squawking. An uneasy silence was all around them as they moved towards the cellar. They reached the cellar door, and down the steps the four of them went, below street level. The red mist shone like a tall sheen of red ice, stretching above them.

Taw said, 'I'm ready. Here goes. Stand back from me.'

Taw put his hand out and pushed the door inward. As it opened, Taw walked through to a corridor, and the door fell closed behind him. He looked up and saw the corridor was about twenty yards long with a brick wall at the end. There seemed to be no mist that he could see. 'I am going to walk down to the end wall,' he said. He set off very slowly, his heart pounding in his chest. Slowly, one step after the other he took; the sweat was running freely now and was even getting in his eyes and stinging a little. But that was nothing to the fear he felt. 'Courage,' he said to himself. Slowly he made his way to the brick wall.

On the left, just in front of it, were steps made of stone. He started to climb up the steps; there were about twelve in all and a door at the top. Taw stopped at the top and blew a sigh of relief as he sat on the top step, just before the door. Harry, Dina and Earthie followed down the corridor but stopped at the bottom of the steps.

'Well done, Taw. So now we know we can walk under the red mist as long as it is not visible,' said Harry.

'Thank bloody god for small blessings! I've never been so scared in all my life, even when we were caught in the orchard,' said Taw.

Taw looked at Dina and Earthie. 'We are halfway there, so best get on. Just one more door to step through at street level and see what is going on,' Taw said as he stood up.

'When you're ready then, Taw. Off you go.'

'Thank you, Captain,' and Taw pushed the door.

It was stuck solid.

'So, Zing Fan, what did you do to me?' asked Eric.

'I make you not here anymore, magician. I sent you into the spirit world, so blue shadow cannot hold onto you, so it float in air looking for new body to possess. I opened chest, and blue shadow returned to jewel, and I close chest.'

'Ah, that's good, but why did it not go to you?'

'I think because I not touch before or because I was casting spell.'

'So, it is sealed in the chest now?'

171

'Yes, magician, that is true, but what is also true is that when you open the chest to get jewel out to defeat dragon, blue shadow will be there waiting.'

'Oh, I see,' said Eric. 'But that's a problem for another day. For now, my little friend, you have freed me from my blue shadow, and we still have much to do. We need to go and find Prince Marcus.'

'Yes, magician, but we leave shadow here, yes?' as Zing Fan started to laugh.

Prince Marcus was with the Lord Marshal, Edmond, and Lord Sandbite, Sandy. They were talking about plans for the city.

'Ah, young Eric Vantor. It is good to see you without your blue halo and equally good to see you, Master Zing Fan.'

'Thanking you kindly, Prince Marcus. I was seeing a little blue,' Zing Fan said with a big smile on his face.

'We need to plan who, where and when we take on this dragon and return it to sleep. Perhaps if Zing Fan and Eric can brief us all and Her Majesty this afternoon, after mid-day meal in the anteroom?' Prince Marcus said.

'No, we can't,' said Eric, 'it is too dangerous. We do not know who or what is about. May I be so bold as to suggest we meet in the catacombs and in the anteroom there, as it is the most protected.'

'Yes, of course, Eric, forgive me. I forget sometimes what we are dealing with.'

Taw placed both hands on the door and pushed again. Harry was behind him. Taw pushed at the door yet again, but it would not open, so he tried the handle, but this did no good either. He then pulled the door towards him, and it moved; slowly, the sunlight drifted in the more Taw opened it.

Taw said, 'Wait here. I'll be back,' and he stepped through and closed the door behind him. He stood for a moment while his eyes adjusted to the bright sunlight. He looked up, and there was the wall of red mist rising from the ground. Except this time, he was on the inside. He slowly turned as he followed the red mist wall, but then it met another wall. This wall was not red, though; it was gold, great big plates of gold, layered on top of each other.

Taw was between two walls, one red and the other gold, reflecting the red from the other. Taw followed the gold wall, which covered any view he might have had of what was going on. To his left, the gold curved around to the right and lowered in height. Then, like a bolt of lightning, it struck him. He staggered backwards; his mouth was dry. Swallowing hard, he composed himself and looked around. Satisfied that the dragon had not seen him, he retreated back through the door.

Once he was inside, he ushered the others down the stairs. He then took the biggest drink of water ever. They all looked at Taw.

'What is it?'

'The dragon,' he said.

'Yes, Taw, what about it? Did it see you?'

'It is as big as a city itself, made of gold plates, each one as big as a house roof.'

'We'll go and look in a minute,' Harry said. 'Are you alright, Taw?'

'Yes, Captain, I'm good. It did not see me, as it had its back or side towards me. But, Captain, it is absolutely huge.'

Harry and Dina went up first to see after Taw. Dina did her best not to scream at its size when she realized that the gold wall she was looking at was the dragon. Harry was calm and took a good look at the dragon and the surrounding area. Anyone approaching from the other side would be seen by the dragon and most likely become food for it. The others in pairs all went and had a look.

Once they had all looked, Harry said, 'Right, Troop. We need to withdraw to the first safe house and discuss what we have just seen and what next to do.'

The troop set off and were moving in and out of the streets and alleyways, making their way back towards the safe house, when a figure darted from an alleyway to a house about two hundred yards ahead. Dina, who was leading the way, called a halt.

'Hide! Move!' she said to the troop, and they obeyed instantly. She sat for a moment, thinking about what she had seen. It was moving really fast. She was not sure; it looked human-shaped, but it was moving just too fast for a human.

'Dragmen,' she whispered, then two more, moving just as swiftly, entered the house.

'Dragmen,' said Taw, 'and I'll wager there are a lot more of them.'

'I think they have been watching us,' said Harry. 'We could go back to the other safe house, or we move forward and attack them.'

'No,' Juliet said. 'We need to do something different. I don't know why, but we do.'

'If they have been watching us, they will know about the safe house near the wall,' Josh was saying. 'We need to lose them somehow, but they are so quick.'

Sam and Earthie were chatting, then Sam said, 'We've got an idea, Earthie and me. Quickly, follow me,' and he entered one of the houses of a long row, all along the street. When they were all inside, he asked, 'Did they see us?'

'No,' said Harry. 'I was the last. So, what's this plan?'

'We go upstairs, and somewhere, there will be a loft hatch. Once we get in there, we should be able to go all the way along to the end of the street in the lofts, as there are no walls in the lofts. When we get to the end, we will have passed them, hopefully, and be on our way, but we must be like mice; not a sound, or we could all be dead, I think.'

'That's a good plan, you two,' said Harry. 'Go!'

They went upstairs.

'There, that square, push it up. We will need to help each get up, but be careful: only stand on the main wood supports; otherwise, you will fall through.'

Sam was the last up and put the cover back.

Earthie was going to lead the way. 'Just follow me. Remember, quiet as mice. If they hear us, we've had it. Also, if anyone hears anything, call a halt.'

'Is the hatch back?' inquired Harry, 'As they will think we have disappeared. Good, by the time they figure it out, we will be well gone.'

They set off. House to house they went through the roofs as silently as they could; the odd squeak from the boards did not help. After some time, Earthie called a halt. They stayed perfectly still; they could hear someone shouting orders.

'They are not down this end, you idiots. Start from the blue house up there. They are up there somewhere, so find them, or I'll have your heads for break fast, you jesters.'

The troop stayed still for a few more moments and then set off again house to house through the lofts, quiet as mice. Earthie reached the end house and called a halt. He listened for a few seconds.

'Dina, have a quick look through the hatch and see if it's clear.'

Dina did, then opened it and dropped down into what was once a bedroom. They followed her quietly until they were all down. Taw approached one of the windows and peeked out. There was nobody about, not a sound at all, no birds, no wind, just an eerie silence.

'Listen up,' said Harry. 'We are about ten to fifteen minutes away from the safe house, the inn, but it will be difficult. We have to cross a dozen streets in the open and cross at least one square. We have to get back and get a message through to get a magician here, and tell them what we are facing. They have no idea! The biggest dragon ever.'

Chapter 22

'If you would be so kind, Eric, please erect the shield, and we can begin.'

'Of course, Prince Marcus. With your Majesty's permission.'

The Queen nodded her approval.

'I will begin. This spell is far more complicated and infinitely better; it just takes a little longer.'

A small see-through pearl started in Eric's hands and began to grow and grow like a big bubble. Soon it engulfed him.

'Don't be alarmed,' he said as it continued to grow. Soon it had engulfed them all, nearly filling the huge cave in the catacombs. Eric said some words and moved his arms around, then he stopped, and so did the bubble. 'It's done,' he said.

'I am impressed. I did not be thinking you remember words so well, magician. Then I would have to rescue you again, before you turn all people blue,' Zing Fan said, with a big grin on his face, and some of the others laughed at Zing Fan's joke.

'Your Majesty,' began Eric Vantor.

'Please dispense with the formalities whilst we are in here. It will take all day reading all the titles out. Let's get on with the issue at hand, shall we?' the Queen said.

'Yes, of course. The gods were very clever when they imprisoned the dragon using the four forces of nature: Earth, Wind, Water and Fire. They also knew that, should it ever escape its imprisonment on this earth, the gods would be no longer here to do it again, which brings us to the present day. They have left clues all over the earth. In the passing of time, much has become legend, folklore and miracles of a great history. However, in all of this, there is some truth, which, with Master Zing Fan's help, we have, I think, been able to piece together. We have, though, some serious clues missing before we can challenge the dragon out in the open.'

Gasps came from around the room, together with: 'Are you mad? You're crazy, magician!'

Master Zing Fan stood, and everyone looked and was quiet. 'Most of you not know me or I you. Do not know from Kingdom I came except far from your lands, and yet this dragon is known in my lands. We need it in the open, so we can imprison it once more.

'If, like its last prison, it was made by Earth which covered the dragon, then fired by the wind of the gods to super-hot, much as you would encase a clay pot or casting a sword. At the maximum temperature, Water, instantly cooling forming a solid mass. A prison for a dragon, a mountain of fired clay, then dragon will sleep for another thousand years, or awake again by two of the forces of nature.'

The little man sat down again, and the room was silent.

'Thank you, Zing Fan. We are two vital parts missing, and how long we have, nobody knows,' then Eric sat down.

Marcus stood. 'So, Eric, what you are saying is that we are nearly there, but not, and we might never be in time!!'

Eric stood. 'We have at the moment too many maybes and not enough yeses. As we answer one question, two more come with it, or we solve a problem, and an even harder one surprises us,' he said. 'Marcus, you were talking about protecting the city and its people. Zing Fan and I are working on a spell, an enchantment, but it is so huge, we could, instead of protecting the capital and palace, utterly destroy it.

'We don't even know whether it will protect us from the red mist or, should the worst happen, we will be unable to protect us against an attack by the dragon.' Earl Eric Vantor sat down and took a glass of water after his brief.

Zing Fan stood up. 'Magician and I have make decision to go down to this Mons Harbour where dragon is.'

Eric stood up, too, and said, 'We believe we may be able to gain more relevant information that we require, with, of course, your permission, my Queen.'

'Eric and Zing Fan, I think when this is over, we will owe you both a great debt, but also in saying that, it seems we have no choice if we are ever to defeat this dragon. We trust your judgement, but you will leave our defences sadly lacking here if the dragon should attack,' the Queen said.

'I fully understand the situation, but we really have no other choice. We could die either way, but our best chance is to travel to where the dragon is now and gain what we can, Your Majesty.'

'I see, Eric, and what do you think, my son? Which way do we go?'

'At present, we can do nothing, Mother. All the armies we train will mean nothing. It will utterly destroy anything in its path. We have to have information if we are to prevail against this foe, so I agree, Mother, we need to let them go, and at very short notice, they can be back. Which is why I am going with them.'

'I know if I say no, my son, you will stay but not be happy, so, therefore, go with my blessing. We will all meet again, once they have returned. Thank you all for attending, and good luck, gentlemen.'

The Queen stood and left the room; shortly after, so did the trio.

Harry took over leading the way from Dina. 'I want you, Dina, to cover with your bow. This next bit is tricky.'

They scanned the square, but there was no sign of anything.

'Taw and Juliet, I want you to go first. Once across, cover and wait for us, then we cross in pairs.'

Taw and Juliet set off and crossed with no problems. Next were Sam and Josh. Again nothing. Dina and Harry next. Dina shot an arrow, then another a split second later; it sped towards Sam and the others. Harry could only look on, stunned. The first arrow flew between Sam's head and Juliet's shoulder to punch home in a man creeping up behind them unseen. The second arrow took him in the head. As he started to change into a Dragman, the body fell to the floor.

Harry shouted, 'Everybody, move!' They ran as fast as they could to the next street and met up at the corner. 'Everybody here and not injured?' asked Harry.

'Yes, we're all here,' said Sam.

'Good. Let's get to the safe house now.'

Dina led the way. Five minutes later, they arrived at the safe house, all glad to be somewhere safe for the moment.

'Back to normal routine, all. You know the drill. Briefing after supper, everyone.

Harry sat thinking about the day's events. 'We were lucky a couple of times, but it will not last. Eventually, we will meet with the Dragmen. We need to know how to defeat them at close quarters, when they are shadows,' he was thinking.

Juliet came and sat next to Harry. 'We don't get much time to talk anymore, brother,' she said. 'What's on your mind? I know this look.'

'There is so much going on, and so much we know that needs passing to the others at home. We need to get word to Earl Vantor to get a magician down here, or even him to come. He needs to know what we have learned and, more importantly, tell us how to defend ourselves against these Dragmen.

'It will not be long before they find us, so we have to leave and try and make it out of the city.

'Listen up, everyone,' he commanded.

Dina, Taw, Earthie, Sam and Jackus gathered around.

'We have a real situation, the Dragmen are hunting us, and they will eventually find us here. We can't defend ourselves against an army of them. Although I reckon we'd give them a good fight, we would all die. We have important information for the Queen, Marcus and Vantor, and we need a magician here. Our choices are simple: we leave in the morning as a troop, fight our way out together and find the nearest town, or we send two groups out, hoping one or the other gets out of the city. We cannot stay here much longer, though, so anyone got any ideas?'

'I did not come all this way to run away,' said Dina, in an abrupt voice.

'Me neither,' said Taw, shortly echoed by the others.

'I know,' said Harry, 'but we don't have much of a choice.'

'That's no choice,' said Sam.

'Why can't we hide on the other side of the mist? We need more information, and we can find a place to hide. They will not expect that. So, do we run like scared children, or do we move on like soldiers?' said Joshua in a matter-of-fact tone. Everybody looked at Joshua with surprise on their faces. 'Well?' he said.

'That's an interesting proposal, Josh, one, at least, I had not thought of,' Harry said. 'It does, though, give us now three options to choose from, so will it be one, two, or Josh's three? What's it to be, Troop?'

Chapter 23

Prince Marcus felt a little light-headed as they arrived; Vantor and Zing Fan were fine and looked about. There was nobody in sight.

'Quickly, we need to find cover,' said Marcus.

They moved towards what looked like an old tailor's shop. They made their way inside through the front door and into the back room. There were an old table and chairs against the wall and some other bits of furniture around the room. They sat at the table.

'How do we find them?' enquired Marcus. 'They are most likely in hiding themselves, only moving when they need to.'

'Question, Prince Marcus. Are you good with your sister? Do you love her?'

'What sort of question is that, Master Zing Fan? We do not ask that sort of question of our royal family,' Vantor stated.

'I need Prince to answer me true. If it is so, then we may have chance, but if no, then we search through city for them.'

'Master Zing Fan, the answer is yes, I do, but I do not see how this may help us.'

'If all work, Marcus will take us to find the group.'

'Are you crazy? Is he mad, Eric?'

'We must hurry, Prince, come stand with me.'

Prince Marcus stood and walked over to Zing Fan, a look of bewilderment on his normally regal face.

'We kneel, Prince. Take my hands.'

They both knelt facing each other, hands joined at waist height, Marcus looking more unsure each minute that passed.

'Prince, I want you to follow my instructions to letter, or this will not work. Understand me, you must.'

'Yes, Zing Fan.'

'Close your eyes, picture your sister, better if you are children again. See her face, laughing, smiling, can you see her face?'

'Yes.'

'Where are you?'

'We are in the royal garden playing. There's Mother.'

'No. Concentrate on your sister, only her, picture her face again, smiling. Can you see her?'

'Yes. How young she looks!'

'Reach your hand out to touch her; you want to hold her hand. Reach, go on, reach for her hand and call her name.'

'Juls! Juls!'

'Marcus, Marcus! He's here! Marcus! I'm here, here! No! Look out! Marcus, Marcus, no, noooo!'

A huge gust of wind from nowhere blew Marcus and Zing Fan across the room with formidable force, crashing them into the wall and breaking some of the old furniture. Vantor just managed to stay on his feet. Marcus had his sword drawn ready for a fight, but nobody was there except the three of them.

'What happened, Prince? What did you see?' enquired the little man.

The troop were starting to get themselves up off the floor. They had all been flung across the floor by a tremendous wind. All of them were looking at Juliet.

'What in Heaven's name was that?' exclaimed Harry.

'Marcus is here in the city, trying to find us. He is with Vantor and Zing Fan. He was calling to me, I answered him, and then it was there, heading for Marcus. It had a curved sword, and it was moving fast. Marcus had not seen it. All I could do was to, to…'

'To what, Juliet?'

'I forced it away with my mind, or at least I think I did. Something built up inside me, some sort of force, as if all the wind in the world was in my hands, and I threw it at them.'

'Yes, you did; that's what happened to us, too. One minute we were all talking away, and the next thing, we were getting blown across the floor,' said Harry.

'Marcus, Zing Fan and Eric Vantor are here in the city looking for us. The shadows and Dragmen know that they are here. I told Marcus where we are, but in that, I may have told the Dragmen, too. If they try and get to us, they will walk into a trap and possibly die, but also, if we try to get to them, we face the same situation,' said Juliet with a sigh.

'I doubt that,' said Harry. 'I doubt that very much. Two bloody good wizards and my brother – I'd love to watch 'em try.'

By all that is holy! A flash of light and a loud bang.

'Greetings, brother and little sister,' Marcus said.

Marcus, Zing Fan and Eric Vantor were in the room in the safe house with them.

'We are here, little troop,' Zing Fan said with a cheeky grin. 'Eric, erect a shield.'

Without a moment's hesitation, Vantor began the chant, and the air shifted with a very slight breeze.

'There, it's done, one inside the other.'

'We were just about to decide what to do next. We needed to get to you or get the information to you. I'm glad we don't have to make that decision now. We have so much to tell the three of you. We have discovered much in the last few days, but things here are now getting a little complicated.

'The Dragmen have our scent, they nearly had us yesterday, and it will be only a matter of time, brother,' Harry said. 'We were out of options, and Sam and Earthie came up with a brilliant plan, which worked perfectly. Then Josh surprised us by suggesting we hide on the other side of the wall with the dragon, which was one of our choices, but not one I thought of.'

'Don't worry too much, Prince Harry. I have placed a double shield around us here, and they will not get through that,' said Vantor.

'It is nice to see you all. My, how you have all grown, taller, stronger, but how have you been bearing up? You've done a marvellous job, but, again, there is much more to do before this is over,' Marcus stated. 'You mentioned that we can get to the far side of the red mist. Is this possible? And how do we manage it?'

'Yes, we can, is the answer,' Harry said. 'The red mist covers a complete circle, trapping all those inside to their fate. However, the red mist does not penetrate below the surface. A tunnel, catacomb, large pipes and even cellars are conduits underneath it; we passed under it without any effects.'

'I was first to go through via a cellar,' said Taw. 'Once I emerged on the other side, I was greeted with two huge red walls, but then realization struck me: there were not two red walls; one was the red mist wall, the other was huge gold plates that looked like a wall of red. But the gold was reflecting the original red mist wall. The gold wall was, in fact, the gold dragon, and the dragon was *enormous*,' concluded Taw.

'I'd like to see this dragon,' Eric remarked.

'I would,' said Zing Fan.

'So would I,' said Marcus.

'It will be tricky getting there with the Dragmen now on our trail. They know we are here somewhere, but as yet have not found us. Once out on the street, we are open to attack and ambush, and there are a lot more of them than us. And the speed they move at!' Harry said.

'What about the dragon? Did it know you were there? Was it moving?' asked Marcus.

'Brother, as far as we could tell, the dragon was asleep or resting, as there was no screaming. The best time to go is probably after mid-day meal when the sun is at its hottest.'

'Thank you, Juliet. Then tomorrow after mid-day meal we will go', Marcus stated.

'We have been busy too,' said Vantor. 'We know we need four swords of the elements. These need to be placed in line with the compass, North, South, East and West, but the swords need to be in the hands of a person who can command that element. That is why Zing Fan and I are going to test some of you. We believe that, unknowingly, you have these abilities, or you know and do not use them as well as you can. So we will do this tomorrow morning after we have all fed and rested tonight.'

'Joshua, keep hold of the log. You must concentrate, boy; grow the fire in your mind.' Zing Fan was attempting to help Josh control the amount of fire and heat he applied, but the log would suddenly burst into a massive ball of flames, and Josh would drop it.

Meanwhile, Eric Vantor was having more fun with the twins, Earthie and Jackus. He was trying to talk to them while they were under the water; they obviously could not hear a thing he said.

He would pull them up and say, 'Did you hear what I said?'

'No', they replied, 'we were under the water.'

Marcus and the others just laughed.

'Juliet, how did you make this wind?'

'I don't know, brother. I just felt so angry and hurt; it seemed to burst out when you were in danger. I saw that thing and just, just... I don't know.'

'However you did it, we will need it if we are ever to defeat this dragon.'

'We will never defeat it, brother. You have not seen it; it is as big as half a city, and that's crouched up. God only knows when it stretches out its wings.'

Zing Fan came in with Josh in tow and said, 'At least we have had a little success.'

Josh was holding, or more like it, keeping suspended, just above his hands, a burning log, and it was spinning slowly.

'Oh!' said Juliet and Marcus. 'Great stuff!'

'Put log in fire now, Josh. Lesson for today finish,' the little man said as he sat down.

They all gathered together in the main room and had their mid-day meal, chatting about their newfound skills and how they needed to get better at them.

'Let's get ready, then,' announced Prince Marcus. 'About time we went and saw this red wall and dragon. Get armed up quickly, and be ready to move. Eric, will you remove the shield?'

'The shield is done, Marcus.'

'Dina and Taw, you two scout ahead at the front and lead the way; Earthie and Jackus, take the rear. The rest of you, stay between them and keep your eyes peeled. Any sign of trouble, alert the troop.'

They went out at a cautious pace, moving from cover to cover until they were about a street away and Dina called a halt.

'I don't like it, Taw,' she said. 'Not one of those Dragmen. I wonder whether they are waiting in the safe house for us?'

'They could do that, but we will know because they would have tripped the booby traps, and that would leave a big mess.'

'You're right, Taw. But there is something not right.'

Marcus closed up to Dina. 'What's the problem?'

Dina explained to Marcus the situation. Dina was an excellent hunter and had a sixth sense when something was amiss.

Taw said, 'Dina, you cover me, and I will move slowly down the street towards the house on this side. Then, when I'm ready, I'll cross over the street. Wait till I signal to follow.'

He set off crouched down, moving slowly down the street. Dina spotted someone in the window opposite and drew her bow. She wondered whether Taw had seen them, but he was continuing to move down the street. There was someone else in a doorway, too, a bit further down. Dina fired her first arrow and took the one in the window, but the one in the doorway was across the road in a flash to attack Taw.

Taw had seen it and was waiting. As the Dragman got to him, Taw spun backwards away from the wall, swung his sword and took the Dragman clear in the back of its neck, removing its head.

The second blow just about carved it in half as it attempted to change into a shadow. Taw crouched down again and gave Dina a thumbs up. He was about to set off again when he saw the Dragmen at the bottom of the street. There were about twenty of them, filing out across the street.

Marcus said, 'Let's move! Half that side, half this side. Go!' and the troop moved.

Marcus grabbed Eric and Zing Fan. 'One of you on each side – can you do anything?' he asked.

'Oh yes,' replied Zing Fan. 'Do not risk your troop, Prince. Magician and I do these with pleasure,' and he smiled.

Marcus turned to see even more coming down the street towards them; they were trapped unless they could get down the side street on the left.

'Gods, no, that's out. They are there, too. We are trapped!'

Eric walked past the troop into the middle of the road.

'Stay there,' he said as he faced the ones at the bottom of the street. Two bowmen fired arrows at him.

'Look out!' shouted Sam, but Eric just held up his hand and the arrows fell to the ground. Now he started to chant and wave his hands and arms around; slowly, the chant got louder, then he stopped. He looked up from the ground at the Dragmen, then his arms came up and levelled at them.

'Usque emarcescunt et pereunt,' he said to them.

Nothing seemed to happen at first, then one by one, they started to scream, crouch into themselves, wither, fall to the floor and die. The troop looked on in awe at what they had just seen. But it was short-lived, as the others coming down the street started to charge, now at a running pace, shouting battle cries.

Zing Fan looked as if he was doing a slow-motion dance in the street, hopping from one foot to the other. Then he held his arms out and began to spin. Faster he went, then even faster, his arms folded into his body, and faster still. Everybody was now looking at Zing Fan and not the charging men, but they, too, had been dragged together and were now spinning in one big group. Faster they went into a tornado shape, faster and faster, and up they went in a tornado.

Then it suddenly stopped, and they crashed to the ground in one big heap of bodies. Zing Fan turned and said, 'I love a good dance. Ah, magician, what did you do?'

'Master, I used Wither and Die.'

'Excellent, my favourite student.'

'What about the ones in the side street?' said Marcus.

'They have all fled,' said Earthie. 'Should have seen their faces!'

'To the safe house, then. Dina, carry on, but again be cautious,' and they set off.

Dina reached the corner of the safe house five or six minutes later and called another halt.

'We can still get into the house if we are quick,' she thought, 'but we will be trapped.' She scanned the road towards the red wall; there were hundreds of soldiers, Saracens. As she waited, Marcus moved up again to where Dina was.

'What's the matter now, Dina?' he asked, concerned.

'Look, hundreds of Saracen soldiers,' she said. Then they heard shouts from behind as even more soldiers came marching down the street. 'At least two hundred of them,' said Dina.

'Surrender now,' came a voice. 'Throw your weapons down and walk out with your arms raised. You have one chance to do this; then I will order your death. Do it now,' the voice commanded.

Marcus, Harry and the others looked at each other.

'We surrender,' said Marcus. After all, they were allies.

They put down their weapons and stood up with their arms raised; the troop followed suit. They were quickly surrounded by lots of soldiers from the Southern Kingdom, Saracens.

'On your knees,' an officer barked.

The troop kneeled down. Except Master Zing Fan.

'Only Emperor and my master do I kneel for,' he said and stood with his arms crossed. The officer looked over at a huge Saracen and nodded to him.

The soldier drew his curved sword and headed towards Zing Fan, saying:

'You will kneel before your betters.' He swung his sword towards the little man.

Zing Fan waited until the very last second, then moved with lightning speed. The soldier was face down on the floor, and Zing Fan was sitting behind the officer on his horse with the soldier's sword held at his throat.

'You want I cut your little head off and use as a flycatcher, and your big idiot soldier there for big doggie food, fat man?'

'There will be no need for that; put your swords away. They are friends. Welcome, Prince Marcus and Harry. Nice to see you again.'

Marcus looked up and saw General Aziz.

'I am also pleased to see you and your men. We have come to clear the city of bandits, thieves and these Dragmen things.'

'Come join us, all of you, as my guests in my new headquarters. We have much to discuss, Prince Marcus.'

'Indeed we have, General. Please lead the way.'

The general dismounted and walked with Marcus, the rest of the troop and the two magicians following.

The afternoon went quickly, with Prince Marcus, Vantor, Zing Fan and Harry talking with the General. Much was spoken in whispers, and Vantor had erected a small shield.

Eventually, Harry came over to the rest of the troop.

'We move out first thing in the morning, same mission, gather information. Oh, one other thing to look out for. If you see anyone with a blue aura about them, let one of us know immediately. It is vital.'

'What's an aura, then?' asked Jackus.

'It is like a glow, but not as bright. Get some sleep now while you can and it's safe.'

'Yes, Captain.'

Chapter 24

'Are you awake, Taw?' said Dina.

'Yes, I have been for a while; just waiting for the sun to rise.'

'Me too. Do you think we will ever get home, or even get to kill this dragon?'

'I don't know, but they say it cannot be killed, only put back to sleep again by some complicated ritual,' Taw said.

'So that's why Zing Fan and Vantor keep testing us; the four elements are needed,' put in Juliet.

Josh said, 'There are three of us here: me, the Fire, the twins, Water, and Juliet the Wind. We just need to find the fourth, Earth.'

'There is also one other we need,' interrupted Harry. 'The person who can hold the blue stone; they are vital. As we believe, it calls to the dragon, but only a special person can hold the stone. That's the one who will have the blue aura, and they will need to hold it to the dragon while the rest get in place. Up time now! Break fast and move out in thirty minutes,' said Harry. 'Let's go then, Troop!'

They set off towards the safe house. There was no need to duck in and out of doorways or alleyways. There were soldiers everywhere, but with their escort, they had no problem getting to the safe house and then on to where they had found the cellar door. The escort then left them there as they all entered the cellar, with Josh leading.

Once they were all down in the cellar at the bottom of the steps, Harry called them all together.

'Dina, Sam, you two go and have a quick look around and see what's happening. Go! The rest of us will wait until they return.'

Dina edged out first into the daylight, followed by Sam.

'What a scene,' said Sam. 'Nothing but rubble everywhere, smoke and flames.'

There were people lying dead, others still alive, just wandering around as though they were asleep.

'Wait!' said Dina. 'Where is the dragon? Where has the dragon gone? Oh, horse crap, where is it?'

They returned downstairs and reported. Everyone then came upstairs and outside to look. The devastation was complete, nothing stood, but the dragon had gone. Silently, it had vanished. Marcus looked at the two magicians and Harry.

'So, gentlemen, where is the dragon now?'

Then a touch of fear passed over them all as if a silent word had been spoken.

'Eric, call your brothers, now. Put everyone on alert. Let them know we have no idea where it is or where it is going.'

The troop had split up and tried to talk to the people trapped inside, but it was of no use; they were all mind-dead. Eric contacted his brothers about the dragon not being there anymore, but they had not seen it either, and there were no reports of it in the kingdom. As requested by Marcus, a full alert had been called across the Astel Kingdom. Soldiers were everywhere, although truth be known, they would not be able to fend off a dragon. Marcus had sent Sam to alert General Aziz about the missing dragon. He came with a hundred soldiers to gather up the people inside and take them to safety.

'What of us, now?' asked Eric Vantor to Marcus.

'We need to know where the dragon has gone first, and we need to return to the city, with the element people, if you will, so they can train for what's coming.'

'I can only take three to travel with me,' said Vantor. 'I'll take Joshua, Juliet and Earthie. Zing Fan will be able to do the same. He will take Jackus, you and one other; the rest will have to travel normally. That leaves Harry, Taw, Dina and Sam.'

'Harry, you and the remaining three will have to wait for Eric's brother, David, to come for you. I don't know how long that will be, but if you make tracks back towards Astel,' said Marcus.

'Joshua, Juliet and Earthie, with me,' said Eric, and, flash, they were gone.

'Zing Fan, are we ready?' said Marcus.

'We be one short, Prince.'

'Who's coming with us?' Marcus asked.

'We are going to stay together, brother,' Harry answered.

'Let's go, Zing Fan,' said Marcus, and a few seconds later, flash, and they were gone.

'Just us now, guys,' said Dina, looking at Harry, Taw, and Sam.

'That's right. Let's see whether our friends will lend us some horses,' Harry said as they walked towards General Aziz.

They arrived at the keep in Astel. The young group took a moment as the dizziness wore off.

'I am going to pay my respects to my mother. Juliet, would you like to come with me? But we must be quick. We need to get them all into the catacombs and protected, as we do not know where the dragon is, and you are all valuable,' Marcus stated.

Eric said to Marcus, 'I will take the rest and ensure the shield is intact. Tell no one of their return. Master Zing Fan, will you collect the swords and meet us in the crypt down in the catacombs? We will need to see what happens when they take up the elemental swords.'

Zing Fan nodded and was gone.

The pulse was still there, very faint; occasionally, it would shout then fade again, calling to her from afar. She was not strong enough yet; more time was needed. She had gained in weight, and she had just eaten very well, but it needed time to build her strength. But soon, she would seek out her stone and take it for herself. Nothing would stand in her way, and she could leave this dreadful world on which she was imprisoned.

Before she left this world, they would pay; she would devour and destroy everything that had done this to her. Now was not the time; this time was for resting and building her strength. 'Then another full feed, and rest, and I will be ready. I will take my stone, destroy and then leave forever,' she thought. The pulse continued very faintly, getting fainter as she drifted off to sleep, nestled in the heart of the Rajh mountains.

'Hello, Mother, said Marcus, 'look who I found while I was away.'

'Juliet, my darling, look at you! Come here and give your mother a hug.'

Juliet ran to her mother and gave her a big hug.

'Look at you,' the Queen said. 'You look fit and a little like a boy,' she remarked as she laughed.

'Mother!' exclaimed Juliet, with genuine horror in her voice.

'Sorry to interrupt,' said Marcus. 'Things move very quickly, Mother. The dragon has moved, as you know. We need to move with haste and get everyone who knows of any plans into the crypt.' In an urgent voice, Marcus said, 'If you and Juliet, Mother, could make your way there now, I will get word to the others to move as well.'

'Walk with me, Juliet,' said the Queen, and they set off towards the catacombs. 'I don't really like your hair like that; it is too short. It looks very boyish, and you are so pretty.'

'It's not that short, Mother. It is mostly tied back and up out of my way while I'm doing this. Look, I'll show you!'

'Ah, I see! That's better. Alright then, about time we got you into some Princess clothes.'

'No, Mother, I have a job to do, and I am working with my comrades on defeating the dragon. Are you aware that I am... Oh! I can't say here... Not safe, according to Marcus and Vantor. Enough to say, I am vital, and I have to practise with the others, so you'll have to forgive me, Mother, but I must go.'

'I know of your... your talent, Juliet. I'm sorry, I just thought I'd have my daughter back for a while.'

'You will soon, Mother, I promise.'

She kissed her and set off to join the others.

Harry and the others were making slow progress towards home. They had been given horses, food and water by General Aziz, and one other thing so they got home safely: the General had insisted on an escort of three hundred mounted knights and lancers. They were to follow Captain Harry's instructions, but their own captain was a young captain called Ashoo, a young-looking, skinny chap with a wisp of a beard that made him look as if he was still in schooling.

They had reached Lake Blue and were making their way north along the western edge. The area was patrolled by many Southern troops, not that they had any issues with them because of their escort, but the area, in general, was more secure now. Harry had reminded Dina, Taw and Sam that there were still Dragmen out there and that they were above the others as targets, so to be vigilant.

'I wonder where the dragon is,' Taw said to Harry and Dina.

'I don't know,' said Dina, 'and I'm not sure I want to,' she added as she looked up.

'Once we get to the top of Lake Blue, it's pretty easy going from there; hopefully, we will reach there by tomorrow evening.'

'Halt!' shouted Harry as a command. 'We will rest here tonight in this makeshift fort, Captain Ashoo.'

'Yes, my Prince,' he answered.

'We stay here tonight. Get your men and horses fed and watered, and we will set off at first light in the morning. Please ensure you set sentries around the perimeter.' Harry, Dina, Sam and Taw sorted their horses out then set about making a meal. There was not much but enough to feed the four of them.

After their evening meal, Harry went to find Captain Ashoo. Sam, Dina and Taw sat around for a while talking about home and family and what they would do if ever they survived the dragon. Finally, there was no sign of Harry, so they got into their sleeping kits and bade each other pleasant sleep.

She could see it plainly now, although the edge around it was faded. Its face was of a purple colour but had no distinguishing features. Round black eyes, no nose, and a mouth like a small beak. That's strange, she thought. Wait, there was another behind him, playing with something on the floor. What a very strange, funny dream. What are they playing with? And that one seems to be laughing. There they go again, playing with something on the floor and laughing again. Dina moved a little closer. Oh! My god, it's Taw!

They are choking him, then releasing him and then doing the same again. Taw was thrashing around on the floor but could do nothing to fight them off. Then they saw her. They, too, just looked at first, then realisation struck. Dina froze for a second; so did the Dragmen. For the first time, she realised she was on the floor too. Where was her weapon? She felt around. Earth, soft earth beneath her fingers and hands, feeling the cold ground. Just like before, she released an arrow. Time was really slow; she felt the soft earth beneath her, the ground teeming with life. She saw the figure leaning over Taw, the other moving towards her, with its round, black eyes. Fear, colossal fear, struck her like a bolt of lightning.

She pulled her fingers slowly to a half fist as if pulling on something. She was. The ground responded to her calling. 'Grow,' she said, 'grow,' and the plants did, at lightning speed compared to everything else, wrapping around the two figures, holding them. Then an arrow flashed over her head and struck the first figure straight into its heart, and it disappeared. Dina's eyes turned towards the second. It was still standing over Taw, but it was unable to move with the plants wrapped around it. Another arrow flashed above her head and hit its target. Like the first, it disappeared. Dina turned to see who had shot the arrows, expecting to see Harry or Sam, but no. There stood a woman in black flowing clothes, her long, dark, curly hair blowing in the wind. Her face was as white as pure marble and stunning to behold. She held in her hands an ornate bow; it was the same as Dina's, except this one was slightly bigger.

The women said, 'You are safe now, child of ours. Wake, wake up, wake up child!'

Dina awoke with a start. Taw was sitting up, coughing, trying to catch his breath, rubbing his neck. Dina stood and went to him.

'Are you alright, Taw?' she said.

'They had me, Dina! I was so afraid. I have never, ever been as frightened as I was. They were choking me, then I would pass out, but they'd then let me go and start again, all the time laughing. I tried as best I could to fight, but I could not get them off me. What about you?' said Taw. 'Are you alright?'

'Yes, I am,' and she told him of the women and how she had shot the arrows after Dina had held them with the plants.

'What about Harry and Sam?' said Taw suddenly. They both ran over to Harry first. 'Harry, Harry!' they called, but it looked as if he was still asleep. Dina reached down to rouse him; then she noticed the blood.

She pulled back the cover to find Harry had a knife or sword wound to his right side. Dina moved him gently and blood bubbled from his mouth, but he was just about able to talk.

'I tried to fight,' he said, 'but another caught me from behind and punctured my lung.'

'Taw, quickly, check Sam!'

Taw rushed to Sam. Again, Sam seemed to be sleeping, but he was unconscious; he had a large lump on the back of his head.

'Don't move, Harry. We'll get some help. How's Sam?' called Dina.

'He will be alright; a nasty thump on the back of his skull. He will have one mother of a headache, though.'

'Go and see if there is a physician for Harry in the old makeshift fort.'

There in the fort, all seemed normal, as if nothing had happened. Taw found the surgeon and bought him to Harry. Captain Ashoo came over and apologised, but there was nothing he could have done or could do now.

'We will have to wait here,' said Dina, 'at least until Harry is able to travel or we can get word to Astel.'

Sam staggered up to where they all standing. 'What has happened?' he said. 'My head hurts so much; I think the world fell on it last night.'

'That will need a couple of stitches,' said Dina. 'Sit down here before you fall, and I'll try to explain what happened.'

Chapter 25

Marcus arrived at the crypt; the others were already there.

'Where is Earl Vantor?' he enquired.

A young soldier said, 'He is in that room over there, Your Majesty, with someone.'

Marcus forgot his manners and just walked off from the soldier towards the room. As he entered, he saw Joshua holding a sword of flames. His hands around the base were on fire, too. Joshua was practising some basic moves with it.

'Ah, Prince Marcus!!' said Vantor. 'Look, Josh has managed to bond with the sword of Fire.'

'That's good news. Well done, Josh! What about the twins?' Marcus enquired.

'We just cannot seem to get it right yet. Every time they touch the sword, it turns to water and lands on the floor, where it reverts to the sword again. Your sister, Juliet, is with Zing Fan in the other room, if you wish to see them.'

'No, thank you. That's great work, Eric, but we need to hurry, or the dragon will be upon us.'

'Marcus, Juliet can manage a slight breeze with the sword of Air. Zing Fan is teaching her the seven katas of basic sword skills, according to the ancient master's teachings. It is hard and taking time.'

'But Eric, it's time, and time we do not have.'

The Queen arrived with Lord Sandbite and Edmond, the Lord Marshal. 'Your Majesty' could be heard from around the hall and from the other rooms as she passed them. Marcus called everyone into the anteroom.

'Be seated everyone,' said the Queen as she herself sat.

The Queen addressed everyone: 'We are, we believe, in the final stages. All garrisons are on full alert; most of the people across the empire are now hiding in underground bunkers or cellars in their own homes. We are protected here with the magic shield and the catacombs. So, for the moment, we are safe. Prince Marcus will now take over.'

'We are very close to solving how we put the dragon to sleep; however, we lack essentially two major things. We have the four swords of the elements, but sadly we have only three people who can wield the swords. We are missing the Earth person, so, it will be impossible to cast the spell of sleep. More importantly, we have not found the stone wielder.'

'Stone wielder?' went around the room in whispers.

'Quiet, please! The Dragonite stone is red but glows blue and gets hotter the closer the dragon is, and only the chosen stone wielder can hold it out before the dragon.

'The stone places the dragon into some sort of trance, half-sleep, according to Earl Vantor and Master Zing Fan, whilst the sword wielders get into position, North, South, East and West, and the same use enchantment to return her to her sleep. First, we must find the stone wielder and hope and pray that they are brave enough to hold the stone out in front of the dragon.'

Gasps and chatter filled the room.

Prince Marcus held up his hand for silence. 'We are going to open up only the outer chest containing the Dragonite. We require that everyone walk past at a swift pace, but not too quickly, to see if anyone has any reaction. We cannot keep it open for long, as we believe that the jewel calls to the dragon.

'Everyone, line up here by this table, where we will start, and each person will file past. Earl Vantor, if you will, please open the outer chest only.'

Everyone in the room filed past, but the jewel did not change, nor did anyone start to glow blue. Eric shut the chest as the last person went past.

The Dragon stirred in its sleep; it felt the pulse grow stronger. 'I will come for you soon, my Dragonite. Be still; we will have all of eternity together,' and faded off to sleep again.

'That is all we have for now, ladies and gentlemen. With your permission, Mother?' The Queen nodded. 'You may all take your places and return to your duties. Thank you, all.'

After the meeting, Zing Fan, Marcus and Eric Vantor sat in the throne room with the Queen.

'The facts are, Your Majesty, that without these other two, we have no way of standing up to the dragon. The most vital part is this person who can wield the stone. I held it for a while, and it turned me blue, but it was burning me, and no spell could prevent it. Second is the person to wield the sword of the Earth. We can hold the dragon with the stone, but without the fourth element, we can't put it back to sleep.'

'How do you suggest we attempt to find these persons, Eric, and how do we get them here?' asked the Queen.

He was about to answer but said, 'Excuse me, Your Majesty,' and left the room. 'Yes, Alice, I hear you; what can I do for you? I'm a little busy at present. I'm with Her Majesty,' he said to his ex-wife, Mother Superior Alice.

'I have an important message from Queen Sienna. Harry, Taw, Sam and Dina were attacked by Dragmen in the night; Harry was seriously hurt, but the others survived and are unhurt. Dina is the Earth person; she is the last one. You need to get them all to safety. That's all.'

Eric stepped back and almost staggered. 'Marcus!' he called. 'Marcus.'

He came out to Eric. 'What is happening?'

'I have just spoken to Alice, Mother Superior,' and he told him what Queen Sienna had told her.

'We have got to get them out!' said Marcus.

'I know we do, but we don't know where they are. We can't just zap to them; we need a place to go, a picture in our minds.'

'Find out now, Eric, by whatever means we have available.'

'Yes, Marcus, I will,' and he called Zing Fan out of the room, too.

Marcus went back into the throne room to inform his mother about Harry and that they had found Earth.

Harry's wound was serious. They had stitched and dressed it, but this was no ordinary wound; this was a shadow-wound, stuck in him whilst they were in shadow form. They had managed to slow the blood loss on the outside, but where it had punctured his lung, they were helpless. The blood was slowly filling his lungs, and he would either drown in his own blood or die of loss of blood. Either way, if they did not get some sort of magical help, Harry would be dead by mid-day.

'Saracens do not do magic, as far as I know,' said Dina, 'so we have no choice; we have to wait.'

Eric called David and Luke and explained the situation to them and how Harry and the others been attacked by Dragmen but had been protected by Queen Sienna.

'They were en route from Mons Harbour. They may be at Lake Blue, but find them you must. Harry is gravely injured; you must try and save him. When you do find them, bring them to the keep, and then we will bring them down here to us. You understand all this, brothers?'

'Just one thing, Eric. There is a quarter gap around the city which will have nobody magical watching for the dragon.'

'Don't worry; Zing Fan will cover. Go now, as soon as you can. Time is of the essence, and it's imperative we find them.'

'We cannot travel with Harry,' said Taw. 'The movement of the horse will tear his wound apart, if he doesn't bleed to death or drown first. But what else can we do? We can't stay, hoping he will get better, because he won't. One of us could go on alone, or even two, and try and get help, but I'm afraid that will take too long.'

'I know,' said Dina. 'I don't know what to do. I'm afraid, Taw. I don't want Harry to die,' as tears filled her eyes.

'It will be alright, Dina', said Taw. He put his arm around her as she cried on his shoulder. Sam had a tear for Harry, too, as the young warriors watched as their Prince, captain and, most of all, their friend lay dying. Their tender moment was interrupted when Harry coughed up a spray of bright red blood. Dina went to Harry; he was barely conscious and very pale.

'If he does not get help very soon, he will be dead within the hour,' said Dina, with tears in her eyes again.

David and Luke appeared in Mons Harbour. Luckily, they were not seen appearing there. They walked into the street, and they were instantly surrounded by Saracen soldiers. David and Luke both put their hands up in surrender and got to their knees. A soldier asked them something, but David did not hear what he said; again, the soldier asked them, but they did not understand what he said this time. The soldier walked over and stood in front of them as he drew his sword. David began to say something, but he was hit from behind, and all went black. Luke followed the same fate seconds later.

David opened his eyes to find his head thumping. He tried to move, but he was tied. His hands had been tied behind his back and to his feet. Luke was next to him, exactly the same; he, too, was just waking up.

'Ah, you both now awake. No fun taking your heads while you are asleep. What do they call you both, so I can record your passing, infidels?'

'I am David Vantor, and this is my brother, Luke, and we are from Astel Kingdom. We are searching for our friends, but we got lost.'

'It is not a good place to be getting lost, my David and Luke; lots of bad people about and these Dragmen. So tell me how you got here, as we already searched that building and there was nobody in it, then you walk out. Answer, if you not Dragmen, and if you are, I take your heads.'

'No, I am not. I am a magician from Astel Kingdom, and we are looking for our friends.'

'So you claim to not be Dragmen; you are magic man. Ha ha!' and a chorus of laughter started. 'We will soon see, magic man, when my commander comes and I cut off your heads from your bodies.'

Another chorus of laughter boomed out. David thought for a moment. He could just disappear, but he would still be tied up, unless he went back to Astel.

'I don't have time for this,' said David, and with a flash and a bang, David stood up free of his bonds. 'I am from Astel Kingdom. I am friends with your Empress Shulla and your High General.'

Just then, riders rode up. 'What's the problem?' the lead rider asked.

'Commander, these are the Dragmen I told you about that we captured. May I have the honour of taking their heads?'

'David, David Vantor, is that you and Luke?'

'Hello, General Aziz. It is good to see you. Forgive us for not coming and shaking hands, but our heads may be chopped off.'

Luke stood up too. He had released himself.

'Release these men immediately!'

'But General, I...'

'Release them immediately, or I'll have your head decorating this sorry city.'

'We were getting ready to do a disappearing act before we lost our heads, General. It is good to see you, but, alas, we are in a hurry. We need to find Prince Harry and the others.' David explained why and what had happened in the attack.

'There are two locations they may be at; the first is about halfway between here and Lake Blue, the other is on Lake Blue just near the bottom, an old fort. It is too far for them to have reached the one at the top, given the time. It will take you several hours on fast horses to reach the first and another full day's travel to reach the other one at Lake Blue,' said the General.

'We do not have the time for that amount of travel, General. We travel another way.'

'Another way, David? What do you mean?'

'Sorry, General, but time is short.' David took hold of his arm, and he, Luke and the General were gone.

They reappeared in the garrison between Mons Harbour and Lake Blue. General Aziz staggered slightly, but David kept hold of him. His head was a bit fuzzy, too, as if he'd had a few to drink.

'What happened?' he said. 'And where are we?'

'You will be alright, General. We are at the small garrison.'

'Allah be blessed,' the General said. 'You there, soldier!'

'Yes? Er, yes, sir?'

'A mounted troop came through here, when?'

'The day before yesterday, sir.'

'Well done. Now carry on with your duties,' he said to the soldier.

'Ready again, General?'

And before he could say anything, they were gone again. This time, General Aziz fell down on his bottom as the dizziness swamped him.

'Stay there for a moment,' said David.

'I feel sick,' the General said.

'You'll be alright soon.'

They had appeared just outside the old fort. Lots of people and soldiers were coming and going; how nobody saw them just appear, they didn't know. David recognised the place; they were at the base of Lake Blue. Two soldiers walking past saw the General and instantly saluted him.

David, wanting to waste no time, said to the soldiers, 'Fetch your commander, the garrison commander. Now!'

The soldiers ran off into the building.

General Aziz stood up, shaking his head. 'That hurts. Next time, do me a favour,' he said. 'Don't ever do that again.'

'I'm sorry, General Aziz. If they are here, we will not have to, but needs must.'

The garrison commander rode out of one of the buildings, flanked by two other officers, at a slow walking pace, chatting away about his darn sleep being interrupted by two stupid soldiers, but he would have them flogged later in the morning for it. He pulled his horse up in front of General Aziz.

'So, you'll be the so-called general I've been dragged out of bed for,' said the round, fat captain from his horse. 'I don't know what part of the kingdom you come from, boy, but I am...'

General Aziz was about to explode when a troop rode out of the fort at pace, with Captain Ashoo in the lead. He stopped in front of the General and dismounted. He bowed and then saluted.

'General Aziz, it is an honour and a pleasure, sir. I have only just been told of your arrival.'

'Thank you, Captain Ashoo,' then he turned to the garrison commander, still sitting on his horse, and said, 'You have two seconds to get off that horse before I drag you off myself by your ears.'

'Er, yes, General. I ...er, did not know it was you, sir. I...'

'Be silent. Captain Ashoo, are Prince Harry and the others here?'

'Yes, sir, they are,' he said. 'They are in one of the rooms in the fort. Harry is badly hurt; one of those Dragmen things attacked them in the night.'

'Quickly, show David and me where they are. David, take that horse there; I'll take this captain's. You, so-called garrison commander, don't go anywhere. I will deal with you soon. Lead the way, Captain Ashoo,' and they set off at a gallop to find Harry and his small band of soldiers.

Chapter 26

Juliet was practising hard with Zing Fan. Slowly she was beginning to control parts of the air, but any slight lack of concentration would alter the power ratio: a slight breeze, then a wrong movement, and Zing Fan and everything else was blown across the room by a hurricane. The twins were not much better. Mostly, the sword would turn to water, hit the floor and return to a sword.

Marcus watched their progress from the doorway. 'We have a long way to go,' he said to himself. 'If the dragon arrives here within a month, we're all doomed.'

'Prince Marcus, the defences around the city are complete; the huge crossbows are in position, some horizontal, but most vertical. The catapults also, with the fireballs. The large crossbows are ready on the hills, hidden under canopies – they can fire across the top of the city from two directions. The steel netting is also ready and will be in position by the morning.'

'Thank you, Lord Sandbite and, of course, the Lord Marshal. Have you got a minute, Sandy?'

'Yes, of course.'

'Let's go and get a drink, Sandy; I think I need one.'

Prince Marcus sat with Lord Sandbite and poured them both a goblet of rich red wine.

'What's going on, Marcus? It is not like you to be like this.'

'Sandy, we have no idea where the dragon is or where it will strike. What we do have is woefully lacking in skill. We do not have the most important bit, someone to hold the stone, and now, to top it off, Harry is gravely injured somewhere in the Southern Kingdom. I think that about sums it up.' Marcus picked up his wine and drained the goblet.

Sandy picked his up, too, and did the same. 'Better pour me another one, too, Marcus. Marcus, we are grown men, leaders of other men. They look up to us; so do the people of this kingdom, from the children to the old and feeble. They look to us to protect them from whatever it may be. This time, yes, it happens to be a dragon. It does not matter what it is, we have done what we can, and we will do our very best to make things right. We may die trying, but all of us will die.

'We have to believe that we can, and make others believe we can, and you never know, we might bloody well just do it and put this dragon back to sleep, which, incidentally, I think we are both lacking. When did you last sleep, Marcus?'

'Erm, I think a couple of days ago.'

'Then no arguments, it's off to bed with you, Your Majesty. Any arguments, and I'll tell your mother,' he said with a grin on his face.

'You're right, of course, Sandy. I must go and see Mother first, and then I'll get some sleep. Thank you, old friend.'

Marcus walked off towards the throne room in the catacombs.

He walked into the room, and his mother, the Queen, enquired, 'Marcus, is there any news of Harry, yet?'

'No, Mother, we are working on it. I have sent David and Luke Vantor. They have a large area in which to try and find him, but I have faith in them, and Harry is a lot stronger than you think.'

'I need to know what is going on, Marcus. Where is Eric Vantor?'

'I will find him and send him to you, Mother, so you will have knowledge when there is news.'

'Thank you, Marcus. I am worrying about poor little Harry.'

With that, Marcus left and walked into the main hall.

General Aziz and David Vantor arrived at the room where Harry was with Taw, Sam and Dina.

'Hello,' said David as he entered.

Dina said, 'Oh, thank God you're here, David. I think Harry's dying. I tried to do what I could.'

'Yes, very good; now everyone out. Send Luke to me. Out, all of you; I must get to work. This is no ordinary wound, and if we are to save him… Eric, can you hear me?'

'Yes, David.'

'We have found them. Harry is nearly ready to cross over. I will try my best to keep him alive. He has a shadow-wound to his chest, and it has punctured his lung. He has also lost a lot of blood. The others are all well and uninjured. I will need your skills here. One of us will have to keep him alive, the other needs to fix the wound, and Luke must fend off the spirits who will come for him.'

'I am on my way, David.'

'Eric!' called Marcus, but he had just disappeared. 'Of all the bloody gods, Eric!' and Marcus stormed off.

Eric appeared beside David.

'Good, you are here,' said David. 'We need to work fast. Eric, if you can merge with him in a trance state and keep him alive. Ah, Luke, I've called Queen Sienna; you'll both need to fend off the sprits. I fear they are close. I will enter and heal the wound from inside and stop the flow of blood to the lung. Eric, if his heart stops for more than ten beats, get out, or you'll die with him. Are we ready?' asked David. 'Let's go.'

Eric sat and closed his eyes, seeking out his spirit form, ready to merge. He was surprised to see Harry.

'Eric, thank God you're here! Where am I, and why do I have a body of smoke? Oh, you do, too. I must admit I am a little afraid. Am I dreaming?'

'No, Harry, you're not dreaming; you're dying. You are dying from a shadow sword wound to your side that has punctured your lung.'

'So what happens now, Eric? I'm afraid. I don't want to die. I love Dina, and I have not told her.'

'Calm yourself, Harry,' said Eric.

'Arghhh, my side, arghhh, really hurts. How can I feel if I'm dead?'

'Because you're not dead yet, Harry.'

'Arghhh,' and Harry doubled over.

'That will be David trying to heal your wound. You must return to your body and hang on, Harry.'

'Arghhh, it hurts so much! Arghhh, my strength is going. Someone is pulling me, Eric; they have got my legs.'

'Hold on to me, Harry!'

'Luke, Luke, get them away,' David was saying.

'I'll help,' said a female voice from nowhere. 'Hold on to me, Harry. Don't let go; stay with me. If you let go, you will die,' as Queen Sienna appeared next to Harry.

'I'm trying; it hurts so much. Arghhh. Eric!'

'Harry, hold on, keep hold,' and that was the last Harry heard.

Eric checked in on Dina, Sam and Taw. 'Are you all well and no injuries?' he asked.

'Yes, we are all doing good. How is Harry getting on?'

'Well, for the moment, he is alive, and that's about all we can say. David is a skilled healer, and without him, Harry would be dead. David is with him now, helping his body to heal; Luke and Queen Sienna are protecting his spirit. We will know in a few hours, and it will be light by then. We must travel back then to Astel as it is unprotected here.

Hopefully, Harry will be able to make the trip. Tell me, Dina, Queen Sienna said you are a child of the Earth much like her mother?'

'So that's who she was! I recognised the bow, and she seemed very familiar.'

'We need to know how your skills in Earth are used and controlled.'

'I don't know what happened. Ask Queen Sienna; what did she say?'

'I have not been able to speak with her yet. Tell me what you know,' said Eric.

Dina started to tell Eric of the so-called dream and the attack on Taw.

'They were choking him to unconsciousness, then letting go and starting again, laughing each time.

'We did not know that Harry had been stabbed at this time. We thought he was still asleep. Then they saw me and the plants came alive, growing and wrapping themselves around the Dragmen.'

'Have you ever used these skills before, Dina? Be honest with me; it is of the utmost importance.'

'No, I never even knew I could do it. I love the forest, the land and all animals, be it sunny, raining, snowing, it does not matter,' she said. 'I just love it all.'

'That is why you are a child of the Earth, and it chose you,' Eric said.

Marcus found his mother in the throne room, pacing up and down.

'Marcus, is there any news of Harry?'

'No, Mother, but Eric disappeared just before I could talk to him. I hope it's good news and he found Harry. That's all I can tell you.'

'I suppose no news is good at the moment. How is everything else going?'

'Well, Mother, the kingdom is still on full alert; crossbows, fireballs are all at the ready. The people are in bunkers or cellars for their protection. You and Edmond, the Lord Marshal, have done wonders with getting the city, the people and all the weapons ready, Mother.'

'Yes, we have, Marcus. However, it was Sandy, Lord Sandbite, who helped the most. Edmond is getting old now, Marcus; he must be nearly eighty or even more now. In fact, if it weren't for Sandy, we would never have got it finished.'

'That is good to know, Mother. Do you want me to talk to Edmond?'

'No, Marcus, Edmond knows himself, and when time permits, he will tell you himself he is retiring.'

'Very well, Mother. I am going to get some sleep, which I've been lacking over the last few days. If I hear anything, I will come.'

Marcus walked off towards his quarters, sleep on his mind and his stomach rumbling. 'Maybe eat some food first then,' he said and diverted towards the kitchen.

Chapter 27

Master Zing Fan called the four together.

'Juliet, Josh and twins, we maybe have one chance to return dragon to sleep; it need four elements and stone wielder who will face dragon. Stone wielder will entice dragon out into open area. Stone wielder will have to keep dragon there while you four elements move in from North, South, East, West. When you all in place, we not sure what will happen. We think you will hold up sword and say your words for your own element. With the gods' help, maybe we live to talk about it.'

'This is all a bit hit and miss, with our lives and our people's lives on the line, when we have not got a clue what to do. Who is the Earth? And who is the stone wielder?' asked Juliet. 'What if the dragon attacks first, and we are not ready? What if the dragon eats the stone wielder?' Juliet was full of questions.

'We do not know answers yet. We did not know you had powers; you did not know either. We will prevail. So it is time for rest. Get some sleep; you will need it. Tomorrow very hard day.'

Twice Harry had slipped into the realm of the spirit world, but thankfully Queen Sienna and Luke were able to guide him back. By morning, David and Luke were exhausted, as were Eric and Queen Sienna, the four of them having taken turns through the night to keep him safe.

Taw and Dina turned up at first light and asked how Harry was, fearing the worst.

'He is not bleeding internally now, and the loss of blood has ceased. Two or three times in the night, we almost lost him, but he is strong, so at this stage, I would say he has a good chance of pulling through and making a full recovery,' said Eric.

'That's great news. We'll prepare break fast,' said Taw. 'Earl Vantor, how long do you think it will be before he wakes?'

'I would think maybe mid-day, but we need now to get some sleep, so you three need to look after him. Anything strange, or anything happens, wake us immediately. His life will depend on it, do you understand? He must not at any time be left alone, you understand?'

'Yes, Earl Vantor, we understand. Nothing will happen to him.'

'Good. David and I are going to sleep until mid-day. Luke is travelling back to inform Prince Marcus and the Queen. If Harry wakes, give him sips of water and maybe a little broth.'

Prince Marcus was sitting in the main room with Sandy, sipping a cup of tisane and chatting about defences, when Luke came walking in. Marcus stood, as did Sandy, and Luke made a beeline for them.

'Sit, man, you look exhausted,' said Marcus. 'Have a cup of this tisane. What news have you? Is Harry alive?'

'We found all of them, and Harry was near death. We fought through the night to save him and keep him alive; this morning, he is recovering. We closed the internal wound to his lung and stopped the bleeding. We nearly lost him a few times, but he is young and strong and will make a full recovery. Eric and David are resting, and then they will bring them all back. For myself, I too need to rest, so can you tell me where?'

'Sandy, can you show him to the officers' mess quarters? He can sleep there. I will go and tell Mother the news. Thank you, Luke,' and Marcus was off.

'This way,' said Sandy. 'It's only a short walk, and it's safe. Tell me, Luke, did you see my grandson, Taw? How is he?'

'I did see him, sir, and he is in good health, as are his companions.'

'That is good to hear. Here we are. Just say the Prince sent you.'

Marcus arrived at the throne room, and the Queen was busy with people.

'Mother, I have news,' Marcus announced.

'Out, everyone, out now,' commanded the Queen.

She sat on her throne. 'Well?' she said, waiting for the bad news. 'Is he dead?'

'No, Mother, he is alive. It was close a few times, according to Luke, but he pulled through and is now, as we speak, recovering.'

'Thank you, Marcus,' and the Queen got up and retired to her chambers. She closed the door, then sank down and cried a mother's tears.

Marcus went off to find Zing Fan and the others. They were training when he found them.

'Good morning to you, Prince,' said Zing Fan.

'To you all, too. Just to give you some news. Harry is alive and recovering; Taw, Dina and Sam are all well. So, Zing Fan, how goes the training?'

'Truth be told, Prince, Juliet can only manage a breeze under control, the twins, one holds the sword, and the other has to control the water, but is not work all time. We will need mountains of time before we ready; I fear we do not have it. The stone grows stronger each day. We might need another chest. It calls to its master, the dragon; soon, they will find each other, and the game will end. The dragon will consume all in its path, and having once laid waste to this world, it will be free to travel to others and do the same. Sorry, Prince, I am not good at hiding truths, but I see very little chance of us winning this battle if we don't have more time.'

'Time we do not have, you are right there. Every second counts and must be used to the best. One can only hope and pray we are ready when the time comes.'

'Yes, my Prince,' said Zing Fan. 'Stop standing with mouths open, and no practise; keep going.'

The group turned and carried on with their practice.

'Prince Marcus,' Luke said as he approached, 'I have some more news. Harry is stable but is a little weak to travel yet. By early evening he should be ready to travel. They may take a little longer than normal, but they will be here by then with the others, too.'

'Thank you, and well done, Luke. I will go and inform the Queen. She will be waiting for any more news.'

His breathing felt easier and not as if he was trying to breathe underwater. His side was extremely painful, and his head felt as though he had been kicked by a mule. Harry tried to speak, but his mouth was too dry. He opened his eyes to see Dina sitting next to him.

'Water,' he tried to say in a croaky voice.

'Oh, thank the gods you're awake, Harry. Here, sip this water slowly. You're so lucky to be alive; we thought we had lost you. I had thought I'd lost you,' she said.

'I seem to recall I was fighting in a dream, then a sharp pain in my side; it burned like fire.'

'You were in the realm of the dragon men, the sprits. They came for you, Harry, and stabbed you.'

'How is it that we are...'

'Enough, for now, Harry. Save your strength. I'll get you some food as we need to travel later today.'

David was walking back to where Harry was, and there seemed to be an awful lot of activity about. He stopped an officer. 'What is going on?' he enquired.

'Fighting, sir.'

'Where is the fighting?'

'Mons Harbour, sir.'

'Mons Harbour? There's nobody there; there isn't anybody to fight.'

'Excuse me, sir, we're fighting the dragon's army. We move out in fifteen minutes to go to Mons Harbour.'

David hurried back to get Eric, who was already on his way to Harry. 'I take it you have heard the news, Eric?'

'Yes.'

They arrived to meet with Taw, Dina and Sam. 'We have also heard the news and thought we would be ready to move. But what about Harry?'

'David, can you manage Dina, Sam and Taw, and I will take Harry on my own?'

'Yes. Eric, are we ready?'

'I think so. Best not to wait. I will go first with Harry. Harry, can you stand?'

'No, I don't think I can yet; I'll try...'

But Harry was not able to stand.

'Sam and Taw, pick up Harry and place him in my arms.'

They did as he bade, then he was gone.

David said, 'Gather round. Ready?' and they, too, were gone.

General Aziz had given orders that nobody was to enter the city. He sat outside with over two million men, six hundred thousand mounted men and five hundred thousand archers. There was sporadic fighting in the ranks until the order about silver was upheld, and the Dragmen that had infiltrated the army either died where they were or fled back to Mons Harbour. General Aziz sat waiting, thinking about what they would do.

Eric arrived in the Palace, in the throne room, with Harry in his arms. The Palace was deserted after everyone went underground.

'That you, Taw?'

'Yes, me, Sam and Dina, and David.'

'Good. Take Harry.'

Sam and Taw lifted Harry and placed him on the floor.

'Grab that cover there. We can use it to carry Harry.'

David and the three others took a corner each and lifted Harry.

'Follow me,' said Eric.

They made their way to the catacombs and reached them fifteen minutes later. They entered the large room after avoiding the entrapments Eric had set.

'Take Harry over there to Marcus's quarters, and put him to bed, David. I will go and find Marcus and the Queen. The rest of you wait here,' and he was gone again.

'Marcus, there you are!'

'Eric, you're back? What news of Harry?'

'He is here, Marcus; I hope you don't mind, but I put him in your chambers.'

'How is he, Eric?'

'He is good now and will mend fine.'

'Good. We can go this way. I'll see him, then we go to Mother.'

Harry was sitting up, taking some much-needed food from Marcus's servant.

'Good to see you, brother. So glad you're alive. Couldn't bear to tell Mother you are dead, but now I don't need to,' he said with a smile as he walked over and hugged him. 'So glad you're home, Harry. Well done, all of you. Come with me; we need to see the Queen.'

They arrived at the throne room, but it was closed. 'We need to speak with the Queen,' said Marcus to the Master Usher.

'Please wait, Prince Marcus.'

Marcus and the others were called into the Queen's makeshift throne room, where the Queen was sitting on a bench-like seat. She stood when she saw Marcus.

'What news of Harry?' she said.

Marcus was about to answer when the room glowed blue; everybody looked around. There was Taw, standing just inside the doorway, glowing blue too, as were the chests.

He looked at himself. 'I'm glowing blue,' he said. Then in a clear voice, he said, 'Stop this now, I have things to do,' and to everyone's surprise, it did.

Many miles away, eyes opened. 'I hear you. Not yet, soon, soon, I promise I will come for you,' and her eyes closed again.

'What was all that about, and why was Taw glowing blue?' asked Dina.

'Nothing. I just told them to stop, and they did.'

'Told who, Taw?' inquired Eric.

'Whoever was shining that blue light.'

'No, Taw. You are the stone wielder, Taw. You commanded it, and the stone obeyed,' said Eric.

'What stone wielder? What are you talking about, Eric?' asked Taw.

'When we came in, you started to glow blue, and so did the chests. You commanded the stone to stop, and it did. When I glowed blue, Zing Fan had to do a master spell to free me. So, like it or not, you are the stone wielder.'

'Alright,' said the Queen, 'enough of this now. Eric and David, sort this out. First, how is my son, Harry?'

'Harry is safe and is here in my quarters, Mother. The last I saw of him, he was sitting up eating some food, so I reckon he will be up for a visit,' said Marcus.

'I believe I owe you all my gratitude for the life of my son. Without you, he would have died. Thank you. And now I must visit him. Come, Marcus.'

'Taw, you will come with me. Dina and Sam, go and find Zing Fan. You will train with him,' said Eric Vantor.

Chapter 28

The army of the dragon was massing inside the main gates to Mons Harbour but had not moved. There seemed to be no leadership, according to General Aziz's look-outs. The General had issued orders: one in three to rest but to be ready to go in a minute. He would carry on waiting, as they were not going anywhere from here. They were surrounded, backs against the sea and more than two-and-a-half million fighting men in front. Hopefully, he would be able to hold and destroy this army of the dragon here at Mons Harbour and leave the actual killing of the dragon to Prince Marcus and his magicians.

'Time is getting short, and we need all the elements ready, and we need Taw. Master, would you train the four elements, as you are the best qualified with your skills? I will take Taw. This will be very tricky. We might have to have multiple shields, and I'm not even sure that will be enough, and it will still call the dragon,' said Eric.

The two groups had split, and the element students were practising with Zing Fan, as he took turns to train with each of them. Taw was in what could only be described as a large bubble, with Eric and the chests. Taw was holding the jewel and controlling how brightly it shone, and unlike Eric, he was not being burnt. Then Taw stopped, as if he was in a dream world.

Eric was calling his name: 'Taw, Taw.'

But he just looked at Eric with a blank expression on his face.

Eric Vantor was scared; what was going on? 'Taw,' he called, 'Taw!'

'I hear you, childling,' said a voice that was not Taw's. *'We are conversing, so be silent.'*

Eric stood very still. He could feel the sheer power in the jewel and knew that if it wished to, it could wipe all from this world. Then it struck him: the jewel was alive, with a mind of its own. The blue glow stopped, and Taw walked over and placed it in the first chest, then in the other two. Eric remained standing where he was, just looking at Taw. Taw, on the other hand, acted as though nothing had happened at all.

'Are we ready for supper?' asked Taw.

Eric was loaded with questions. 'Do you know what just went on?' he asked Taw.

'Yes, of course I do. I spoke to the stone, and it spoke back to me. You heard it, didn't you?'

'No, Taw, I did not. What did it say to you?'

'It said, "When the time comes, you will have to make a choice, a very big choice. I have been waiting for you and your ilk for a millennium. The time is close, and you must endure the Dragon until the end."'

Eric undid the shields and allowed them to go to supper. A short time later, after he and Zing Fan had discussed Taw's episode, they went to find Marcus, but David found them first.

'I have news,' said David. 'The dragon army is on the move; they're fighting with General Aziz's soldiers.'

They had reached the anteroom where Marcus was sitting with Harry.

'Marcus, we have had word that the dragon's army is on the move; it is surrounded by two million troops under the command of General Aziz at Mons Harbour. Something major is going on; this changes a lot. We have heard of the dragon's army but never seen it, only Dragmen,' said David.

'Oh, my Lord, by the gods! What if this is an army of Dragmen?' exclaimed Marcus.

'Surely not!' said Harry.

'May the gods protect us,' David said.

'If all magic comes from dragons, and from all the soldiers it has killed and are under its magic spell, it could be millions of warriors. This has got to be the dragon; it's much too powerful for a wizard,' said Eric.

'I think the time has come, gentlemen. You all come with me,' said the Queen. 'Boy, fetch all the lords and heads of the war council; we meet in my offices. Now.'

The anteroom soon filled up, but only about half the normal number of people turned up. So word was sent out to them that the meeting had started and everyone was to move into position. The Queen sat at the top table with Marcus. Everyone else stood around waiting. Lord Sandbite was last to attend.

'This is all who will be able to attend, Your Majesty,' stated Lord Sandbite.

General Aziz was awakened by a panic-stricken officer.

'They're coming,' he said. 'They're coming.'

General Aziz rushed out and onto his horse, assessing the situation. The dragon army was facing the gates. Then the army started to walk through the gate, about forty across but hundreds deep.

'Archers, fire.'

A black cloud of arrows flew through the air and landed in the ranks of the dragon army. Not even one soldier fell; they just kept coming.

'Flame the arrows!' shouted the General. 'Fire!'

They still came forward, some on fire. This was unheard of; they were on fire, arrows stuck out of them, yet they still walked forward.

The General pondered for a moment. 'Make a gap through the middle,' he said. 'Let them pass. Mounted men, escort them either side. Let's see where they are going, or whether they attack.'

The army of dragons walked through without so much as a sword straying.

'We stay with them,' said the General, having sent a runner to the Empress and Prince Marcus with news of this latest development.

Marcus said, 'I will be brief, as things are moving. You all know your duties and places, and the kingdom expects nothing less. Good news is we have all four wielders of the elements and, most importantly, the stone wielder, Taw Sandbite. Yes, Lord Sandbite, your grandson.'

Marcus held his hand up.

'Now is not the time for questions. Magicians and Lords Marshall and Sandbite, remain. The rest of you, to your posts and defend the kingdom and its people. May the gods be with you all. Now, to your posts.'

They slowly left the room, chattering to each other as they went.

Once the room was clear of them, Marcus said, 'Glass of wine, everyone?' and a servant brought wine and goblets and then left, too.

'Marcus, how do you know it is my grandson?' asked Sandy.

Eric explained how they had walked into the room and Taw was glowing, and how finally Taw was controlling it.

'By the gods,' said Sandy, 'who would ever have thought it? I found it very strange that these young kids, Taw, Dina, Josh, Juliet, the twins, all more or less from one town at this particular time, are all part of this. With powers, the elements, the stone. It is as if it was written in a book; at this particular time, they all come together.'

'That's a puzzle for another time. We have enough to concern ourselves with. Are the defences ready in the Palace keep?' ask Marcus.

Sandy replied, 'They are, with everything: rocks, fire, archers, spears, boiling oil, as if an army was there, not just twenty men. They are fully rehearsed. At a given signal, they will fire the huge arrows upwards and take to the sewers and tunnels, sealing them behind them.'

'That's just what I wanted to hear. Well done. Eric, we may need to send a wizard south to see first-hand what is going on, where this army is, what it is made of. Whether we, with the Southern Kingdom, can stop it, and what they are doing. We might also need to know where they are heading and when they will get there.'

'Who will I send, David or Luke?' Eric thought to himself.

Eric found Taw, and they began training. After the third time, the stone stopped glowing.

'What is happening?' asked Eric.

'I don't know. It just stopped,' said Taw. Taw approached the chest. Nothing.

'Hello,' said Taw, but no answer.

'Taw, say this exactly: "Dragonite, I am the Stone Wielder. Are you well?"'

'How will it answer?' said Taw.

'Just say it!'

Taw did so, but again nothing happened at all.

'Eric, I am trying to think what I would say and what would make it answer. I've got it! "Dragonite, I am the Stone Wielder. Do you recognise me?"'

The stone pulsed a faint blue glow.

'Great!' said Eric. 'It recognises you. Now we need to move away; it needs to rest, I think.'

They walked away.

'I don't understand, Eric. Why me? I'm nothing special, just an ordinary, normal boy,' said Taw as they walked.

'That is an excellent question, but who could have foretold that all four elements and the sword wielders were in the same kingdom, the same city, and friends, and you, at the top, the stone wielder? Across thousands of years, many worlds, at the precise time the dragon wakens. The odds on that would be interesting,' said Eric. 'As for the now, I am hungry and definitely need some sleep. How about you? It could be a long day tomorrow.'

Marcus found Eric in the dining hall and went and sat down with him.

'Have you sent either of your brothers yet? We need to know what is going on in the south.'

'I was thinking about that myself, Marcus. How soon will they need to go, so I can tell them? I take it coming back will be when they need to, yes?'

'Correct, Eric, and at first light tomorrow, so we can start getting news.'

'Very well, Marcus. I will see to it.'

'How is Taw holding up? Does he understand what will be required of him yet?'

'Yes, I think he does, but he's a brave lad and would not say otherwise. He has gone to meet up with his friends.'

'That is good. They will all need to be so very brave for such young, young soldiers. Thank you, Eric,' and the Prince left the hall.

Taw found his friends in the Prince's special accommodation.

'Taw,' shouted Dina, as she had seen him first, and the others all ran over to him.

'It is good to see you again. So much has happened, and what happened to you? We were so worried when you turned blue in the room.'

They all sat around the big table, telling of their adventures.

'So, who is who?' asked Taw.

Juliet said, 'I'm the Air or Wind.'

'We are the Water,' said the twins.

'I am the Fire, but you know that, Taw,' said Josh.

'That just leaves me, Taw. I am the Earth,' said Dina. 'What about you, Sam?'

'No, Taw, I don't have any special power I know or don't know about. And you, Taw?'

'Me, I have been told that I am the stone wielder!'

'You're not!' said Juliet. 'Please tell me, Taw, you're not the one.'

'Why, Juliet, what's wrong?'

'You are the one who calls the dragon with the stone, then stands before it and commands the dragon, while we get into place with the elements. North, South, East and West. You have to hold the dragon there until we are in place and ready to start the enchantment.'

'How do you know all this, Juliet?' asked Taw.

'I asked Master Zing Fan how we defeat the dragon. He told me we can never defeat or kill the dragon, but we can put it back to sleep again for thousands of years, and this is the only way we can do it, or we all die.'

Everyone fell silent for a moment, then Sam said, 'We could all be dead by now, but we're not, so let's all have a drink, and one for the day after tomorrow, as it is the Day of the Dead. And what a good day to go to the gods on, if we must, so let's charge our glasses.'

Chapter 29

General Aziz had ordered a retreat to Lake Blue by the old fort. They had attacked the enemy three times, and three times they had been pushed back. The men's courage was failing. After the first two attacks, the men had withdrawn.

Ten minutes later, their dead were rising and joining the ranks of the enemy. Behind them were the Dragmen, with their black eyes peering out, not moving to engage in the fighting. They just waited and watched. General Aziz sent riders out, one to his Empress and the other to Astel Kingdom.

'There is a man here to see you, General. Says he was sent by the Empress.'

'Send him in, then. Make sure he is unarmed.'

'No need of that, General, my friend,' said David Vantor. 'How are you?' As they met, they raised forearms in a salute to each other.

'I am so glad to see you, my friend. Have a seat. Are any of the others with you? We could do with their help. Our dying soldiers are getting up and joining the ranks of the enemy, and those Dragmen things stand behind them, doing nothing, just their black eyes staring out. My men are all but ready to flee. I myself don't know what to do. Can you help, David? Please say you can.'

'The honest answer is I don't know either. I only came to gather information, as we heard there was an army of the dragon. I will need to talk with Master Zing Fan to ask whether anything can be done. Your Empress is on her way to Astel Kingdom to stay with our Queen in safety underground, which is, we believe, the safest place to be. I will go and speak with Zing Fan and see what action we can take. I will be back soon, General,' and he walked off.

The troop, now back together, sat around chatting about all sorts of other stuff, rather than the tasks they were to perform when and if the dragon came. Taw was sitting with Juliet. She was explaining that she could not get the sword to work properly; it was either a breeze or a harsh gust of wind. Taw was saying the last gust of wind he had was after his dinner.

Laughing, Juliet gently slapped his arm. 'Don't be so rude,' she said.

'What do you mean?' he said, pushing her back on the bed they were sitting on, and began a little play fight. The others just looked and carried on talking and laughing among themselves. Laughing, Taw held Juliet down by the wrists. Then the laughing stopped as they looked into each other's eyes, and they kissed. It was a very brief kiss at first.

Taw blushed and said, 'Sorry, Juliet. I just –'

Juliet kissed him. This time it was a long, meaningful kiss.

Dina was the only one who noticed, but she said nothing.

'I was so glad when you turned up again, Taw, but now I have to contend with your facing that dragon and not seeing you again,' said Juliet.

'I will be fine. Eric has said that Master Zing Fan will be with me, so I won't be alone, and if it goes wrong, he's the best to get us out. We will all have someone with power with us, as they have words to say, too. We will do this, Juliet,' and they kissed again.

'Eric, it is David. Can you hear me?'

'Yes, brother, I am here with Zing Fan and Marcus. What news do you have?'

'It is worse than we thought,' David said and explained what the General had told him and what he had seen. 'I feel we need to help. Can we do anything, Zing Fan?'

'This very powerful magic, to have the dead live and fight. I think Dragmen behind army are the controllers, or intensifying the magic somehow. Still no sign of dragon, David?'

'No.'

'In that case, get the General to target the Dragmen with mounted archers, in and out only. Don't stay there; try in one place and then observe. Try that tactic,' said Marcus.

'Is there anything I can do, Eric?'

'You could try probing to find the source of the magic. But be very careful, David, as they may track you, too.'

'Yes, brother, I will speak with the General and speak again tomorrow.'

Across the sky, a low sun was rising, a golden orange filled the sky, and all seemed to be at ease, birds merrily singing their songs. The four elements were in place: Josh, Dina, Juliet and the twins, Earthie and Jackus. All set in their places, and Taw was standing South East. Eric and Zing Fan were drilling them, saying the words, but without swords. They did not want any accidents, so the swords were wooden. All the best planning can always go wrong, as Josh found out when his sword burst into flames.

He was waving it about until he dropped it. Everybody was laughing; it was so funny, then Zing Fan did an impression of Josh, which was even more hilarious.

Prince Marcus and the Lords Marshall and Sandbite were walking around the City and Palace, inspecting the defence's positions and armour placements.

'These are Lord Sandbite's idea: the last defence, large catapults pointing upward, the arrows super hard. They are fixed to every other house and can be set off in sets. Hopefully, they will pierce the dragon's skin,' said the Lord Marshal.

'These are extremely good defences, Edmond. Both of you are to be congratulated. Well done,' said Marcus.

Marcus went to see his mother, the Queen. 'I need to call a meeting, Mother. The time will be tomorrow; we must make the first move.'

'Perhaps you are right, Marcus, but are we ready?'

'The truth, Mother, is no, but we have to be. The army of the dragon will be at our border in the morning. We need to take on the dragon first to destroy it or send it back to sleep.'

'Very well. Call the meeting.'

'This is a select meeting,' said Marcus. 'The dragon first. So, the three wizards, Queen Sienna, Zing Fan, the four elements and the stone wielder will deal with the dragon. Lords Edmond and Sandy, and, of course, Mother and the Empress, will all assemble underground in the catacombs, in the throne room, and deal with the defence of the city.

'My plan is to draw the dragon out into the valley of Lady Lake, then move the elements into place and then pray we can send it back to sleep. We will muster our forces along the southern border, south of Yorker, which will be as my command. We will also have the Southern army north of the border facing the dragon's army. I will be in Yorker. You will all have your places. The plan is to be executed tomorrow, which, I might add, is the Day of the Dead.'

'How ironic,' said Sandy, and a small ripple of nervous laughter echoed.

General Aziz marshalled his forces but did not attack; the sun was getting low, and he wanted to get to the border before the dragon's army. They had amassed nearly three-and-a-half million troops, and the High General was coming from Manch City with another two million mounted troops.

He decided he would send in five hundred thousand mounted archers directly to the front, running in a huge circle to target the Dragmen in one place. That way, they would have to walk over the ones in front. The main army would continue north to meet with Astel Kingdom.

General Aziz ordered the attacks.

'Marcus, I would very much like to have a dinner tonight, before tomorrow begins. Just listen for a moment. You, me, Harry and Juliet, Eric, David, Luke and Zing Fan. Sandy and Edmond and his wife, our cousins, Aron and John, Queen Sienna, Mother Superior, Baroness Verna, and of course your special troop. The Empress will be here by early evening and, of course, will be there too. I want this to happen. Everything has been already arranged. People just need to be told.'

'But, Mother, how can you do this the day before? We could all be dead tomorrow.'

'Exactly, my son. That is the very reason I want this. So, it will happen. You will see to it. Dress is formal, an hour before sundown,' and the Queen walked away.

'As if I have nothing better to do at this time in my life. You there, go and fetch me six squires. Now.'

'Yes, sir,' and he was gone.

Marcus sat and quickly wrote the invitations. Just as he finished, the squires appeared. They looked so young, he thought.

'Take these invitations to the people named. They need to be delivered in the next ten minutes. Off you go.'

There was some noise outside, and Marcus went to investigate. He looked out and saw Empress Shulla and her escort of six Saracens.

Marcus stepped out. 'Greetings, Empress', he said and bowed slightly.

She, in return, said, 'It is an honour to see you again, Prince Marcus.'

'You too, Empress. The Queen is expecting you in the throne room.'

'Will you be joining us?'

'Later, perhaps, but certainly at dinner.'

'We look forward to seeing you later, then, Prince Marcus.'

'Empress.'

She had become even more stunning than he had remembered, and she so stirred his blood, but he knew nothing could come from it, monarchs of opposite kingdoms.

'Ah! There you are, Marcus,' said Eric, who had Zing Fan and Luke in tow.

'We need a room to talk to David.'

'This way, and you're all invited to dinner this evening, an hour before sundown, formal dress. Before you say anything, by order of the Queen.'

'Ha, ha. Thought you would like that, so you will be there. Here we are,' said Eric with a big grin on his face, as if he already knew about the dinner.

'Hello, David, can you hear me?'

'Yes, Eric.'

'How are you?'

'I am tired, Eric. The tactic on the Dragmen worked. Not enough, but it has slowed them down. They are, at the moment, just standing, waiting, for what we do not know, but when they move, it will be hard to stop them.'

'I have a plan,' said Marcus. 'Do not try to stop them, but fight a retreat. Guide them towards Chester Cira on the border. General Aziz knows the plan. Once at the border, we will meet them there, where we have surprises for them.'

'I tried to probe, brother, and was hit with a powerful mental blow that knocked me off my feet.'

'Well done, David. Time to come home,' Eric said. 'We have dinner with the Queen an hour before sunset.'

'I will leave soon and be there,' said David.

'So, Juliet, are you going to wear our uniform, or are you going as a Princess of the Crown?' asked Dina.

'I don't really know. What I should do, Dina? What do you think? What about dress, boots, sword and backpack? That will make them laugh, not to mention my mother's face,' said Juliet.

'Very funny. You know you will have to go as a Princess.'

'I know, Dina, but we can wear the colours of the uniform and a shawl. That's a great idea. What are you waiting for? Grab your stuff. We'll go and get sorted in the royal chambers where we can have a bath.'

'Oh, how lovely, Juliet! Let's go.'

The girls set off to get ready.

The boys were all ready, with their new uniforms, dark navy, with the gold piping and edging. They looked so smart.

'Eric, Eric, it is David. The dragon's army is on the move and they are heading north. They are ignoring us and moving around us, rather than fighting.'

'Marcus said he thought they would do that, as long as they head north. You have done well, brother. Come home.'

'I am now, brother.'

The diners were standing behind their designated chairs, awaiting the royal family and the Empress. Prince Marcus walked in first, with Princess Juliet and Prince Harry, and they took their places.

'My lords, ladies and gentlemen, Her Majesty the Queen of Astel Kingdom, and Her Royal Highness the Empress of the Southern Kingdom.'

They both walked in and seated themselves; everyone else then followed. Waiters began serving the wine. Prince Marcus then stood, and the room became silent.

'My lords, ladies and gentlemen, the Queen wishes to address you all,' and he sat.

'I wanted to take this opportunity to thank each and every one of you for your sterling efforts up until now, and for those yet to come. Without such, we surely would be wiped from the face of this earth. Yet I say with regret, this could still happen, and to prevent it, we must place people, and also ask people to place themselves, in grave danger, for the benefit of us all. To these brave people, we salute you.'

The Queen stood and raised her glass; the room stood too.

The Queen said, 'To the bravest of us all, may they prevail and save us all.'

The room echoed the toast, and all sat down.

'Let us now enjoy possibly our last evening together,' and dinner was served.

Taw could not take his eyes off Juliet. She was dressed in a royal blue off-the-shoulder dress, with gold piping and edging, with a shawl the same colour, with the Prince's Elite Troop badge embossed on it. Dina was dressed exactly the same, but Juliet had on her tiara. Apparently, the Queen had had the dresses made, as she hated the ladies' uniform for court. Taw knew it would be impossible to get to see Juliet tonight. Sam was doing his best during dinner with Dina, but her eyes were fixed on Harry. Harry did his best to not seem to notice, but Marcus did. His own eyes were on the Empress.

'What a hopeless lot of love that cannot be,' said Josh to Earthie and Jackus.

'I've got my eye on that Empress,' said Jackus.

'Not before me,' said Aron, and they all started to laugh. 'But it's alright, boys,' Aron said, 'my brother John has always got his horse. That's about the best-looking filly he is likely to get,' and the laughter continued.

Chapter 30

The sun was rising on the Day of the Dead. The dragon army had continued to move north through the night, not stopping. General Aziz did what he could, constantly sending in mounted bowmen to attack the Dragmen. Overall, it had little effect, but at least he was not losing any more men to feed the enemy. At their current rate, they would reach the border at mid-day.

At the border, the High General would be there with another two million mounted archers and pikemen, Prince Marcus with another two million, and the three-and-a-half million with him now: a total of seven-and-a-half million mounted fighting men.

The Dragon opened her eyes, blinking in the bright sunshine, adjusting to the light. She raised her huge head. She still felt a little groggy; she yawned wide and shook her head a little. That felt better, and she stood, standing on all four of her giant legs, her claws stretching out. She opened out her huge wings, feeling the cool, crisp air against them. She stretched and relaxed them, fluttered them, feeling the wind under them. But not yet, need to think. Who are these insignificant little insects running around? Never before have I had need of an army to protect me while I rest after feeding. I also need to get my stone; its voice has gone, not calling me anymore. It is silent. I can't even feel a slight pulse. Where are you, my Dragonite?

Marcus and Eric stood with Taw by the chests.

'Remember, Taw, when I open the last chest, you must stop it from glowing, as we think that's the way it communicates with the dragon, and we don't want it here with us.'

Eric opened the last chest, and there was the stone, just a plain, ordinary blue jewel by the look of it.

'Place the stone into this little travel box if you can, Taw. Last time, it was getting very hot.'

Taw reached in and took the stone and placed it in the small travel box.

'It's not hot, Eric; it's cold.'

'Now,' said Eric, 'you must go. One hour after mid-day, Marcus. They must be in place exactly at that time. I will be north of Taw with Juliet.'

'Master Taw, we go now,' said Zing Fan.

'Goodbye to you. I wish you –' Taw began, and they were gone.

Eric and Marcus walked into the throne room where the Queen was sitting in her chair.

'First part done, Your Majesty,' said Eric.

The twins, Earthie and Jackus, were standing in full fighting uniform with Luke Vantor and the sword of Water. Next to them was Dina, with Queen Sienna and the Earth sword, and now Dina knew, their bows side by side, they were twins of the Earth. David Vantor was standing with Josh and the sword of Fire. Eric moved over and stood next to Juliet and the sword of Air.

'We do not know where the dragon is, so we will need to give an hour to Taw and the jewel. Then we must be ready to move and start casting the spell together. That's why we have a wizard or witch with each of you, so we can all say and start at the same time. I need to take Marcus to the border and to his army, to carry out his plan and be returned, ready for when we move,' Eric stated.

'Good luck, everyone. If we are triumphant, I will see you all later. If not, I will see you in Heaven. It has been a real pleasure. God bless us all,' said Prince Marcus.

It was echoed by them all. Then he disappeared with Eric.

Marcus arrived at Chester Cira. 'Is all in readiness?' he asked the captain of the guard.

'Yes,' he replied.

'And where is General Aziz?'

'He is just crossing through now, at the end of his men. Just about four million, sire; three hours to cross five miles of border.'

Marcus took his horse and rode to meet General Aziz, and as the two men met, the shout went up: 'Dragon's army spotted!'

Marcus rode forward so he could see. Just as he had expected they would, they were coming straight for the north.

The Dragon stretched out her huge wings and flexed them. Time to fly, she said, and up she soared, leaving the mountains below. It was good to be free, to feel the wind in her face and beneath her wings. On and upwards she flew, higher still into the thermals, where it was warm. Now to seek out my Dragonite. Where are you? I'm coming.

Zing Fan and Taw arrived at the top of Lady Valley. Taw felt a little sick from the travelling.

'It will pass, Taw. We have a little while. Drink some water; make you feel a little better.'

Taw drank some water; it was cool but did nothing for the queasiness.

'How you feel now, Taw?' asked Zing Fan. 'You good?'

'Not really, Zing Fan. I think I am so scared of facing a dragon with just a stone in my hand.'

'Remember your words, Taw. You are calling it to you, commanding it. You must believe it with all your soul.'

'I would, if I was not shaking in my boots and rattling in my armour.'

'Say the words, Taw, say them!'

'*Come to me, mighty Dragon, come to the Stone Wielder. Come to me and obey! Come to me, Dragon of Dragons.*'

'Now the second part, Taw.'

'*With this stone of Dragonite, you will obey thy bearer. You are still, nothing moves, nothing exists, time stands still, time is no more. Look to the stone, look to the Dragonite, Dragon of Dragons.*'

'Well done! How do you feel now?'

'Better, Master Zing Fan,' he lied.

'Archers!' shouted Marcus. Behind him and in front of him were rows of archers, stretching for five miles from the mountains along the only passable part of the border. Seven million bows were ready.

Marcus, General Aziz and the High General were convinced they could hold the advance of the dragon's army. There were three trenches between them, each deeper than the previous one, the first, thirty feet deep and twenty feet wide, the last, forty feet deep and forty feet wide, and they again ran along the length of the crossing point. Each one could be fired at separate times. All they had to do was hold them there while the others put the dragon back to sleep.

'It's time, Taw. We need to start,' said Zing Fan.

'Yes, I know we do,' and he walked and sat on a low stone wall facing down along the valley. He reached inside his pocket and took out the small box. 'I am still scared,' he said.

'You will be good; you have heart of lion.'

Taw opened the box and took the stone jewel in his hand.

'We are ready,' Zing Fan passed to Eric.

'Remember, Taw, as soon as you see the dragon, you must start saying the first part over and over until it lands, then start the next part. I will tell the others when to start.'

Eric said, 'Places, everyone,' and they moved together with their partners.

'Remember, wait for the call to move closer, and start to say your words straight away, as the dragon will have landed.'

The great gold dragon circled high above, feeling free with the wind blowing beneath her, totally unaware of what was about to unfold.

There it is, there the pulse is back, and it's strong. It was calling to her, growing stronger. She headed towards the pulse, so strong now. She shook her head. Why is it so strong now? 'I'm coming,' said the Dragon, 'I'm coming to you now.'

Taw was holding the stone. He was glowing faintly blue, then it and he would pulse a vivid blue, like a beacon. It reached out to who was listening.

There was someone listening, and she was on her way.

The sky turned black as millions of arrows sailed over the advancing army of the dead and into the ranks of the Dragmen. They fell, and the advance faltered briefly but then carried on, walking over the fallen. Another rain of arrows blacked out the sky as the first ranks of the dead army fell into the trench. Another volley of arrows followed. But they kept on coming, and volley after volley of arrows was shot into them.

'It is working, Prince Marcus. The advance is faltering as the Dragmen are killed and the dead fall into the trench.'

'Not fully, General; the Dragmen are rising after a couple of minutes, but we have already thought this might happen,' he said with a smile on his face. 'Fire the arrows!' shouted Marcus.

All across the front, the ranks knelt and lit their arrows with fire.

'Ready. Fire!' and millions of flaming arrows took to the sky.

This time they were not aimed at the Dragmen or the dead army, they were directed at the trench. The trench was nearly full with the dead army, which was now soaked in lantern oil that had been placed in the bottom. The arrows struck their intended target, and there was a mass of explosions up and down the trench as flames erupted everywhere along its line.

'Hold!' shouted Marcus.

They stood watching as the flames burnt the army of the dead. In the distance, the Black witches had arrived and were now attacking from the rear with enchanted arrows, flying in and out.

'Now we wait,' said Marcus, 'and hope the others do as well.'

Zing Fan stood with Taw, who was now glowing bright blue, and the heat coming from him was increasing.

Zing Fan looked at Taw. 'Don't you be afraid, Taw. I am afraid for both of us.'

But Taw just looked at him, then the sky went black, and then shone again.

A red mist descended from above and was encircling them. It was not close, but Zing Fan could see it from the inside. Up the sides of the valley, it stretched for two miles in a big circle.

'Say the words now, Taw, say the words!' but Taw did not answer; he was in some sort of trance.

'Taw!' Zing Fan shouted, but no response.

Zing Fan thought for a second, then held his hand up to his face; he could feel the heat emanating from Taw, and it was starting to burn his hand. Taw needed to say the words, or they were all dead.

Zing Fan walked in front of Taw and looked at him, then said, 'I'm sorry, friend.' He slapped Taw as hard as he could across the face, and all went black.

Chapter 31

Eric Vantor was waiting for news. The only thing he had heard was that the dragon was on its way. They had no way of knowing whether the dragon could sense the elements, or whether it knew what they were planning. Timing was everything. If they got there too soon, they would be caught in the open by the dragon, and it would be all over if the dragon got just one of the elements.

Queen Sienna said, 'We should move now, Eric. My sisters are attacking the Dragmen.'

'Very well, it's been long enough. Keep an open link to speak to Zing Fan. Let's go. You know your positions. God be with us,' and one by one, they were gone.

Eric and Juliet arrived in the north position of the valley. To their surprise, they were faced with a huge red wall of mist.

'Oh, no!' said Eric, 'I did not foresee this. We can't jump through it, as the dragon is on the other side, and we could end up inside it and be dead. Sienna, Luke and David, can you hear me?'

'Yes,' said Sienna, 'but there is a big red wall in front of us. Luke, what about you?'

'We have a big wall, but it is gold and behind us is a red one.'

'Luke, the gold wall is the dragon. Stay very still. We are on the outside. We don't think the chants will work through the red mist, as it rejects spells or magic. I need to think, think what to do.'

She could see the blue glow of the stone, and it called to her. She had sent out the red mist as she homed in on the stone. Closer she came towards the stone. Finally, it would be hers. Something was attached to the stone, but no matter, she would deal with that. Closer she came, time to land. 'What is happening? I feel... I feel dizzy. This is not right.'

"Come to me," *was all she could hear.*

She landed clumsily on the ground with a thump, and the ground shook. She looked half dazed at the bright blue light.

"Look to the stone, Dragon."

The bright blue light was all-consuming. Its vivid blues were swirling, sparkling, beautiful; all was at rest.

"Come to me, mighty Dragon, come to the Stone Wielder, come to me and obey."

The Dragon lay still, her eyes firmly fixed on the dazzling blue light.

'Look, look at that,' came the shouts from the men. 'The dead are staying dead, and the Dragmen are like lost sheep, wandering everywhere.'

'Keep vigilant,' said Marcus. 'This could be temporary. Keep watching and hold your ground.'

But the men had already started cheering and waving to the Black witches, who had broken off their attacks. The flames were still high in the trenches, but nothing moved anymore.

Zing Fan's eyes opened. His head felt heavy and hurt so much it was almost unbearable. He pushed himself up from the ground into a sitting position, holding his head. There, in front of his eyes, was a colossal golden dragon. It was enormous, truly the Dragon of Dragons. Its huge eyes were glowing blue, locked to the stone Taw held.

Zing Fan looked at Taw; he was not glowing blue and had just finished repeating a verse.

'Ah, I see you are awake. Thought you were to help me? Tell the others to start now,' said Taw.

The dragon moved.

'I must repeat the verse to keep it fixed on the stone. *"Come to me, mighty Dragon...,"'* and Taw carried on.

'Eric, look! You can see through the red mist; it's fading,' said Juliet. 'Taw, bless you, lad. You must have the dragon.'

'Eric, Luke, David and Queen Sienna, it is Zing Fan. You must start now.'

'We can't just yet. We need to be through the red mist before we can start. Whatever Taw is doing, get him to carry on, as it is breaking the mist down. Soon we will be through.'

Queen Sienna and Dina were first to step through, then Eric with Juliet.

'We are now through. Just Josh and David... We are ready.'

Suddenly the ground shook. The great golden dragon stood up on its four legs, her massive wings spread out, blocking out the light. Zing Fan looked at Taw. He was exhausted and barely able to stand, the light from the stone fading. The dragon was breaking free of the magic blue light's hold on her.

'Wizards, start your chants now! The rest of you, get ready. Taw can hold her no longer,' said Zing Fan.

The wizards started their own chanting, with magic intertwined in the words:

'I call on the magic of the land on this Day of the Dead. Bring your magic to bear on this unholy Dragon. We call for the Sleep of Dragons combined with the Power of the Earth.'

A bright green light shot out from Dina's sword straight upward, then a blue light, a red light and a pearl light.

'We command you, sleep the Dragon's Sleep. Draco somnum aeternum, draco somnum aeternum.' They all spoke at the same time.

The earth started to tremble, rocks dislodging, the ground heaving.

Taw was glowing bright blue; he could hardly stand. Zing Fan attempted to hold him but was forced away by the heat. The four elements were now starting to merge towards each other, high in the sky. They met above the dragon, and a rainbow of brilliant, coloured lights shone down in a dome around the dragon and Taw. All lights stopped, all the wizards and witches, the sword wielders of the elements. Even Taw fell to the floor exhausted and looked up at the dragon. The dragon was not controlled by the blue light anymore but encased in this rainbow of lights with Taw.

The dragon held up one of her huge claws and said, *"Stand little thing."*

Exhausted as he was, Taw staggered to his feet. Zing Fan looked on but could not move at all. The dragon lowered her head down to Taw.

Looking directly at him, the dragon said, '*I am the last of my kind upon this earth; I was here when it was born, many thousands of years ago. I've lived thousands of years, and I have slept thousands, too. But I am immortal, I cannot die, and I cannot sleep the Dragon's Sleep again. It can only be used twice, and this is spent.*'

Taw felt his heart sink. They had failed, and now all would die beneath this huge golden dragon.

'*You do not know this, Stone Wielder, but you are the one. Across the universe, it was told of your coming and that of your companions. I thought it would never come to pass. When I am gone, Stone Wielder, take this egg and the stone. Cast them in the deepest part of the deepest sea. They will surface when the three planets meet in a millennium.*

'*You have not put me to sleep, Stone Wielder, but freed me from the chains that have held me here, so I thank you and leave you a name and a gift. The name is Merlin; the gift you will discover yourself.*'

With that, she extended her huge wings, then she began to glow, brighter and brighter. Taw and Zing Fan shielded their eyes. The others, too, around the dragon shielded their eyes. The army on the border saw it, like a sun, then it was gone, and so was the dragon. Zing Fan blinked and looked around. It was all gone. No dragon, no mist; all that was left was a golden egg, about two foot in length. Zing Fan looked for Taw. He was just about standing, looking at the stone in what was left of his hands.

The stone was now just a burnt piece of deep black rock. Taw fell to the floor next to Zing Fan, who could now move.

'You have done it, Taw. The dragon has gone forever; it will never return. It's not asleep; it's gone forever.'

But Taw did not answer. Zing Fan moved over to him and looked: both Taw's hands were just burnt bones, like fixed claws, and he was not moving, although he was alive. The others came running over to where Taw was.

'We need to return to the keep with Taw,' said Eric Vantor. 'The dragon has gone, but Taw needs attention.'

Eric walked over to the golden egg that lay on the floor, but as he tried to pick it up, his hands passed right through it. Zing Fan came over and tried also, but then just stood over the egg.

'No one but Taw can take the egg. He was asked by the dragon to take it and drop it into the deepest ocean with the jewel,' said Zing Fan.

'What?' asked Eric. 'Take the egg? That I don't know, but we leave it for now.' They all reappeared in the main throne room in the keep. Taw was taken to the sisters, still unconscious.

Prince Marcus and the generals watched as the bright flash of light disappeared. Prince Marcus looked out over the battlefield to see the dead army gone. As for the Dragmen, they were just wandering around confused, asking why and how they were there. General Aziz looked on in disbelief.

'What happened?' he asked Prince Marcus. 'Where did the army go?'

'I think our friends, the wizards, the young soldiers, and Taw have put the dragon to sleep. Hopefully for another two or three thousand years, well after we have gone.'

'May Allah be praised!' said General Aziz.

'This is the time when I lead the army home, General. You are welcome to join me.'

'Thank you, Prince, but I, too, have duties to attend to. Farewell, Prince Marcus.'

'You too, General.'

They both called up their armies, and with a final salute, they headed off in different directions with their armies following.

Word had been sent to the Queen and the Empress that all was safe, and people were making their way back to their homes and villages. The Queen's party was also making its way back to the Palace and the keep. Word was travelling fast about the deeds of Taw and his companions, the heroes, the dragon slayers. Taw was being treated by the sisters, with Juliet at his side. He had not regained consciousness since his talk with the dragon.

'You can't die, Taw, I love you,' Juliet was saying, the words mixed with tears.

The Queen was informed by Harry that Taw had not awakened, and also that Taw and Juliet were in love.

'If he dies, it may be a blessing,' said the Queen.

'What do you mean, Mother? He is our greatest hero.'

'Yes, he is, my son, but he is also a commoner.'

'But, Mother, I am also in love with Dina.'

'That is unfortunate, Harry, but at this time, we have far more important matters to deal with. We are the Royal Family, and it is our duty to look after the kingdom. Go, I'll hear no more of this love stuff.'

'Your Majesty.' The sisters bowed as the Queen entered.

Taw was lying in bed, his hands bandaged heavily, and Juliet sat beside him.

'How is he?' asked the Queen.

'He is unconscious still, and his hands are very severely burnt. They are just black bones, really. David has tried to find him, but he is lost.'

'I see,' said the Queen. 'Leave us,' she commanded and then she sat.

Juliet got up and went to her mother and hugged her, tears flowing freely.

'I love him so much.'

'I know, dear,' was all she said, but the conversation would have to be had if Taw was to live.

'Your Majesty,' came a voice from the door.

The Queen looked up and saw Sandy in the doorway.

'Come in, Lord Sandbite.'

'Thank you. How is he?'

Juliet wiped the tears from her face. 'There is no change; they don't know if he will survive. His mind is lost, and the sisters cannot find him,' she said, almost breaking into tears again.

Before he could answer, Eric stepped in.

'He will survive,' he said.

'How do you know?' asked Juliet.

'That's easy,' said Eric. 'The dragon told the stone wielder to take the golden dragon's egg and drop it in the deepest ocean, with the stone. If he is dead, that cannot be done. Nobody else can pick up the egg, as it is a shadow. So, he will wake when he is ready.'

'Thank you, Earl Vantor,' said the Queen, rising. 'Juliet, come with me.'

Juliet was about to say something when the Queen said, 'Now, if you please, Juliet.'

Juliet leaned over and kissed Taw, then went with her mother, and they walked off.

Sandy and Eric looked at each other. 'Oh, dear,' said Sandy, 'we may have another bigger problem.'

'Yes,' said Eric, 'but he's not the only one.'

'Not the only one?'

'No,' said Eric laughing, 'Harry and Dina too!'

'Oh, God bless us,' said Sandy. 'Join me in a goblet of wine.'

Taw was visited by all the others through the day, but most of all by Juliet.

Marcus was met by David just north of Yorker City.

'Greetings, Prince Marcus. I have been waiting for you. I have orders from the Queen to return you home.'

'Thank you, David. May we have mid-day meal first with my captains?'

'Of course, sire.'

'That's good, and you can tell us what's happened to the dragon. I take it the dragon is asleep. Is there any other news of note from across the kingdom?'

They sat in a rough circle while the meal was being made.

David started to tell them the saga that had befallen the kingdom, the final facts about the dragon and Taw, and the fact Taw had not regained consciousness when David had left. He told Marcus of the dragon's request to Taw.

'It is all brilliant,' said Marcus, 'a complete mess up, but it worked, and we succeeded.'

'Just one more thing you need to be aware of before we return, Prince Marcus, but this is for your ears only. May we take a little walk?'

Marcus and David walked away from the others.

'So, what is it?' asked Marcus.

'Taw and Juliet are in love.'

'Oh! Is the Queen aware?'

'Yes, she is, but not about Dina and Harry!'

'Oh, bloody hell! I'd rather face the dead army again.'

They walked back to his captains, and after the meal, Prince Marcus said:

'It has been an honour, gentlemen, and I'll see you in the keep for a drink when you return.'

They saluted, and Marcus and David were gone.

Chapter 32

Taw opened his eyes: where was he? His last sight was the bright light and sky. 'Taw, you are awake,' came a familiar voice.

He looked over and saw Juliet smiling.

'Hello,' he said, 'how are you?'

'I am great now you are back. How do you feel, Taw?'

'I don't know yet! Aarrgghh!' he said. 'My hands!' They were heavily bandaged, but he could see they were like two claws. 'What happened to my hands?' he said.

'They are badly burnt, Taw. The sisters say maybe, in time, you will be able to use them. But that is only a maybe.'

'That is just great. I won't be much of a soldier or knight, will I? That's all I ever wanted to be, a knight, a glorious knight.' His eyes closed, and tears fell as Juliet tried to comfort him.

Marcus met with the Queen. 'We have much to talk about, Mother. Shall we do that now?' enquired Marcus.

'Yes, I think the sooner, the better. We need to get things back into order.'

They sat.

'To start,' she said, 'each person in the kingdom is to be given two silvers. We will announce a three-day holiday across the kingdom.'

'Yes,' agreed Marcus, 'we need to reward some people for their service to the kingdom.'

'Agreed,' said the Queen. 'I have a list here you can look over, Marcus. You can amend it within reason, but clear it with me first. Finally, Marcus, a slightly delicate matter. You're taking your rightful place as King?'

'I knew you would bring this up, Mother, and I did give you my word. So, yes, I will become King. Mother, just one more thing: Taw and Juliet.'

'That is obvious, Marcus. She will not marry a common boy; she is Royalty.'

'Actually, Mother, he is not a commoner. His father and grandfather are both Lords of the Realm. His grandfather will be the High Lord Marshal, if he accepts it. Therefore, on all accounts, as far as the Crown is concerned, Taw is eligible.'

'But she is my daughter! I want the best for her, to marry a prince or king and be happy, instead of a boy with no hands.'

'He will be a national hero, and have you thought of what reward to bestow on him for saving the kingdom, in fact, the world? We also have Harry and Dina, who are in love and want to marry.'

In the days that followed, much planning was done. At the start of the festival the following month, Marcus would announce that he would be crowned King of Astel, and the Queen would step down. Then it would be up to Marcus, as the king, whether Harry and Dina could marry; Taw and Juliet would marry the following year.

Days later, Marcus was journeying to the valley of Lady Lake with Taw and Eric, to collect the dragon's egg.

Taw's hands were beyond repair, and after this, the sisters would remove the black bones. The egg was still there; both Eric and Marcus tried to pick it up but to no avail.

Taw said, 'I will do it,' and walked over to the egg. He reached down with his black claws and took hold of the egg. Then he began to scream. Marcus and Eric could only look. Taw was glowing blue where he held the egg. He continued to scream, then he stopped. The blue had gone, the egg was still in his hands... hands! He had hands!

They were back to normal, muscles, flesh, skin, and he could move them.

He was about to put the egg down when Eric said, 'I would not do that until we drop it in the ocean, as you may not be able to pick it back up again.'

'Yes,' agreed Marcus, 'can we please go now, Eric?'

The ship was waiting in the harbour, ready to set sail on the forever ocean. They appeared on the ship: it was easier to go straight there, rather than travel across land, and quicker.

'Set sail,' said the Captain, and the ship heaved to, out of the harbour.

The time passed slowly. Taw held the egg for two days, eating and drinking with one hand, silently praying that when he released the egg, his hands would stay as they were.

'This is the place,' said the Captain to Prince Marcus. 'The deepest part we know of.'

The three of them stood on the deck at the rail. With the gentle rocking of the ship and the small swell across the ocean, it was calm, the crew silent, just the creaking of the old ship in the water.

'It's time,' said Eric, cutting through the eerie silence.

Taw stood in the middle, Marcus one side, Eric the other.

'May the gods protect us,' said Taw and dropped the egg and the stone.

It seemed to take forever for them to hit the water. They waited expectantly for something to happen. But no, they hit the water, no bangs, lights, noise, nothing; they just sank below the water. Taw looked at his hands; they were normal.

'Thank the gods,' he said as he turned to Marcus. 'Thank you, both of you,' he said, with tears in his eyes.

Marcus and Eric clapped an arm around him. 'No, it's "Thank *you*,"' said Marcus.

'Can we go home now?' Taw asked Eric.

Marcus turned to the captain. 'Thank you, Captain.'

The three disappeared just as they had appeared.

Epilogue

At the start of the three-day festival, there were Royal announcements to be made, with first, a prayer in honour of all those who had died. The Royal family was seated on the dais. Royal Prince Marcus stood and addressed the huge crowd in the Palace.

He started with: 'Her Majesty the Queen, my mother, Prince Harry, Princess Juliet and I wish to thank the following.' He read out a list of names. 'There are also some special awards to be presented by her Majesty the Queen:

'Firstly, Lord Sandy Sandbite, now the High Lord Marshal, second in command to me

'Lady of the Realm – Her Royal Highness Princess Juliet, and Dina Shield

'Dame of the Realm – Mother Superior Alice

'Baron of the Realm – Henry Shield, Royal Blacksmith

'Earl of the Realm – David and Luke Vantor, Aron and John Smith, Nalt Aron (Innkeeper), Joshua Shield, Earthie Admis, Jackus Admis, Sam Baker

'Next, His Royal Highness, Prince Harry – Commander of the Royal Navy and Army

'The final awards are to Master Zing Fan and Earl Eric Vantor – Lord of the Realm

'Taw Sandbite – Lord of the Realm, and my new Captain of the Prince's Elite Troop.

'As for myself, The Queen and I have agreed that in autumn, I will take the Crown and be your King.'

The crowd roared with pleasure, and the merriment began.

During the months that followed, Taw and Juliet were married, and Harry married Dina the following year, with King Marcus's permission. Master Zing Fan and his friend, blue magician Eric, took a slow trip back to his home.

THE END

Lightning Source UK Ltd.
Milton Keynes UK
UKHW041212230821
389329UK00001B/197

9 781802 271119